"I've come to ask you to marry me, Susannah.

"In truth, this time. Not an extended farce with a decidedly bad ending." He gave her a crooked grin.

Was this his attempt at making things right? Or was it merely a joke in poor taste? She gave her hands a final wrench and set them free. "You are talking nonsense. And I wish you would stop. It's bad form. And moreover, if anyone sees that you are here, then I might as well lock up my shop forever and wander the moors as a beggar."

"I don't care what other people think." Daniel lowered his brows and fixed her with his piercing green gaze. "I only care about—" He broke off abruptly, his expression clouded.

Susannah's heart pounded in her chest. "Of course you don't care about other people, Daniel! You've never had to." Oh, this selfishness. His cocoon of wealth and privilege. When would he ever learn?

Books by Lily George

Love Inspired Historical

Captain of Her Heart
The Temporary Betrothal
Healing the Soldier's Heart
A Rumored Engagement

LILY GEORGE

Growing up in a small town in Texas, Lily George spent her summers devouring the books in her mother's Christian bookstore. She still counts Grace Livingston Hill, Janette Oake and L. M. Montgomery among her favorite authors. Lily has a B.A. in History from Southwestern University and uses her training as a historian to research her historical inspirational romance novels. She has published one nonfiction book and produced one documentary, and is in production on a second film; all of these projects reflect her love for old movies and jazz and blues music. Lily lives in the Dallas area with her husband, daughter and menagerie of animals.

A Rumored Engagement

LILY GEORGE

⟨H⟩ **HARLEQUIN**® LOVE INSPIRED® HISTORICAL

Recycling programs
for this product may
not exist in your area.

LOVE INSPIRED BOOKS

ISBN-13: 978-0-373-28265-4

A RUMORED ENGAGEMENT

Printed in U.S.A.

I praise You, for I am fearfully
and wonderfully made. Wonderful are Your works;
my soul knows it very well.
—*Psalms* 139:14

This book is dedicated to my teachers over the years, especially those who encouraged me to write. I was a terrible student, terrified of school and often absent—I couldn't have been easy to deal with. These women went above and beyond to motivate me at a time when others would have given up on me. I certainly had given up on myself.

Mrs. Liz Ramsel,
Northside Middle School,
Georgetown, Texas

Mrs. Tommie Thompson,
Georgetown Junior High School,
Georgetown, Texas

Mrs. MaryLynn Fernandes,
Trinity School,
Midland, Texas

Mrs. Betty Underwood,
Midland Freshman High School,
Midland, Texas

Chapter One

"Well, here we are." Susannah Siddons injected a false note of cheeriness into her voice. After all, it fell to her to convince her sisters that she had matters well under control. Not always an easy task when one was only twenty and the head of the household. "It's not much, but we'll give it a good cleaning and it will look much better."

She turned to face her sisters, Hannah and Rebecca, whom she had long ago nicknamed Nan and Becky, her stair-step sisters, as she called them. Becky two years younger and Nan four years younger—yet despite that difference, they clung together close as twins. Their faces, as alike as two profiles on the same coin, reflected doubt and disgust as they glanced up at the tumbledown building before them.

"It's awfully small," Nan ventured, biting her lip in a distracted fashion. "Where will we live?"

"On the top floor, silly," Susannah answered with a bright smile. "There are two rooms up there and a small kitchen in the back of the shop area."

"It's rather far off the main road, wouldn't you say?" Becky scanned the street with a rapid glance. "How can we attract shoppers if we don't have anyone strolling by our windows?"

"Well…" Susannah hesitated. Becky had a point. They were at the far end of the main road, where the gravel path trailed off into the nearby meadow. The hustle and bustle of a daily market crowd—or as much of a crowd that ever gathered in a small village like Tansley—would be down at the end of the road. Still, this shabby storefront was all her slender purse could afford. "We'll just have to give them a reason to seek us out. We'll make our windows so alluring, so stuffed with beautiful goods, that our shop will become a destination."

She tucked a stray lock of deep auburn hair back under her bonnet and leaned forward to get a better look at the store through the dirty glass window. But all that she saw was a reflection of herself—the dark circles under her gray-green eyes, her pale skin with its light dusting of freckles. No one, looking at her, would be deceived. Her life was a shambles, and though she might try to hide it from her sisters, 'twas writ plain across her face and her person.

She drew back from her reflection sharply. It didn't matter. No one cared what she looked like, anyway. "Shall we go in? Father's solicitor said he'd leave the key under a stone."

Becky dropped her satchel on the grass and pushed back her bonnet. "I don't see a stone."

Nan walked up to the front doorway and parted the long moor-grass with her fingers. "Neither do I."

Perfect. How absolutely, positively, perfectly perfect. They had been traveling for weeks now and finally reached the end of their journey—only to find the door locked. 'Twas a metaphor for her entire life. Tears stung the back of her eyelids and a hysterical desire to laugh bubbled within her. What could they do? The solicitor lived back in Matlock, a day's journey away. The mail carriage they'd ridden in on was long departed. People came and went down at the other end of the street, their faces and forms blurred by the distance.

She could go and ask one of the other shopkeepers for assistance, or one of the townspeople. But a sudden and unreasonable wave of stubbornness assailed her, holding her in its grip. She was here to start a new life for her sisters, and it would be intolerable for anyone to know she was making such a poor start. She would find a way to open that door on her own. "I'll look around back. Perhaps there's another door to the shop, and he hid the key there."

With masterful nonchalance, straightening her spine and holding her shoulders back, she marched around to the rear of the building. There was another door, to be sure, but no key there, either. Nothing even remotely resembling a stone graced the back porch. She clenched her fists and bit her tongue, willing herself not to lose her temper completely and utterly. 'Twould be a blessed relief to roll about in the long moor-grass and flail her arms and legs as she had as a child. But it would do no good. Giving vent to her temper wouldn't change their present circumstances.

There was only one thing to do.

She returned to the front of the building, where Becky and Nan stood waiting. "I'm going to break in," she announced.

Her sisters gasped in unison. "No," they breathed, their eyes widening in shock.

"Oh, yes, I shall," she snapped. "I'll break out one of the door panes. You'll see. We'll be in quick as a wink."

Of course, since there was no rock to be found, she'd have to improvise. She opened her valise and withdrew her sturdy boots with their lovely curved heels. One blow from those heels would surely do the trick. Tapping it against her palm, she walked over to the doorway and raised the boot in the air.

"What do you think you're doing?" A man's voice, rich and deep, boomed behind her. She dropped the boot and swung around. There, beside her sisters on the tapering path, were two young gentlemen. Her breath came in quick gasps as she studied the form of one of the men. Surely that wasn't Daniel Hale. No, it couldn't be. And yet—those mischievous green eyes, the tousled black hair—she squinted, taking a closer look. Daniel wasn't as tall as this fellow when he left, but then, that was several years ago.

Her sisters were staring at her, openmouthed and silent. Both gentlemen awaited her reaction. The dark one who looked like Daniel appeared amused, if one could judge from the upturned corner of his mouth. The man beside him, with dark brown hair and brown eyes, merely looked confused and a trifle bored.

"It's my shop," she explained, coming toward them with her palms turned upward in a defensive gesture. 'Twould be horrid to begin life in Tansley marked as a woman who tried to break in to a building. She must defuse the situation. "We're just moving in. But I cannot find the key and so I thought I could break the glass with my boot heel."

"Good thing we came along," the green-eyed man said

with a chuckle. "'Tis mighty hard to find a glazer in the village. You'd have a broken door for weeks."

There was no doubt about it. This man was Daniel. An older, more rugged version of the boy she'd known, but it was him. Her heart pounded so that surely everyone in the little group could hear it. Better to cover her nervousness by concentrating on the problem at hand. "I don't know how to unlock it. Without the key, I have no way to get in. And I can't go back to Matlock to beg the key from the solicitor. We've only just arrived." She indicated her sisters with a jerk of her bonnet.

"I can help you." He stepped forward, dusting his hands on his breeches. "Give me a hairpin and I can pick the lock."

She nodded. Of course. If only she'd thought of that herself. She tugged her bonnet off her head, pushing some of the curls back off her shoulder. As she removed a hairpin, her hair finally broke free of all restraint. It tumbled around her shoulders and she pushed it behind her with an impatient hand. So many women had hair that behaved perfectly well. Why couldn't her hair be more ladylike?

His intense gaze searched her face and lingered on her hair as she held the hairpin out. He no longer looked mischievous or amused. His mouth was pressed into a firm line and his green eyes no longer twinkled. They—Well, they overwhelmed her, truth be told. As he took the hairpin from her palm, his fingertips brushed against her glove. She suppressed any reaction to his touch. He probably didn't even recognize her. Better not to let on that she knew all too well who he was.

He turned his attention toward the lock, straightening the hairpin. Kneeling in the moor-grass, he leaned forward, working the lock with the bit of wire until a click sounded. "There," he exclaimed, and twisted the latch until the door eked open. "Of course, you'll have to have the locksmith come out and assist you with finding a new key. But I wouldn't worry. Tansley's a safe place. No need, really, for a locked door."

"Thank you." They had no money left for a new key. They'd just have to leave the door unlocked until she could write to the solicitor and beg for the old key back.

"You're welcome...?" He paused, midbow. Of course. Where were her manners?

"Sus—I mean, Miss Siddons." Gracious, what a blunder. 'Twas mere habit, but still—her face heated to the roots of her hair. He would never want to know who she was. He'd merely helped her out once.

He peered at her with hooded eyes. Did he remember, after all? "Mr. Daniel Hale." He finished his bow and indicated his friend, who tipped his hat. "This is Paul Holmes, my friend." He turned back toward her. "Is there anyone here who can help you? Your father... your uncle, perhaps?"

Was there a heavier emphasis on those last words? No, she must have imagined it. "No one. We are on our own. But I do thank you for your help." She waved her hands at Becky and Nan, beckoning them inside the building. Better to cut this interview short. It had rattled her more than she cared to admit. She was ready to be safe behind those walls, where she could breathe again.

"Ah, then, I shall check on you in a day or so."

She opened her mouth to protest, but he cut her short with a shrug of his powerful shoulders. "No, really. I don't like the idea of three women living alone without any male protection. I have a place not too far from here, Goodwin Hall. I come to the village often and shall stop by."

With that, he touched the brim of his hat. He gesturing to his friend, and the two men strolled down the path as it narrowed and was overrun by long grasses and wildflowers. She pressed her back against the stone facade of the building, watching the two men as they grew smaller and smaller in the distance. Wiping her clammy hands on the worn fabric of her faded gown, she glanced down at her boot, discarded in the grass. Looking both vulnerable and ridiculous. Just like Susannah Siddons.

Once again, a desire both to laugh and cry seized hold, threatening her with madness.

She'd run away from the past. And here it was, claiming her once more as she ventured out on her own.

"I had no idea you were so deft with a hairpin, old fellow," Paul remarked as they strolled across the pasturelands toward Goodwin Hall. "Something you picked up during your days as a pirate, no doubt."

"I wasn't a pirate." Daniel rolled his eyes. "I was on a merchant vessel. Any man worth his salt knows how to help a lady in distress. I was merely following my instincts." He kept his tone light and bantering. He didn't want to talk about meeting Susannah again. She must remember him. But pushing her recognition with his best friend and her sisters standing there, watching with avid interest—no, thank you. He would hate any display like that, and so—if he remembered the lady correctly— would Susannah. But the unanswered questions would gnaw away at him until he finally was able to satisfy his curiosity.

"She's very decorative, that Siddons gel." Paul slashed

his riding crop at a particularly large clump of moor-grass. "But I thought the sisters were pretty, too. Should have asked them to tea."

"Well, since they've moved into the village, I am sure you shall have a chance to be formally introduced." Daniel scanned the horizon, willing his heart to resume its normal pace. He didn't like hearing Susannah referred to as a "gel" and he certainly didn't care for the admiring tone in Paul's voice. 'Twas all well and good for Paul to behave the way he did around women Daniel didn't know. This was a different matter altogether.

"You sound rather prim, like an old schoolmaster," Paul said with a laugh. "I can tell, after all, that you found Miss Siddons rather attractive yourself. Didn't you help her right away? Never even asked to see a deed for the building. You just took it on faith that she was telling the truth. She could have been burgling the place, for all we knew."

"It's highly unlikely that a young lady would set about burgling a vacant building in broad daylight. Have some sense, my good man." There, perhaps now Paul would cease his constant babbling, if he knew he couldn't draw Daniel out.

Paul looked up, scanning Daniel's face. "All right, all right. I know when I am invading on precious turf. I shan't say another word about the lovely Miss Siddons."

They strolled the rest of the way to Goodwin Hall, as the late-summer sunshine gilded the hilltops. Daniel breathed deeply of the scent of the grass as it swayed in the wind. He stifled the feeling of dread that crept up his spine as he looked out over the moors. Soon they would be mowing the hay at Goodwin, and like his father and brother before him, he would be expected to supervise—

or at least pretend an interest in the matter. He swallowed convulsively. He was no master, not really. In fact, he had run from any hint of obligation or duty since he was a lad. 'Twas mere fate that brought him back, not a desire to settle down. Some fellows might call it the hand of God that brought him here, or took him anywhere, for that matter. But he'd relinquished his faith long ago. And pretending he was a happy, fulfilled master merely brought on that insatiable thirst, the kind that would only be quelled with a few stout scotches.

He just glimpsed the Hall on the horizon, the sunlight turning it a bright shade of slate. The turrets that flanked the main hall were squat and modest compared to some of the grander homes of Derbyshire. David kept the Hall just as it should be while Daniel was off gallivanting on the high seas, and after Father's death he hadn't helped David as he should.

Now that David had passed, it fell to him to keep Goodwin Hall and adhere to family traditions and customs as he should have done long ago. And he was certainly not equal to the task, as much as he tried to conceal it.

"You're awfully silent company today, Daniel. I suppose I shall see you tomorrow for dinner?" Paul paused at the park gates and leaned against the balustrade.

"Yes, of course. You're always welcome, you know. Sorry I haven't been much company. Got a lot on my mind…." Daniel forced what he hoped was a casual smile.

"Ah, chuck your cares in the bucket. Come back to London with me when I return next. We shall tear the Town apart, and no debutante's reputation shall be safe." Paul chuckled at his small joke with appreciation.

"I'd like nothing more," Daniel rejoined with bravado. But even as he spoke the words, the memory of his boyhood promise flitted across his mind. He would never be free of it. Never. They were both pretending at a farce, Paul and he. Paul would never be free of the sorrow of his first love, try as he might to satisfy himself with light skirt after light skirt. And he himself would never be free of the unhappy shadows of his past, try as he might to drown them with scotch.

He bade goodbye to Paul at the gate and stood, for a long moment, looking at Goodwin Hall and the hills beyond, so green that they looked black. The way the hills rolled beyond the horizon was like the waves undulating on the sea. They called out to him in a way that the sea had once lured him, beckoning with promise.

If only he could feel that way about Goodwin Hall and all it represented. But it remained a prison, reminding him of what a shambles his life had been and become, beneath his swagger.

Alone at last, he allowed his mind to drift toward Susannah. Her auburn hair was as lovely as ever. He'd caught his breath when he saw the length of it tumble from beneath her bonnet. And those eyes—the sea had that same caste when a storm was brewing. She was as lovely as the day he'd become engaged to her. How long ago was that? Three years now?

She'd asked for his help once, and he'd promised her all he could offer—his name. They were no longer children then, and yet at that age, time seemed infinite, unending. There was no definite promise between them, just an agreement that she would marry him when he returned. And then he ran away to sea, to follow his dream. Together, they'd given each other the most precious gift they could think of at that time. Freedom. For Susannah, that meant freedom from her tyrannical uncle. And for him, it meant the freedom to forget his familial duties and run away from his dismal past.

The gift they'd given each other had proved hollow over the years. Here he was, back in Tansley, trying to ignore a home he hated. And here Susannah was, toiling away at building a poky little shop. Well, there was no repairing his own life, or changing his own wretched fate. But he could maybe make life easier for Susannah.

He clenched his jaw. As a matter of fact, he would find a way to help Susannah Siddons.

She was, after all, his betrothed. 'Twas the least a fiancé could do.

Chapter Two

Susannah's new building, which the solicitor had described in such glowing terms, was not much better on the inside than on the outside. The three sisters had slept in the upstairs quarters, squeezed together on the humble mattresses. Susannah awoke with a stiff neck and sharp hunger pains gnawing at her belly. 'Twas time to assume control of her pitiful situation, no matter how difficult it was.

Careful not to disturb Nan and Becky, who still slept, she crept into her serviceable lilac gown and her sturdy boots. Then she descended the back staircase and struck out for the shops at the other end of the main road. Surely there was something to eat in one of the shops. She was famished.

The street was empty, and a hush had settled over the dewy moor-grass. Even her footsteps on the gravel path were silent, for the road was also damp with dew. She paused a moment, gazing up at the pale sun as it climbed over the rolling hills. Tansley was such a beautiful place. Was it this wild and picturesque when she was a girl here? If it was, she'd been too unobservant to note.

They'd moved to Matlock when she was fifteen, and it had become home to her, not Tansley Village.

She turned and scanned the cluster of shops before her. A boot maker, a dry-goods store—a bakery. Oh, how lovely—a bakery. She darted forward and opened the door, causing the bell to swing merrily. She breathed deeply of the scents of flour and yeast. She hadn't eaten a bite since luncheon yesterday. Hungrily, she devoured the case of sweets and breads with her eyes until a plump, rosy-cheeked woman with graying hair stepped up to the counter.

"Well, then? And what can I get for you today?" She smiled and dusted her hands on her apron, sending clouds of flour dust into the air.

"Oh, I'd love one of everything. It all looks so delicious." Scones…muffins…biscuits… She heaved a sigh. "But my slender purse must dictate my purchase. So I shall take a loaf of the cinnamon bread and three of the scones, if you please."

The baker chuckled and tucked the sweets into brown-paper wrapping, tying the packages with a bit of string. "Here, try this marble cake. I made it this morning and I cannot tell if it's any good. You'd be doing me a favor if you gave your honest opinion."

Was this charity? She shouldn't have mentioned her lack of funds. She didn't want to beg for food, but…the kindly baker pressed the warm slice into her outstretched hand. At this point, it would be beyond rude if she said no. So she took a small bite. Oh…it was delightful— chocolate and vanilla swirled together. She finished the rest in two large bites.

The baker laughed. "I suppose it passes your test."

Susannah nodded, wiping the crumbs from her gloves. "By far the best I've had anywhere."

The baker nodded. "Good to hear that I have most of the kingdom beat." She handed the parcels over to Susannah. "Are you new to the village? You look a little familiar."

"My sisters and I bought the building down on the corner. I'm setting up shop as a milliner. But my family was here for a while before that. We've just moved back from Matlock Bath."

"Three girls on their own? That's worthy of applause. When I started this bake shop, I was only sixteen. I'd lost my mama and papa within a year of each other and had to support my brothers." She extended her hand, grasping Susannah's in a warm grip. "My name's Bess. So happy to welcome you back to Tansley."

"Thank you, Bess. My name is Susannah—Susannah Siddons." It had been years since they'd lived here, of course, but still—perhaps the name would ring a bell.

"Siddons? I thought you looked familiar. You must be part of that Siddons family that used to live here. A gentleman and his wife." The baker tilted her head, drawing her brows together. "Your mama and papa?"

"Yes. We moved away five years ago." She hugged the brown-paper parcels against her chest.

Bess nodded, the confused look still clouding her eyes. Susannah took a deep inward breath. That was enough reminiscing and chatting for the moment. No need to explain why the gentleman's daughter had returned home to work for her living. Another moment and she would be howling her woes onto Bess's ample floury chest. "I had better be going. My sisters are as hungry as I am, I'm sure."

anyone's help again." 'Twas better to stick to the facts of the situation—if she did so, perhaps she could keep her emotions in check. He had never written to her, and the knowledge that he had forgotten her so carelessly burned deep embarrassment and anger into her very soul.

"The last I heard of you, you were still living in Matlock. Why did you leave?"

"My aunt and uncle died in a carriage accident, two years after my parents passed away. While I stayed with them that last year, I became an apprentice milliner." She paused, unsure if she should tell him the whole truth. It was rather a ridiculous, sad little history. "My father left us a small inheritance. I bought this building with it so we could start a milliner's shop of our own." Thank the good Lord above, they were nearing the shop now. Her sisters would be awake and hungry, and the time for living in the past was over. "I hope all is well at Goodwin Hall."

"My brother died," he responded briefly. "I am master of Goodwin now." His face was still turned away from her, but the slight catch in his voice spoke of misery.

"I'm so sorry." And she was. Daniel and his brother had never got on very well, but his brother's death must have been a shock to him all the same. He'd certainly fled from his father as often as he could, and his brother, too. It would be difficult indeed to be called home to assume control of everything he'd cast aside. After all, Daniel had always lived as though there would never be any consequences to any of his actions.

And that was precisely why she was in her current position. Daniel simply couldn't be trusted to live up to his promises. So while she could sympathize with the loss of his brother, she could never let herself forget that she must earn her own way in the world. She must never trust anyone again—certainly not Daniel.

His expression had not changed, but he clenched his jaw at her words. "Thank you."

"Well, I should be going." She extricated her arm from his clasp and reached up to get her parcels. The time for reminiscing was over, and she must move on with her life.

He held on to the packages, looking down at her with eyes so green they took her breath away. "What are we going to do about this other little matter? You are my betrothed, after all."

As soon as Daniel said the words, he was ready to take them back. Susannah's face paled, and the freckles that marched across the bridge of her nose stood out in bold relief. He never meant to anger her. But dash it all, his head pounded like a big bass drum from last night's drinking bout, and thinking of the delicate way to phrase things had simply fled.

'Twas easy enough to ignore their engagement when an ocean separated them. But now they lived in the same village. He must acknowledge the truth now.

Susannah trembled, and he fought the urge to steady her. This was not maidenly fear—Susannah was in the grip of her formidable temper. Her hazel eyes had darkened to a deep grayish green hue, a sure sign of the storm to come. "There's no need to do anything about our engagement. Only my uncle and aunt knew."

"Even so…" He hesitated. A smart man would leave now. Susannah would likely throw something at him in a moment. But he rather enjoyed tangling with her; she always put up a jolly good fight. "Can't I do anything to help you? Anything at all?"

"No." She made another grab for her parcels, but he grasped them tight. As long as he had the bread, he held her there with him. He wasn't ready to let go. "You helped me escape Uncle Arthur by proposing to me. A letter every now and then would have been nice, since I thought we would marry some day, but I suppose you were too busy." She spat out the words as though they left a bitter taste in her mouth.

"What about you? You never wrote to me." He took a step backward, putting more distance between them. Would she follow? She took a step forward, still intent on retrieving her parcels. "Perhaps you were the one who jilted me first, Susannah. Is it better to be making bonnets for a pittance?"

She raised her chin in a defiant manner, a flush stealing across her cheeks. "There is dignity in all work, so I'll thank you not to mock me. And besides, I did write to you. You never wrote back. I should thank you, Daniel. You taught me the value of independence well. I shan't ask anyone else for help again."

What a hash he'd made of that.

But at least they were starting to speak, to discuss the problems that had plagued their engagement for these three years. He'd ignore the letter-writing for the moment—'twas ancient history, after all. And he must stop riding roughshod over her pride. He might try reason instead. "But surely, as the daughter of a gentleman, you're ashamed to live in such a place, and to earn your living by your hands." He looked down at her—how could he soften her temper? If only they could speak to each other without anger, as they did when they were children. "And your sisters? What of them?"

She drew herself up, throwing her shoulders back.

"My sisters will do quite well, thank you. In fact, we are all doing splendidly, so long as we are together."

He nodded. "I must confess I am jealous of your closeness with your sisters. Never really understood the closeness of other families." His mouth quirked with bitterness. His dour, domineering father and staid, lethargic brother certainly held no charms for him.

His admission helped. Her eyes had lost some of their hard, glittering light. "I truly am sorry, Daniel. And I appreciate your offers to help. But I just can't prevail upon you for assistance the rest of my life. Independence is everything to me now. I must find my own way."

Behind her, the door opened and one of her sisters poked her head out. "Is everything all right, Sue?" she called.

"Yes, I'll be in momentarily. Start brewing some tea, will you, please?" Susannah tossed the words over her shoulder.

He handed the parcels back. Their interview was now over, and he must surrender with as good grace as he could. Once he rid himself of this wretched headache, he might be able to think more clearly. Susannah spoke as though she released him from any obligation, but was that really the best thing for both of them? And did she really mean it?

"Come to Goodwin Hall for tea sometime," he offered. "You and your sisters are always welcome." It was a mere social gesture but all he could think of at the moment.

"Thank you." She glanced up at him uncertainly. The fire had gone out of her, and when it left, the traces of her fatigue remained. "You were always a charmer, Daniel."

Something in her tone made him pause—allure of any kind was apparently not high on the lady's list of male virtues. One auburn curl had pulled loose from under her bonnet, and he resisted the mischievous urge to reach out and grasp it. He shook his head. "No. I'm not as charming as you think me."

He touched the brim of his hat and walked away. He refused to look back at the ridiculously run-down cottage that was her stab at independence or at her trim, lovely silhouette as he continued his stroll. Three years he had been engaged to Susannah. Three years. Somehow, in the back of his mind, he had planned for it all to work out. But after hearing nothing from Susannah, he'd pushed the thought of marriage further aside. And it wasn't until he'd received word that his brother died that he'd had to bow to obligation and come home. The thought of marriage to Susannah was rather daunting; he hated the thought of becoming as violent and grim as his father had been. Or as dreary and drab as his brother had been. Why not avoid the inevitable as long as possible?

And that made sense at the time. Unhappy relationships were his lot in life. He had no idea how a couple in love should act. He'd certainly never seen it for himself.

His mother had died when he was still quite young— hounded to death, so village rumor ran, by her sour and cruel husband. By the time Daniel was old enough to think and feel for himself, Father had lapsed from abusive to merely domineering, while his distant brother sat dully about the house. He hated everything about family. Family meant duties and obligations. Family meant silent meals, recriminations over one's personal foibles, absentminded reminders that he really never had lived up to anything in his father's estimation.

And falling in love meant marriage. And marriage led

to families. And that would merely start the miserable process all over again.

That was precisely why he'd run away.

The Hall loomed in the distance. Its solid presence nothing more than a stark reminder of his family and his failings. Small wonder he shirked his duties to seek fun and adventure. And now, in the bitterest of ironies, he was in charge of everything he'd once cast aside. And Susannah had returned, too, another link to his regretful past. He craved the abyss that drinking a bit more than he should would bring on. Good thing Paul was coming this evening. He would have someone to drink with, and that was decidedly more cheerful than being alone.

He strode up the drive, his boots crunching on the gravel, preparing to at least get a bit of a head start on Paul.

But—of course, there was a slight hitch in his plans. Paul stood on the front steps, his angular face alight with laughter. "What ho, man? Been to the village to check on Miss Siddons? That's a gentleman for you."

"I walk to the village every morning," Daniel responded evenly, refusing to take Paul's bait. "You know that." He brushed past his friend, taking the steps two at a time. He opened the front door and removed his hat and coat. "To what do I owe this dubious honor? Come early to steal a march on me?"

"Ah, well. Life at home is most awfully dull. I decided I would head back to London this week, so I thought you might not mind some early company. Is that all right?"

"Certainly, certainly. The earlier the better." Daniel ushered Paul through the front door.

"So, if you are determined to stay here, what may I bring you from Town to amuse yourself? A new horse, perhaps? Or a new wife?" Paul cast his hat on the hall bench and stripped off his gloves.

Daniel spun around. "What?" Most of the time Paul's teasing was tolerable, but now—it struck a bit too close to home to be amusing.

"Here you are with a big country home. Plenty of money. It's positively un-British that you aren't seeking a wife." Paul shrugged his shoulders. "Watching you with Miss Siddons yesterday, it occurred to me that the pair of you made quite a picture."

"You're as bad as an old maiden aunt, Paul. Why are you so intent on marrying me off? Are you trying to narrow the competition for the ladies?" He slapped his friend on the shoulder and led the way to the library.

"No, of course not. I'm enjoying the bachelor life whilst I can." Paul fell silent for a rare moment, a moody expression crossing his face as he settled into a leather chair. Perhaps he'd overstepped his teasing with Paul— perhaps Paul was still really upset about Ruth Barclay. But no, in a blink the expression had vanished, and Paul leaned forward, an incorrigible gleam in his eye. "Though, I must say, Miss Siddons does rather make a fellow want to change his mind."

Paul was never going to stop nattering on about Susannah. He thought her pretty and would likely try to court her if Daniel didn't put a stop to the silliness. He eyed his friend as Paul settled back against the cushion. Could he be trusted with a secret?

"You can't have Susannah Siddons," he replied evenly. "She's already spoken for." There, perhaps that would be enough to throw Paul off the scent.

"Really? How fantastic. I shall have to nose about until

I find the fellow. Of course, I could always court one of her sisters. They're quite tolerable, too."

Nose about? Paul really was like a hound on the trail. There was nothing for it but to confess the truth to his friend. Only then would the matter cease to worry them both.

"I'm the fellow. Congratulate me, Paul. Susannah Siddons has been my betrothed for these past three years."

Chapter Three

"Indeed?" Paul quirked an eyebrow with amusement. "If it's true, then why haven't you married? And why isn't she here with you, in Goodwin Hall? Why is she staying in a hovel?"

"'Twas meant as a way to keep her uncle Arthur from forcing her into a marriage she didn't want. We concocted the plan." Daniel's fists clenched at the memory. "Her aunt was browbeating her into marrying some fat, doddering fool of a country squire. And the blackguard spent all their money. She went from being a gentleman's daughter to an apprentice milliner. Her family left Tansley when she was still a young lass. And her parents died soon after. So within a couple of years after their passing, her life turned upside down." He heaved a deep sigh.

"And you never married?" Paul shrugged his shoulders. "What happened that kept you apart?"

"We never had a formal plan." There was no excusing it, or even explaining it. "I never received a letter from her, so I assumed she had found another way out. And I was enjoying my life on the sea. It was a passion of mine."

"You'll forgive me for saying so, but you were passionate about the wrong thing entirely," Paul replied in a tone so dry that Daniel winced. "So, if she's not your fiancée in truth, then she must be fair game."

"She's not one of your light skirts, Paul. She may have to work for a living, but she's not what I will allow you to consider fair game." He stalked over to the decanters and began pouring out the rich amber liquid.

Paul gave a short bark of laughter. "I don't think of every woman in that way."

Daniel slanted his gaze over at his friend as he handed him his drink. "Don't you, old fellow?"

"I may have been unhappy in love, but I declare that a lady like Susannah could make a chap believe in the theory of marriage again. Those magnificent eyes…that Titian hair…"

"Enough." He didn't appreciate Paul cataloging Susy's physical attributes. He couldn't suppress the proprietary feeling that arose from deep within. Whether she admitted to it or not, he couldn't stop thinking of her as his fiancée. And there needed to be a sense of propriety about that fact. "Anything more about her beauty and I'll be hard pressed not to plant you a facer."

"Fine, fine. Truce, and all that." Paul held his palms in the air in supplication. "I shan't say another word." The secretive, absorbed expression on his friend's face showed that, though he would refrain from speaking about Susannah, he'd not cease in thinking about her. "What do you intend to do now?"

"When I spoke to Susannah this morning, I alluded to our problem," he admitted. "But she indicated that she had no interest in renewing even my friendship, to say nothing of our engagement. She's proud, Paul. Very proud. I have to step carefully if I am to keep from offending her."

"How did you broach the subject?" Paul took a long sip of his scotch with nary a shudder.

"Well, I…uh…" How embarrassing to rehash the disastrous conversation. Better to keep it short. "That she could come to tea here at the Hall."

Paul shook his head gravely, rolling his eyes. "I am sure she leaped at the opportunity," he mocked, his voice dripping sarcasm.

Daniel shrugged, concealing his annoyance at Paul's tone. "What? I couldn't very well profess my undying love for her. She's got brains and is quite acute, Paul. She'd know it was a lie. I'm not going to insult her intelligence."

"And so, instead, you invited her to a tea party?" Paul set aside his empty glass and made an impatient movement with his hands. "I quite understand that you couldn't very well sweep her into your arms. But what of romance? Surely you should woo the lady a bit first."

"I wouldn't even know how to start. I don't love her, you know." Daniel rubbed a weary hand over his brow. How extraordinary to court one's own fiancée. Most fellows went about it the other way around. "And I have no knowledge of happy marriages. Or of romance."

"Plenty of marriages have been built on less." Paul narrowed his eyes, predatory as a panther. "What do you want from her, anyway?"

"I want to help. When I went to sea, old man, I had much to keep me occupied. I had no idea where Susannah had gone, or what happened to her. I never got any letters from her, you see. So I just—" He broke off a moment, fumbling to find the right words. "I never forgot her. I just let the matter go. As I have with everything else in this blighted village."

"I know your family life was rather awful." Paul stood and helped himself to another tumbler of scotch. "I have been unhappy in love, but at least I grew up in a loving home. In fact—if you want my advice—don't think of her in terms of love. Don't seize control of anything. Simply be kind to her. It never hurts to have a pretty gel's favor, you know."

"Being friends. That sounds rather nice." He cleared his throat and began anew. "How should I start?"

"Remember what she likes. Poetry, flowers and whatnot. Women like jewels, too, but that could be considered too forward if your intentions are honorable." Paul settled back in his chair. "And if they aren't, you certainly don't need my advice for that."

Daniel scowled at Paul. "Of course my intentions are honorable."

Befriending Susannah Siddons would be no ordinary task. She wasn't like other women, not even when she was a slip of a girl. She was sharp and bright and had a disconcerting habit of laughing at you when she thought you weren't being sincere. So, giving her jewels and silks would be quite out of the question. He'd have to be more original than that.

"They're most dreadfully poor, you know. From a gentleman's daughter, she's gone into trade," he muttered. "Rather painful to see that. Perhaps I could help. When I saw her this morning, she was buying food."

"That's easy enough to handle. Send her a hamper. Load it with every delicious morsel you can think of." Paul waved his hands as though the problem had been decisively solved.

"A good idea." He'd ask Cook to put something together. Susannah would have something to eat. And maybe she would think kindly on him. And they could be friends.

Life wouldn't seem so bleak then.

"Hear, hear. Go on, then. Ring the bell. And while you're ordering the Siddons dinner, make sure to ask for something for us, too? I vow, I am feeling my liquor far too quickly, and it's due to this empty stomach." Paul slapped his midsection and groaned.

Daniel nodded and headed for the bellpull. Yes, this was a good plan. 'Twas the only way he could begin to bridge the gap of the past.

"We won't accept it. Take it back." Susannah scowled at the maid before her, drawing herself up to her full height—small though that was. "While we appreciate Mr. Hale's generosity—"

"Sue, please." Nan popped her head around the door frame and eyed the basket of food hungrily. "It's a hospitable gesture and nothing more. Don't be so missish."

Susannah glared at her younger sister, who responded by widening her already large brown eyes appealingly. Then she swallowed, for the tantalizing smells drifting up from the basket the servant held were almost too good to endure. They'd finished the cinnamon bread at luncheon, and after a hard day of scrubbing and putting the cottage to rights, all three sisters were famished.

"Mr. Hale said he must insist." The maid shifted her weight from one foot to the other and placed the heavy basket on the front stoop. "I'll just leave it here and be on me way. I'm late for me own tea as 'tis." The maid rubbed her palms on her apron, and with a cheeky wave, set off across the dwindling path toward Goodwin Hall.

Nan scooped up the basket. "Becky, there's food," she called indoors. "Oh, 'tis heavy. Susannah, grab hold and help me carry it."

Susannah unfolded her arms and grabbed one of the basket handles. Oh, gracious, was that chicken she smelled? A roast chicken? Her stomach grumbled in appreciation.

"Food? From whom?" Becky hastened forward to help, and together, the three sisters plunked the basket on the table. Susannah took a step backward as her sisters plundered the basket. As they dug out dish after dish, a scrap of foolscap fluttered to the bare wood floor. She grasped it and unrolled it carefully.

"Pies—meat and fruit. Oh, Becky, it's fairly oozing berries. I cannot wait to try this."

"Nan, do look! Bread and cheese, and a tin of tea. It's too much, I tell you. We shall feast for a week on this."

Susannah eyed her sisters as she opened the parchment. They were too busy to take any notice of her, so she strolled over to the firelight to better read the note. Good gracious, Daniel's handwriting had grown wobbly over the years.

Dear Susannah,
I thought perhaps you'd have few provisions laid in and thought I would send a few things from the Hall. Perhaps this will help make your first few days in Tansley more enjoyable.
Please do not hesitate to call upon me if you are in need of anything.
I am, as ever,
Your humble servant Daniel

"Whatever are you reading, Sue?" Nan demanded, a loaf of crusty bread in each hand. "Come, sit down. We shall have a feast worthy of all our hard work."

"She's reading a love letter from her fiancé, no doubt," Becky answered, giving Nan a wink. "After all, we owe this largesse to him."

"Hush. Both of you." Susannah cast the foolscap into the fire and folded her arms across her chest. "My engagement to Daniel helped us out of a dreadful situation. 'Tis no cause for levity."

Becky bit her lip and cast her eyes down at her plate. "I'm sorry."

Susannah sighed, looking at them both. They had worked hard all day—and they had earned a decent meal. In fact, until Daniel's servant showed up at the door, she'd had no idea what they were going to eat for dinner. So… she would merely have to swallow her pride on this one. Let the girls enjoy a real feast. It was terribly kind of Daniel to think of them, after all.

"Enjoy your feast," she said quietly. "You've earned every mouthful."

"You, too, Sue." Nan patted the chair beside her. "You'll feel much better after you've had a bite to eat." She bowed her head and led them in prayer.

And the remarkable thing was—she did. 'Twas amazing how a dinner of chicken, bread and cheese could take the edge off the harshness of life. And there were apples, too. She crunched into the bright red fruit happily, relishing its sweet juice. Even the thinness seemed to go out of her sisters' cheeks and they looked positively rosy.

As darkness fell over the cottage, illuminated only by a few candles and the firelight, even its rough edges appeared more attractive. Susannah sat back in her chair, meditatively twirling the apple core on her plate. They might—just might—do quite well in Tansley. The baker had thought so, and she was a woman who had her own shop. She had started young, too. So perhaps this was no chance meeting this morning. Perhaps it was a good omen. A sign of His blessing, even.

She glanced across the table at her sisters. Nan had pushed her plate aside and laid her head down on the burnished wood. The slow rise and fall of her shoulders indicated that she was sleeping deeply. Susannah shook her head and a smile lifted the corners of her mouth. She'd have to move Nan soon, or her sister would awaken with a terribly stiff neck.

"Susy?" Becky murmured softly. "What made you decide to marry Daniel Hale?"

Susannah stopped toying with her apple core. "You know why. Uncle was going to make me marry that lout Sheppard. And so I asked Daniel for his help."

"Yes, but why Daniel? There were other boys living near us. Why did you go to him above anyone else? Why did you seek him out instead of running away?" Becky tilted her head and gazed at Susannah intently.

"Well, if I had run away, I would have had to leave you two behind. So that would have been a foolish idea." She sighed. Why had she asked Daniel? It had seemed like the natural decision back then. She hadn't even questioned it. "Well, he was there. He had come to Bath to visit some of his family, and we could meet each other that way. It all just fell into place, you see. And I suppose I asked Daniel because he always knew how to get out of tricky situations. That was his charm. I knew I could depend on him to help me out of that mess."

Becky leaned forward, resting her elbows on the table.

"That's nice. So why don't you think you can depend on him now?"

Susannah flicked a glance at Nan as she lay cradling her head on the table. "Shush. You'll wake your sister." In truth, she didn't want to think about the matter, much less hash it over with Becky. She couldn't focus on the past. She had to plan for the future.

"She's sleeping. She'll sleep for hours like that if we let her." Becky wound her shawl more tightly around her shoulders. "Doesn't it seem…odd…to you that we should come home to Tansley only to find your fiancé here? Almost like fate or destiny." Her tone grew shivery and romantic.

Susannah resisted the urge to roll her eyes and crush her sister's romantic visions. Becky had always been the dreamer of the three, the most inclined to moon over Byron. Susannah, with her iron fist of practicality, had learned the difficult way to rein herself in around Becky over the years and not ride roughshod over Becky's girlish ideals.

"It's not fate or destiny. Both of our families are from the village. It's just…common ground." She rubbed her eyes with a weary hand. What an exhausting day it had been. "I think I'll rouse Nan enough to help her upstairs."

"Wait. You never answered my question." Becky was nothing if not persistent. "Why can't you depend on him now? Can't you become Daniel's wife in truth?"

"Don't be absurd. He never thought about me in all those years. Why do you persist in making our engagement something it wasn't?" She rose stiffly, shaking out her skirts. "He helped a long time ago because I asked for his assistance. What kind of woman would I be if, years later, I showed up on his doorstep begging for help again? I must earn my own way in this world. True independence is my only hope for freedom."

"Hmm." Becky smothered a yawn with her palm. "All this talk of being alone…I don't know. He's awfully handsome, Susy. So tall. So formidable and yet approachable. And he's your—"

"No, he's not." Time to put an end to this. She had no desire to investigate her past any further. She'd already spent far too much of her day on Daniel Hale. Time that should have been spent devoted to her shop. Susannah shook Nan gently and helped her to her feet. "Take Nan upstairs and you two go on to bed. I'll tidy up down here, and then I will be along." She needed a few moments to compose herself.

She tucked away the leftover food in the tiny larder adjacent to the kitchen. They'd have enough to eat for a few days at least. She would never accept charity again, but in this case—well, it was certainly going to go to good use.

A sudden chill ran through her body, and she clasped her arms across her chest. She strode over to the hearth to warm herself. She could never prevail upon him for help again. Her words to Becky rang true. She couldn't very well presume upon a relationship that obviously meant nothing to him. After all, he had never written her. Not once in all his travels around the world.

And there it was. That was the truth. She couldn't trust him because a tiny, bitter part of her resented the fact that he'd never once checked in on her during those long years. After her first few letters went unanswered, she knew the harsh truth. Daniel was away on the high seas and had simply forgotten her. That was his way. He was as mercurial as quicksilver and would never conform to any sort of stability. Over time, the raw, impotent rage she felt at being left behind had callused over. She would never count on him again, not for anything important.

But…perhaps she could count Daniel merely as a friend. She would never venture to be more than that, and it would behoove her to keep him at arm's length. But after being alone in this world and taking care of her two sisters for so long, it was nice to have someone one's own age as an acquaintance. She didn't feel quite as miserably alone now.

She dusted her hands on her apron and blew out the few beeswax candles that hadn't burned too low. Lit only by the flickering firelight, the dining room was warm and cozy. She sat on the hearthstone and surveyed her little kingdom with pride.

She said a quick prayer of gratitude.

The trip to Tansley, which had started so poorly, was looking much brighter.

Chapter Four

Some creature was dealing severe hammer blows to his head. Daniel lay with his eyes squeezed shut, willing the pounding to stop. At least for it to lessen enough that a fellow could turn his head. Baxter's discreet knock on the door was as loud as cannon fire, and his footsteps across the wooden floor might as well have been anvils dropping from the sky.

"Have mercy, man," Daniel groaned. "Why are you here, anyway? It's before dawn and you know I don't wish to be awakened before ten."

Baxter gave a subtle cough. "It's nearly noon, sir."

Daniel opened his eyes, but the sunlight seared them, and he closed them again. "Are you sure, Baxter?"

"Quite sure. I do have your breakfast tray. Cook sent up bacon and eggs." The mattress squeaked in protest as Baxter set the tray down.

"Oh, all right." Daniel slowly pushed himself to a sitting position, holding his head as still as he possibly could. Perhaps a little bacon would ease the throbbing of his brain. "Don't open the curtains, I beg you."

"As you wish." Baxter stood at the end of the bed, facing his master expectantly as Daniel pulled the breakfast tray into his lap.

"Well?" Daniel bit into a slice of bacon. The smoky taste of it gave him an uncertain moment. He'd either toss his accounts or be hale and hearty in a few seconds. He chewed carefully, waiting to see which way his body would react.

"Mr. Donaldson is here, waiting in the parlor. Your estate manager." Baxter coughed again, and Daniel shot him a rueful glance under his brows. That sound was like nails on glass, especially after one had imbibed a bit too much the night before. "I told him that you were having a bit of a late start but that you would meet with him within the hour. He has some account books, which I gave him leave to spread out on the table."

Account books. Estate managers. Parlors. His head gave another painful throb, and he bit slowly into the bacon once more. He was doing better, but still—the thought of meeting anyone to discuss business right now put him off. "Did I have an appointment with him?"

"You did, sir. I mentioned it to you yesterday, when Mr. Paul was here."

"I don't remember much of anything after Paul arrived, Baxter." There had been a lot of scotch, hilarious conversation and japes, of course. But practical conversations? No, he didn't recall a word. "Well, let the man cool his heels in the parlor. I'll have a bit more breakfast and make myself presentable. This bacon is just what I needed." He sipped at his tea, a potent, bitter brew so strong that the tannin left a film on his tongue. *Bracing* was not the word for Cook's tea. No, she boiled it for so long that you could use it to scrub the decks of a ship. Perfect.

"Very good. Mr. Paul is still sleeping in the guest room. Shall I awaken him?"

"Don't be absurd. That fellow has no responsibilities, no estate agents waiting upon him. Let him sleep it off. I'll meet him later, at dinner."

Baxter bowed and quit the room, shutting the door with a decisive snap. Daniel took another burning sip of tea and struggled to remember all that happened after Paul came over. What had they done? They'd spoken of Susannah and her sisters….

The throbbing in his head was easing. Now it just felt like annoying little birds giving his head an occasional peck.

Well, he couldn't very well sit here forever. Donaldson was downstairs waiting. He'd only communicated with the fellow a few times by letter—never met him in person. Why was Donaldson here, after all? He was the expert on running the place. Daniel knew nothing of managing a farm.

He pushed the tray aside and sat up, every movement a small agony. Baxter had laid his clothes out for him— the typical country squire attire. Breeches, shirt, jacket. Cravat. Bother the cravat; he was not in the mood to be slowly choked by a piece of fabric today. He tugged and pulled, getting dressed to boots but draping his jacket over the chair as he strolled to the washbasin. The thing fit so tightly that it was impossible to properly wash one's face with it on.

He gazed in the looking glass, running his hand over the rough stubble on his chin. He needed a shave, and the bags under his eyes spoke volumes about last night. When Donaldson left, he'd enjoy a nice hot bath and a shave. That would be his reward for making it through this meeting when he would much rather sleep.

He splashed tepid water in the washbasin and lathered his hands with a cake of soap. He paused. This wasn't his usual soap, the one that smelled of fresh green herbs. What on earth was this?

He paused, breathing deeply for a moment.

Orange blossom.

Just like Susannah.

The certainty of what he'd done yesterday speared through him. Paul had dared him. Dared him to send something nice to his sweetheart. And he'd ordered a huge hamper of food to be delivered to the Siddons girls because Susy had been so hungry when he saw her last.

He groaned, rubbing his damp palms over his eyes—but as he drew them away, he could smell nothing but orange blossoms and could think of nothing but Susannah. Would she be offended by his gift? She would be if she'd known that it was done as a dare.

The sick feeling that had begun to ease over breakfast now hit him, full force, in the gut. He clenched the side of the basin and bowed his head.

When the room stopped spinning a bit, he trusted himself to make it over to the bellpull. In short order, Baxter entered the room. "Yes, sir?"

"Why do I have orange blossom soap?" Daniel jerked his head toward the basin and pitcher.

"The maid must have made a mistake. Usually we have your bay rum." Baxter crossed over to the basin and picked up the offensive bar. "I'll have it changed out."

"See that you do. Orange blossom is far too feminine for a chap." Daniel rubbed his brow. How best to broach the next subject?

"Donaldson is waiting, sir. Are you on your way down?" Baxter stood, soap tucked discreetly in his fist, beside the basin. "Is there anything else you need?"

Yes. He needed just a little more information—just some insight into how great of a fool he had been last night. "Did I order a hamper of food to be sent to the village?"

"You did. The basket was delivered by Nancy in time for supper."

Daniel suppressed a groan. There was nothing he could do now. It was too late—the hamper had already made it to the Siddonses' home. The girls had either partaken of its contents or—as was more likely—it was now floating in a nearby stream, chucked there by an angry and proud Susannah.

Fine. He would go meet with Donaldson and then he'd have to think of a way to make amends. He'd have to cut back on his drinking with Paul tonight, and he'd have to watch his friend closely from now on, when it came to accepting dares. After all, Paul thought it was a fantastic joke that he and Susannah had been engaged. But it was no laughing matter.

He shut off his thoughts with a click. After all, if he stood there brooding, he'd need a drink. And once he started drinking he lost all sense of reason. And he needed all his wits about him if he was going to find a way out of this mess. "I'm on my way out now," he informed his butler, his tone rough and brusque.

He quit the room, striding down the stairs with purposeful steps. When he flung open the parlor door, Donaldson glanced up from a stack of books, an expectant look on his face.

"You must be Mr. Donaldson." Daniel offered his

hand. "Good to meet you in person. I'm afraid I haven't had time before, but now…" He trailed off. He really had no excuse at the ready for his lack of interest in the Hall. Not when his head was pounding and his wits had flown.

"Yes, sir." Donaldson shook his hand but then bowed respectfully. "I am grateful for the chance to meet with you at last."

"Well, then. I see you've brought a library with you." A little joke, but really—they must hasten the interview. He had to see Susannah, see if she was really furious with him—

"Yes, well, I had tried to talk to your brother about this, but he had fallen ill and could not make any decisions. The tenants are in need of some assistance, and there are some improvements that could be made on the farm. Improvements that could better the lives of your people here and can bring in more income. Make the place more prosperous." Donaldson indicated his account books with a wave of his hand. "If you like, I can show you. I need your approval before I can start."

Tenants. Improvements. Income. The old stifling feeling of obligation began to well inside Daniel, and he took a step back. By distancing himself from the account books, could he distance himself from his duties? "Yes, well, Goodwin Hall has always been reasonably profitable. We don't want for much here."

"I do understand, sir. But if you'll allow me to speak frankly—I feel I would be remiss if I did not say anything. The tenants' homes could use some repair, and the back fields could, if they lay fallow for a season, produce even better next summer. Or we could try planting a different crop there, to give the soil a rest…"

Donaldson nattered on, showing him a line of finely

scripted numbers in a column in one of the account books. Daniel clenched his jaw and nodded, but even as he feigned interest, his gaze and his mind wandered. He could walk down to the village and try to speak to Susannah. Yes, that was the best plan. Speaking to her directly was the only way to address the matter. She always responded better to directness than to subterfuge.

"…and I believe all these improvements could be implemented over the course of the year." Donaldson closed the account book and glanced at Daniel, an expectant smile on his face. "Well, sir? What do you think?"

"I…uh…" Daniel cast around for something intelligent to say. "I—I can see you've put a lot of thought into this."

"Well, it is my duty." Donaldson stacked the books one on top of the other and shrugged. "So, I should, of course, prefer to have your thoughts on the matters, as well."

He had no thoughts on any of these matters, beyond the growing feeling of dread that he would be chained to them forever. He had no mind for any of this, and yet these obligations were his. "I don't know, really. Do I need to reach a decision on any of this today?"

"No, certainly not. I am sure you need time to think things over." Donaldson stuffed the account ledgers into a worn leather satchel. "However, I would recommend implementing these improvements as quickly as possible, as we are nearing the end of summer. Shall I meet with you again next week?"

"No, not next week." He needed to shake free of these duties. He was never meant to be the one in charge. That was his brother's job—and he had been far better suited to the role than Daniel. "I may be out of town then. I shall have to see. I'll contact you, and we can discuss matters at that point."

Donaldson nodded, his youthful face wearing the expression of one resigned to the inevitable. "Of course, Mr. Hale. I shall wait to hear from you then." He grasped the satchel and strode toward the door. "Thank you for your time." He left without a second glance.

There was no trip out of town, of course. Living out as far as he did, a journey to Bath or London would be a rare excursion indeed. But it was the only way to get the man to stop talking—to leave. Daniel sighed and strolled over to the window, gazing out across the rolling pastures that surrounded Goodwin Hall. These were the pastures he'd played in as a child, the pastures that he'd cantered across on his favorite horse as a youth. And they undulated before him, like waves on a sea.

The sea had called to him, beckoning with promises of adventure. These lands rolled before him, reminding him of all he'd shirked. How he'd left his brother to die alone.

He needed a drink. Or he needed to fix one problem.

A choice, really—to drink oneself into oblivion again or to try to repair one bit of damage.

"Becky, those curtains are lovely. You're really outdoing yourself this time." Susannah glanced over at her sister with a smile as she rubbed at the windowpane. "Once we hang them up, the whole character of this room will change."

"I've never seen this much dust in my life." Nan gave a hearty sneeze. "When was the last time anyone lived here?"

"I don't know," Susannah admitted, stepping back to admire her handiwork. The panes of glass sparkled in the late-afternoon sunshine.

"Judging by the condition of these floors, I'd say it was at least ten years." Nan sneezed again.

Susannah turned to her sister, frowning. "Here, let me sweep. You shouldn't be breathing in all that dirt. I've finished the windows, and when I'm done with these floors, we shall stop for a little while."

"For the day?" Nan asked hopefully, handing the broom to Susannah.

"For a *while*." Susannah stressed the last word as she grasped the rough wooden handle.

"But we've been working since early this morning." Nan used her most wheedling tone. "Couldn't we take the rest of it to enjoy our handiwork?"

Susannah surveyed the room with a critical eye. Things did look remarkably better. It didn't exactly look like a fashionable millinery store yet, but it no longer reeked of abandonment. The windows, free of grime, allowed the sun to gild their humble furnishings, which Susannah had rubbed with lemon oil. Becky's curtains, made of fine ivory muslin, would soften the room and grace it with a feminine touch. And Nan's sweeping, which had started upstairs and worked all the way down to the front entrance, had done wonders to improve the appearance of the worn wooden floors.

She turned her attention to her sisters. Dust smeared Nan head to toe, and Becky's head drooped tiredly as she worked fine stitches into the hem of the muslin. She didn't dare to glance at herself in the mirror—she must look a fright—but the grime that collected around her fingernails bore mute testimony to the work she'd done. Her heart lurched and she twisted her mouth ruefully. Once again, she'd worked everyone too hard.

"Yes, of course. We could all do with a nice bit of rest."

She brushed the broom across the floor in broad half circles, gathering the last bits of debris into a pile. "I'll just brush this out the door and then we can have tea."

She pulled the latch and the door creaked open. Mustering the last reserves of her energy, she pushed the dust outside with a mighty swoosh.

A deep, decidedly male voice exclaimed loudly and then gave a hearty cough. Gracious, did she just pepper someone with her prodigious dust cloud? Susannah paused on the threshold and stepped around.

Daniel Hale stood just outside, covered in a fine cloud of dust. As she watched, her eyes growing wider, he swatted at his jacket sleeves, trying to rid them of their powdered grime.

"Mr. Hale." It was more of a statement than a welcome.

"Susannah." He straightened and removed his hat. "My congratulations. You are an excellent shot. Indeed, Wellington might have use for you in his army."

"M-my apologies, Mr. Hale." Susannah wiped her suddenly sweaty palms on her skirt. "I had no idea you were out there."

"I believe you." He gave her a slight smile, and for some inexplicable reason, it caused her heart to flutter. "I don't imagine you were expecting me."

"We have been working on cleaning up the store today and did not expect any visitors," Susannah explained. There, that took the personal edge off the conversation. It's not that they weren't expecting him. They simply were not expecting anyone.

"Yes, I can see that." His eyes roamed over her bedraggled form, amusement lighting their green depths.

The old anger and resentment welled in her breast. Who was he to laugh at her? What kind of man paid any calls without even wearing a cravat? "Well, now that I've powdered you with dust, at least we match," she replied in a sweetly tart tone.

Daniel laughed and shook his head. "I should know better than to give you that kind of opportunity, Susannah. You never fail to get the last word."

A light footstep sounded on the threshold behind her. "Mr. Hale! So good to see you," Becky called. "Won't you come in and see our handiwork. We've been cleaning all day."

Before Susannah could turn around and shoot her sister a quelling look, Daniel stepped forward, genuine interest in his expression. "I would, thank you. I wondered how you ladies were getting on." He motioned the two sisters in with a wave of his hand.

Susannah had no choice but to turn and follow her sister. To say anything at that point to dissuade him would be beyond rude. And while she didn't precisely enjoy his company, she had no energy left today to cross swords with him. So she set her jaw and waited, arms folded across her chest, as he surveyed their surroundings.

"I must say I am impressed." He gave a low whistle. "You three have already turned this into a palace. Why, it even smells clean in here. And everything so bright and fresh." He grinned at Susannah with such warmth that she blinked. "You are to be congratulated. All of you."

"I've just finished making the curtains for the windows." Becky held one of the gossamer panels up and gave it a shake. "The room will look much more finished when I hang them."

"Here. Allow me." He stepped forward and took the panel from Becky. "I see the previous tenant left the rods up, so I'll just thread the curtains on." He reached up without even having to strain and removed the wooden pole from the brackets. The sight of his powerful shoulders, framed by the windowpane, made her heart flutter once more.

She gave herself a brisk mental shake. Daniel had always been a very nice-looking boy, and if the boy had filled out into a nice-looking man, then that was no concern of hers. Fine feathers meant nothing if a man never kept his word. And, more to the point, his very presence was a distraction. Her heart shouldn't ever flutter when he was about. She had set her path in life, and it no longer included Daniel. Her life was this shop, and securing the independence of herself and her sisters was her sole purpose.

The sooner he left the better.

Chapter Five

"We were just about to have tea," Nan informed him as Becky handed him another curtain panel. "Won't you stay and join us?"

This time Susannah did shoot a quelling glance at her sister, but Nan turned and busied herself with clearing off the table.

"I'd love to." Daniel snapped the rod in place and moved to the next window. Becky darted over and began fluffing the curtains with an expert hand. "In fact, I was wondering if you got the gift I sent you."

"It was lovely!" Nan exclaimed, and the sisters began chattering in tandem about the vast repast he'd sent over and how delicious everything had been. Watching them together, a cold feeling of loneliness settled in Susannah's stomach. She could not be lighthearted about his gift. Indeed, it was difficult to feel gratitude. All she felt was the same undying sense of betrayal—that she had reached out to him when she needed someone desperately and yet he hadn't come back for her. She had to turn off these thoughts. She could not allow him to see how much she was hurt. After all, it meant nothing to him. Why allow him to see how deeply she had been affected by his absence? She grasped the broom and walked out to the back porch. She propped the broom next to the doorway and sank onto the rough brick, tucking her skirts around her.

She was tired. And hungry. Perhaps she could just rest for a moment, savoring the quiet. She untied her apron and cast it onto the long, swaying grass. The wind ruffled her hair, and she turned her face up toward the sun. Methodically, she removed the handful of hairpins she'd used to hold her hair, and relished the feeling of release as its heavy weight tumbled down her back. Just a few moments of peace, and then she'd put her hair up, tie her apron back on and go pretend to be a hostess to the man who had betrayed her.

The grass looked awfully tempting. She could spread her apron out on it and take a tiny nap, the late-afternoon sun warming her and making her eyelids droop…

"Susy. I brought you some tea."

Susannah snapped back to reality with a gasp. She'd almost fallen asleep where she sat, and Daniel stood over her, a steaming mug in one hand and a look of tender concern on his face. She shook her head to rid herself of the dreamy haze that enveloped her and her hair rippled around her shoulders, a reminder that she was dirty, unkempt and had been caught half-asleep by Daniel Hale.

Her cheeks burning with embarrassment, Susannah accepted the cup from Daniel. "Thank you." She let the use of her nickname pass. For the moment.

He knelt beside her and plucked a blade of grass, toying with it. "You've been working too hard."

She took a careful sip. The tea was strong and wonderfully hot, just the thing she needed to feel revived. "No indeed. I need to work a good deal harder."

"I worry about you."

She glanced at him out of the corner of her eye, but he kept his face turned down. He must be teasing her, just as he always did. "Oh, don't worry about me, Mr. Hale. I am tireless as a windmill." She made her voice light and airy, the perfect rejoinder.

"I'm not teasing you. I have grave concerns about the amount of work you are taking on." He cast the blade of grass aside and faced her squarely. "I want to help. If I keep sending food down from Goodwin, would you accept it? I want to make sure you and your sisters have enough to eat until your shop becomes a success."

"We will not accept any charity." She kept the same light tone of voice, but her hands began to tremble. "But I thank you for your concern."

"It's not charity." With a sudden, swift gesture he took the cup from her and set it aside, then grasped her hands in his. "Won't you let me help?"

She cast a quick darting glance at him, scanning his face for sincerity. Deep shadows ringed the eyes that usually held a mischievous light, and the stubble of a beard darkened his cheeks and chin. Daniel looked older—more worn—than he had in some time. Age might have changed him. He might be sincere. But then—Daniel was always sincere at the moment. The sincerity just didn't stand the test of time.

She tried to tug her hands away and attempted a flighty, false laugh. "Don't be ridiculous. I don't see why you feel you need to watch out for me."

Daniel pulled her closer, so close that she caught his scent of leather and green grass. "I'm sorry for what I did. Can you ever forgive me?"

She forced herself to look up at him. She hadn't been

this close to him since they were sixteen years old, and for some reason, his proximity was playing havoc with her sensibilities. "I am trying," she admitted in a whisper. "But it's difficult. You have no idea…" She trailed off, unable to tell him anything over the painful lump rising in her throat.

"I wish I'd done things differently. I know I have a lot to make up for. Can we…" He paused and swallowed. "Can we at least be friends? I can work on atonement much more effectively if you don't openly despise me every time I stop by."

Friendship. Friendship was neutral and didn't use up as much of her feelings as hatred did. Besides, she was supposed to forgive him if she was to live out her faith. He wasn't asking too much. Not really.

Could she relinquish her anger enough to be friends?

She tugged her hands from his grip and sat back on her heels, putting some much-needed distance between them. "Very well," she admitted. "I will be your friend, and you can be mine, but we must have some conditions for this arrangement."

A half smile quirked the corner of his mouth and the light of challenge shone in his green eyes. "Name them."

"First, you do not call me Susy. Second, you do not send extravagant gifts to my family."

"I don't like the terms, but I will reluctantly agree to them if it means I earn your friendship." He drew his knees up to his chest and wrapped his arms around them. "Anything else?"

"Let's just keep everything…pleasant." She could not give voice to her tumultuous feelings, but somehow the word summed up how desperately she wanted to brush over the past. "I'm starting anew here in Tansley, and I don't want to spend the first few weeks in dread of meeting you, or in dread of reliving the past. Do you understand?"

"I think so." He kept his face turned downward, studying his boots. "I know only too well what you mean about reliving the past. 'Tis an awful practice."

He must be referring to their engagement. He must feel badly that he ever agreed to marry her. Finding out this way was like tripping over a rut in a road you thought was smooth. She regretted the engagement, too, but she would never describe it as awful. Rather, she regretted that she ever depended on anyone else for her happiness. At least now she knew that independence was the only way to be fully happy.

Susannah stifled a sigh. But then, Daniel had always hated being confined to duties and responsibilities. One Easter Sunday he'd run off and spent the day climbing the moors rather than attend services with his father. He'd been nothing but a lad then. She found him later— dirty and unkempt—when she'd taken her sisters out for a walk. And they'd shared a jam sandwich and strolled with him back to the gates of Goodwin Park.

He would never change. He'd always be the boy smeared with dirt, running away to avoid his duties.

Friendship, and never reliance, was the only way to be happy with Daniel.

"Rest assured, I never spoke of our engagement to anyone but my sisters, and, of course, my aunt and uncle. My aunt and uncle have passed away, and my sisters will never breathe a word of it to anyone. So you see—we can pretend it never happened."

She rose and picked up the teacup. "Thank you for your assistance today, Daniel. And for the food, too. It was delicious and much needed. I had better finish up, though. There's still a lot to get done and a few hours of daylight left."

He glanced up at her, his eyebrows slightly raised, as though he was surprised by her words. "Very well. I hope to see you again soon." He stood, brushing the stray blades of grass from his breeches. Then, with a slight bow, he strolled off in the direction of Goodwin Hall, his jacket tossed carelessly over one shoulder.

"Is he gone?" Nan chirped, peeking around the door frame.

Susannah jumped, startled at the sisterly intrusion. "Yes." She placed her hand over her pounding heart. "Nan, you gave me such a scare."

"What were you two talking about for such a long time out here? Did he propose again?" Becky popped her head around the door frame, pushing her cheek next to Nan's. "He looks so dashing without a cravat. More men should follow his example."

Susannah suppressed the urge to roll her eyes. "Rubbish. No, he did not propose. Why would he? Our engagement was a childish mistake. We've agreed to become friends, that is all. And I thanked him for the hamper of food from Goodwin Hall." She shooed her sisters inside with a flick of her wrist. "Scoot. Both of you. We need to work on our displays."

Nan and Becky groaned and trudged back inside.

"I always thought Daniel was handsome," Nan muttered.

Becky sighed. "So debonair."

Susannah propped herself against the door frame, pausing for a moment to gather her wits. One must be very, very cautious with overly romantic sisters. In her case, it was always the two of them against her. 'Twas easy indeed to become outnumbered and overwhelmed. Why, they could lead you to think that a fellow cared, or that a handsome face made up for a lack of character.

She must never forget, even if she did forgive.

"Have another drink, my good fellow." Paul splashed more scotch into Daniel's glass, droplets of the precious amber liquid flicking across Daniel's sleeve. "After all, you lose me to London in a day or so. Off to have a good long debauch before settling down for the winter."

Daniel sipped slowly. The day had started late and brought him into too much contact with too many stark reminders of his own deficiencies. Maybe if he drank enough, he could drown the memory of Susannah sitting on the porch, the late-afternoon sun bronzing the gorgeous waterfall of her auburn hair…

Or the look in her eyes as she assured him their engagement was a childish indiscretion.

"By Jove, man, I might as well be talking to a statue. Why so quiet this evening?" Paul sank onto the settee and grinned. "Will you miss my company that much?"

"Don't be daft." Daniel tried to catch the spirit of camaraderie but failed. He was tired of pretense. "I feel the walls pressing in on me. Responsibility and duty and all that." He took another mouthful of scotch, allowing it to burn like acid down his throat.

"So? Chuck it all. Join me in London and leave it all to your estate manager." Paul sat forward eagerly. "I shall meld daylight slumbers with evenings spent crawling through the worst places imaginable, until my bachelor appetite is quite satisfied."

Ugh. What a disgusting way to waste a trip to Town.

Daniel raised his eyebrows in surprise at his gut reaction. Just weeks ago, he would have found Paul's plan enticing. Why the change to anathema?

"No, thank you. I must be getting old. I'd rather drink at home and fall asleep in my own bed." He swirled the scotch in his glass with a meditative air. "You'll have to accomplish enough degradation for two, I am afraid."

"You do sound old." Paul laughed, a sly look creeping across his features. "Ready to settle down, are you? Perhaps take up where you left off with Susannah Siddons?"

"Stubble it." Daniel willed his temper to subside. "We've agreed to remain friends."

"Easy, easy." Paul held his palm up in a placatory gesture and settled back on the settee. "I take it you saw her today?"

"Yes." Perhaps if he spoke of the work Susannah was doing, Paul would leave their failed engagement alone. "You should see the place, Paul. That tumbledown building has been completely transformed. Those three girls work harder than any laborer here on the farm. I'm quite astonished by all they've accomplished."

"Did she appreciate the gift?" Paul winked.

"Yes, she did." Daniel cast his glass aside and scrubbed his brow with a weary hand. "I can't give her extravagant gifts again, Paul. Not even when I am in my cups. She's too proud, and she works so diligently. I don't want to make life harder for her than it should be. I know you think it's all a grand joke, but I cannot find it amusing. Not when I have so much and she has so little." He faced his friend squarely. "I must ask you to respect our pact. I'm a hopeless drunkard and a shirker, but we need to have deference for all Susannah has done to keep her little family together. Do I have your word?"

Paul pursed his lips, a sheepish look in his eyes. "Of course. Never meant to cause trouble. You know me. Everything—even love—is fodder for comedy. But I will respect your privacy. And raise enough trouble in Town for the two of us."

Daniel nodded, a smile quirking his lips. "That's the best I can hope for."

Chapter Six

In the dim morning light, Susannah peered around her new home. More than a home. This was their hope for the future.

There was nothing more to do, at least when it came to scrubbing and cleaning the place. Even their living quarters upstairs had been scoured—the wood floors sanded, cobwebs swept away, the iron bedsteads freshly painted white. The cheerful quilts that all three girls had pieced on rainy afternoons now graced the beds, and Becky had whipped up a pair of pink calico curtains for their dormer window. Downstairs, in the shop area, the girls had created an attractive window display, framed by Becky's gossamer muslin curtains.

Nan had really outdone herself this time. A collection of their finest hats was arranged in artful pageantry, all on hat stands of varying height. Nan had woven ribbons above the display in a bright, colorful web. From outside the store, one was drawn in by the promise of beauty.

Now, if only the customers would come.

Susannah had painted a sign herself, in graceful script, proclaiming Siddons Sisters Millinery. The sign was simply too heavy for her to hang, so it leaned against the front wall, beneath the window. Perhaps she could hire a couple of lads in the village, sturdy boys who could scramble up on the roof and hang the sign properly. Until then, this would have to do.

She opened the door, letting the fresh air in. "Girls!" she called. "Do hurry, I'm opening the store."

"There won't be a mad rush." Nan yawned, traipsing down the stairs. "It's bound to be slow at first."

"Even so, we must appear professional. No dawdling." She surveyed Nan and Becky as they presented themselves for review. The sisters had agreed to wearing matching dresses in dark blue, with starched white aprons. Susannah and Becky had wound their hair up into chignons, while Nan's dark locks flowed in ringlets down her back.

"I think we look quite nice," Susannah offered cautiously. "Now, do we all have tasks to perform for today? We don't want to fall idle and daydream the morning away if we don't have customers."

"I shall be embroidering a white grosgrain ribbon with cherry blossoms. And Nan is going to work on tatting lace. If we work ahead on trimmings, then we shall have them ready when a new order comes in." Becky smoothed her apron and smiled.

"Very good. And I shall work on making a new poke bonnet in nice autumnal shades. I think we have our best opportunity of attracting new customers by opening as we are, on Saturday. If I recall correctly, this is the busiest day of the week in the village." Her memories of Tansley had faded. After all, she left the village when she was still a lass of fifteen. But Mama and Papa walked into the village every Saturday to do the little bit of marketing they needed. And it was always cause for a great occasion.

She settled onto a low stool by the rough wooden table, wrapping brown taffeta over the bonnet frame. Her hands trembled. She must not expect to see any customers today. Building a successful store would take time. And she mustn't let her sisters see how very nervous she was. Since Mama died, it was her duty to make sure the girls remained sheltered and protected. Even under the direst of circumstances, she could not contribute in any way to making them feel uncertain or afraid.

The taffeta slid easily through the bonnet frame, soothing her ruffled spirit. Having an occupation was a good thing. It kept her mind from wandering too far. If she allowed those thoughts of possible failure to flow through her, she would accomplish nothing. Willing her fingers to cease their trembling, she threaded a needle and started the arduous task of placing tiny, even stitches under the brim to hold the taffeta in place.

She would be a rock for Becky and Nan, just as she'd always been.

But all the same, 'twould be nice to have someone she could talk to, and to share her fears with.

A light footstep sounded on the threshold. "Look at this!" a cultured, sweet voice remarked. "A proper millinery here, in Tansley."

Susannah glanced up, her heart beating fast. A slight, pretty young lady stood in the doorway, a delighted expression on her face. Behind her, two other ladies peered in through the shop window. Well-dressed ladies, ladies who—judging by appearances only, of course—might be gentlewomen.

Susannah rose, her knees quaking so badly she hesitated for a moment before stepping forward. Gracious, one couldn't very well fall flat on the floor before her very first customers. She must compose herself. Susannah offered a slight smile—the best she could under such trying circumstances.

"Yes, ma'am. We've just opened. Won't you come in." Her voice sounded as wobbly as an old cart-wheel, and she cleared her throat.

"I should say so. Annabella! Evangeline! Do come in!" The lady turned to her companions. "It's the loveliest little shop I've seen—thought at first I had imagined it."

Her companions scurried in, giggling. "Oh, Eliza! Isn't it marvelous?" One of the ladies—Evangeline? Or Annabella? At any rate, the blonde one wearing her hair in stylish ringlets—clapped her gloved hands in rapture. "Now we don't have to wait to go to Town for new bonnets."

"I'll take the blue satin one in the window," Eliza's other companion, a regal brunette, stated flatly. "Do you have more ready-made than is in your display?"

Susannah paused. They had crafted very few bonnets—she'd wanted to earn more money before whipping up a dozen or so to have ready for purchase in the shop. The supplies were expensive, after all. But stating that to these fine ladies might make her shop seem small and cheap indeed.

"I beg your pardon, ma'am, but you see our bonnets are made to specification. We work to make sure that each one is suited to the wearer and is a perfect match not just for her clothing but for her features, as well. So, you see, we do not have much stock ready-made."

Nan and Becky looked up from their work, their dark eyes reflecting merriment and respect as Susannah made her bold pronouncement. Why hadn't she thought of this before? Because the thought of a bespoke milliner in a sleepy village was patently absurd. But that was before her first customers proved to be gentlewomen.

'Twas a daring move, to be certain. She clutched the half-finished bonnet to her bosom. Surely those fine gentlewomen could hear her heart pounding like a big bass drum.

"Delightful! So we could order anything we want, and to match our gowns." Eliza waved a hand airily about the room. "I am working on my winter wardrobe with my seamstress, Anne. I should like to have you come up to the house and see what she has planned in the way of gowns, and then you can plan bonnets and hats to match."

"And me, as well." The blonde withdrew her card from her card-case and held it toward Susannah with a regal gesture. "Coombe Hall is my home. Perhaps you could come on Thursday next?"

"Yes, of course." Susannah grasped the scrap of paper and scanned it quickly. The Honorable Evangeline Snowden. Gracious above, the gentry. Just as she'd suspected. "I shall be there with one of my two assistants whenever you wish." She indicated her sisters with a slight lift of her shoulder and placed the unfinished bonnet on the rough wooden table beside her.

"You shan't have her before me," Eliza scolded playfully, tapping Evangeline lightly on the arm. "Miss Siddons is my discovery. I was the one who insisted on coming into the village today, and I saw her shop first." She turned to Susannah, her smile causing her dimples to leap. "Can you be at my home on Monday? After noon, I should think. It's Kelwedge Hall, and I shall send my carriage for you." Eliza held out her calling card, as well, and Susannah accepted it with a curtsy.

"Of course, ma—" Susannah stopped abruptly and read the card. The Honorable Elizabeth Glaspell. Oh, dear. How was one to address an Honorable Miss? She cast her mind around desperately. If she was going to play the toffy milliner, she'd have to learn how to address lords and ladies properly.

Eliza chuckled at Susannah's confusion. "Never mind. Just call me Miss Glaspell. Shall I send the carriage for you on Monday, then?"

Susannah nodded and bobbed another curtsy. "Of course, Miss Glaspell."

"May I still purchase that fetching little blue bonnet?" Annabella began rummaging in her reticule. "It's a display piece, so still a one-off. Will this cover it?" She pressed a few notes into Susannah's hand.

"We had not planned to sell that particular item or any from the display, but since you've taken a fancy to it…" Susannah trailed off. Giddiness made her head swim. If only the trio would leave soon, she could sit back down, calm her trembling knees and have a bracing cup of tea.

"Good." Annabella removed the bonnet from the hat stand with a satisfied air, and Nan scurried forward with one of their precious few hat boxes. Nan tucked the bonnet in with a flourish, tying the box lid on with one of her elaborate bows.

"I share seamstresses with Evangeline," Annabella said, taking the box from Nan. "So when you go to Coombe Park, I will work with you at the same time." She handed Susannah her card.

Susannah glanced over the ivory scrap of paper. *The Honorable Miss Annabella Prestwidge* was engraved upon it in elegant script. Gentry clients—even the fragments of their existence, such as this card—were refined beyond compare.

"Of course." Susannah nodded. "Thursday next."

The three ladies left as abruptly as they had arrived, chattering and giggling among themselves. As the sound of their voices faded, Susannah dropped into her chair. Exhaustion and elation swamped her. One bonnet sold, and the promise of commissions? This was more than she dared hope.

"Susannah, you were brilliant!" Becky rushed over, enveloping her in a fierce hug. "I am so proud of you! You were as cool as could be—— If it had been me, I should have fainted from nerves!"

"Nonsense." Her trembling voice surely belied the forthright pronouncement. "'Twas nothing at all. Becky, you shall watch the store on Monday, and I shall take Nan with me as my assistant. As the second eldest, you should be in charge. Next year, when Nan turns seventeen, then she can watch the store by herself."

"Don't be absurd," Nan countered, but Becky shushed her.

"Think of it, Nan! You'll get to see Miss Glaspell's fine home. And they'll come to regard you as an apprentice." Becky gave her sister an encouraging smile.

"Oh, very well." Nan sighed. She turned to Susannah. "I'll go with you."

"Thank you for your gracious acceptance," Susannah remarked dryly. "Now, back to work, ladies. We may have more customers, and we may not. The best way to make the day pass quickly is to work. And that way, when we do visit Miss Glaspell and these other gentlewomen, we shall have more trimmings with which to whip up dazzling adornments."

Her admonishment proved sound, for though they left the door open and the fine weather drew many people to the village that day, not another soul crossed their threshold. Women would venture down to their quiet end of the street and steal a peep at the shop window, but either out of timidity or lack of interest, they wandered off.

If they hadn't received the attention of the Honorable Misses Eliza, Annabella and Evangeline, she would have felt very low indeed. As it was, their early success made her hopes rise almost too high, even though she'd cautioned her sisters against the same failing.

As the afternoon light faded, she cast her work aside and surveyed her sisters. They were working side by side, chattering away like magpies. They'd always been close. Whereas Susannah had always been like their mother. A pang of something like envy shot through her as she watched them together. How nice it would be to have a confidant. Someone she could chatter on with about the day's success.

Gracious. That was the second time she'd harbored such a thought lately. She stretched, unknotting her back as she reached her arms toward the ceiling. How ridiculous—to be mooning over her lack of close friends. What she needed to focus upon was her own dawning independence. If she relied on no one, then she had nothing to fear. No one could abandon her. No one would hurt her. She would earn her own bread and be beholden to herself only.

But somehow, that old comforting thought had lost its appeal.

She must be tired and hungry. That was all.

Susannah turned her mind to the practical matters at hand. And what could they have for supper? Perhaps she could use some of the profit from the bonnet sale to buy a little celebratory dinner. "Girls, I shall go down the street and see if I can find some sort of repast for us. You two finish up what you're doing, and lay the table. I shall be back directly."

The girls murmured their approval but did not look up from their handiwork. Susannah tucked the money into her reticule and stepped out, slinging a wooden basket over her arm.

As she ventured forth, a strong hand caught her arm, and she gasped. A robber? Set to steal her day's profits? Her mouth went dry as she whirled to confront her assailant.

"Hello, Susannah," a confident male voice greeted her cheerily, and she gazed up into familiar green eyes that sparkled with mischief. "How was the first day?"

Susannah looked as though she was ready to strike him or cry. "Are you all right?" Daniel asked, leaning in close to her. He caught her faint scent of orange blossom and closed his eyes for a brief moment. Ever since she was a girl, Susannah had had the knack of capturing his full attention, of swamping his senses. No other woman, not even in the far corners of the world, had quite the same captivating effect upon him as Susannah Siddons.

Even the headache that throbbed all day, a reminder of the previous night's drinking bout with Paul, had begun to subside when he found Susannah.

"You startled me, that is all." She took a step backward and removed his hand from her arm. "Do you always jump out at unsuspecting milliners?"

"No, this is my first opportunity." He cast a lighthearted grin her way and took the basket. "Wither are you bound?"

"To find food. The bounty you sent from Goodwin has dwindled." Her responses were brief, but some of the brittleness had gone from her voice. That was a good sign.

"You could join me at the Hall for dinner."

Susannah halted in her tracks, staring up at him with an exasperated frown. "How would that be remotely proper?"

"It wouldn't be proper. But it might be fun. And we agreed to be friends." He quirked an eyebrow at her. "After all, what do you care what anyone says? Aren't you your own woman now?"

"I am, but as a working lass with my own business, I should hold myself above reproach." She made a move to swipe the basket from him and he skipped back a pace, grinning. "Oh, do stop, Daniel. You look ridiculous, and people will see us together."

He gave an exaggerated sigh, as though admitting defeat. "Very well, Miss Prim-and-Proper Siddons. I shall conduct myself with great deportment if you will answer my first question, about your first day. And I shall accompany you to any store you desire, so that you may buy food."

"To the bakery, then," Susannah ordered, pointing out the way as though he were a newcomer to the village. He stifled a grin. Susannah always was at ease ordering people about. "My day went very well, thank you. I have three new customers, all of them gentry. I think it shall turn out well. I am cautiously hopeful."

"That is excellent news." His heart surged with pride. Susannah could accomplish anything she set her mind to, that was for certain.

"And how was your day?" she asked, her tone polite and even. She must be adhering to her own inner conscience, reminding her that she had promised to be friendly, after all.

"'Twas…" He paused. While she had toiled at her shop, he'd slept, ate a vast repast, bathed and finally, at this late hour, ventured into the village in the hopes of running into her.

Not that he was seeking her out, of course. But he was interested in her little shop and how well she fared.

"'Twas quite…relaxed." He shrugged. "Not as exciting as yours."

"I doubt that." She looked up at him, a smile hovering around her pretty lips. "With such a large estate? I am certain it keeps you busy morn to night."

She halted before the bakery, the spicy scents of cinnamon and cloves beckoning them in. "I should go. I need to feed everyone and put us to bed in time for church tomorrow morning."

"Church?" He laughed incredulously. "The closest one is St. Mary's. In Crich. Don't you remember? Nearly a four-mile ride."

"Oh." She looked crestfallen, as she bowed her head. "Yes, you are right. I haven't been there since I was fifteen years old. I forgot how far we used to journey on Sundays. Well, I shall have to simply have my own little service in the morning. I've much to be thankful for, you see."

"I see." He handed her the basket and touched the brim of his hat. "Well, I am glad you had such a good day, Susannah. With so much to be grateful for." He turned to go.

"Thank you, Daniel." The warmth of her voice took him off guard. He glanced at her from under the brim of his hat and was rewarded with a smile—the first genuine one she'd bestowed on him since he'd stopped her from breaking her own door down.

He smiled back and struck out across the moor for Goodwin. Paul was gone, so he would be completely and utterly alone. He suddenly hated social conventions with a passion that startled him. How nice it would be to have dinner with Susannah and her two sisters, just as friends, nothing more.

After all, she'd made it quite clear that even friendship was a stretch after the wrong he'd done her.

Chapter Seven

The sun crept over the moors Sunday morning, illuminating their small living quarters with hazy sunlight. Susannah suppressed a shiver as she wrapped a quilt closer about her person. Already the faint chill heralded autumn's approach. She'd have to earn a good deal of money—enough to purchase firewood, and to buy wool to make gowns for her sisters, and—oh, gracious, it was all too much.

She tossed off the quilt and grabbed her wrapper from the foot of the bed and tied it around herself, winding the sash into a tight bow. Then she stole across the wooden floor. Already she had discovered which floorboards creaked, so the process of making it from her bed to the staircase and from the staircase to the stove downstairs was rather like making the figures of a minuet. But she performed the dance wonderfully well, for her sisters still lay sleeping in their beds.

She stirred up the fire and laid the kettle on. How disappointing not to be able to attend church. Of course, St. Mary's had been their home parish when they lived in Tansley so long ago, but one expected that, over the years, a new church would have come to Tansley. She'd have to bring her battered Bible down from the trunk upstairs, and when the girls awoke, they could have their own prayer meeting here, at the kitchen table.

The teakettle whistled loudly, as though reminding her where her duties lay. She scooped tea leaves into the strainer and poured the boiling water over them. Warming her hands around the cup, she settled back into her chair and breathed deeply, savoring the spicy scent of her tea as it brewed.

As she waited, a handsome carriage flashed past. How odd, to have a member of the gentry here in the village on a Sunday morning. Teacup in hand, she strolled over to the display window to have a closer look.

Gracious, how very strange. The carriage stopped just past the shop, and as she watched, a servant in a vaguely familiar uniform alit. She took a step back in shock, and the older man strode purposefully past the window and knocked sharply on her door.

Susannah set the cup on the display table and looked down at her dishabille in dismay. There was no way she could dress herself and be presentable in enough time to answer his knock. And no way to pretend she hadn't heard—he might have glimpsed her spying on him through the window. Well, if gentry needed a bonnet at the crack of dawn on a Sunday, she should not expect her milliner to be dressed to perfection.

Tightening her wrapper around her middle, she opened the door slightly. "Yes?"

"Miss Siddons," the servant said with a bow. "Mr. Hale has sent you his carriage to use today. His understanding is that you wish to attend services at St. Mary's in Crich.

Our instructions are to take you and your sisters there and to bring you home whenever you wish."

Susannah gasped. Should she be scandalized that she would be traipsing around the countryside in a young man's carriage, or should she be grateful at Daniel's generosity? This was so much like the old Daniel she'd known. Scandalously generous. Turning such a blind eye to society's dictates that he had no concept of the havoc he could wreak.

"Thank you, but—" she managed to say weakly.

"Mr. Hale said we were not to leave until we had fulfilled our duties, miss. So if you'll pardon me, we shall just be waiting in the carriage until you and your sisters are ready." With a bow that put paid to any further argument, the servant walked back to the carriage and clasped his hands behind his back with a dignified gesture.

Susannah shut the door and leaned against it, her head swimming. If she continued to refuse, then soon the rest of the village would be treated to the sight of Daniel's carriage waiting, immovably, before her shop.

A scuffling of sisterly feet cascaded down the staircase.

"Susannah! Whatever is happening?" Becky panted as she and Nan scurried into the room.

"Daniel sent his carriage for us. So we could go to St. Mary's for services." Susannah crossed her arms over her chest and leaned against the door.

"Wonderful! How lovely of him to think of us." Becky clapped her hands. "I can be ready in two shakes of a lamb's tail."

"And I can, too," Nan added. "After all those years at Uncle's and no church services, how nice it will be to attend a proper Sabbath service."

"We can't go," Susannah stated flatly. "We can't very well be seen traipsing all over the countryside in a young bachelor's carriage. What would people think?"

"It's not as though we are going to Vauxhall Gardens," Becky chided, a frown creasing her lips. "Going to church is perfectly respectable."

"And if we send them away, it could hurt Daniel's feelings. He is trying to be nice," Nan reminded Susannah, her most wheedling "baby sister" expression on her face.

"They won't go away. His servant just assured me that they would not leave without us." Susannah sighed, exasperation welling in her soul. "What am I to do? They'll cause a scandal if they stay, and we'll create a scandal if we go."

Her sisters fell quiet, contemplating the matter. Nan twirled a long, dark lock of hair around one finger, as was her habit when deep in thought. As Susannah surveyed them, her old feelings of protectiveness surged within. No matter what happened, her sisters had to be protected and sheltered from anything bad that could happen. Even if harm befell her, 'twas her duty to protect them.

'Twas the only thing keeping her from storming outside, nightgown and all, to inform that smug servant just exactly where he could drive that carriage.

"Perhaps we could ask him to come along," Becky finally ventured, raising her dark, soulful eyes to Susannah's. "We could ask him to come with us, and then no one would think a thing of it."

"Yes!" Nan's head snapped up. "And if you are still worried about scandal, we could tell him to bring a maid along to chaperone. Our families were old friends, after all."

"I don't know…" Susannah murmured. It did make a

kind of sense. And Becky's plan served two purposes. It allowed them to remove the carriage from the outside of the store, and it allowed her the chance to give Daniel a choice little piece of her mind. But still—attend services with Daniel? She stifled a laugh at the thought. He'd never attended services before, not even in his youth. 'Twas unlikely indeed that he would start doing so now.

So if Daniel didn't come, she could at least be rid of his carriage, and she could give him a right talking-to for sending it over to begin with. "Very well. I agree, it's the only solution we can find, given the terribly short notice." She motioned to her sisters with a wave of her hands. "Let's hurry and dress. If we're to drive out to Goodwin Hall, collect Daniel and then drive out to Crich, we mustn't dawdle."

Nan rushed out of the room, her footsteps echoing two at a time as she climbed the stairs. But Becky stayed behind and fixed Susannah with one of her rare, pointed looks.

"Promise me you'll be kind to him. He offered his carriage out of politeness and nothing more."

And nothing more! Susannah bit back a bitter chuckle at that. There were a hundred reasons Daniel would have sent his carriage—to tease her, to worry her, to make a joke, to make sport of her religion. None of them were kind. He was always so mischievous that his jokes had, as a child, bordered on rudeness.

"I'll keep a civil tongue in my head," she agreed.

But she refused to agree to more than that.

Daniel stirred, his cheek brushing against something that crackled painfully. There were noises in the hall. Terribly loud, cackling sounds like an enormous chicken leading two baby chicks. He forced his eyes open, wincing at the pain of the action. He'd fallen asleep in the study. With infinitesimally small movements, he pushed himself up to a sitting position. The ledger book had been his pillow last night. As he raised his hands to steady his spinning head, he caught a glimpse of a long ink smear across one palm.

Well, he had tried, after all, to do something about those ridiculous accounts that Donaldson had pestered him about. It's just, well—he couldn't do it. Account books meant obligations, and obligations would turn him into a dour old man. Better to have a drink…or two… or three…than to try to master something beyond his comprehension.

The cackling sound grew louder. He opened his mouth to protest but could manage naught but a hoarse whisper.

Before he could wipe the ink from his hand, the door to the study slammed open, and Baxter bustled in as though he was being pushed from behind. "Miss Susannah Siddons, sir," he managed to say before Susannah swirled into the room.

"That will be all," Susannah assured Baxter, who bowed with something like relief before quitting the room.

Daniel blinked twice, slowly, as he gazed at Susannah. Her sudden appearance, gowned in a dark purple dress and a fetching bonnet that did little to conceal the bright glow of her hair, gave him the impression that he was being granted a favor from a queen.

And then the queen spoke.

"Daniel, it smells like a gaming hall in here." She cast her wrap aside and untied her bonnet ribbons, placing the confection on the settee. Then she stalked over to the windows, drawing the curtains and flinging up the sash of each in turn. Fresh air and sunlight poured into the room, and Daniel fought the urge to be sick. He couldn't be sick in front of a lady.

"Susy…don't…" he begged, his voice cracking.

"I'm glad I left my sisters in the entry. They shouldn't ever have to see a man looking or smelling like this. And I told you not to call me Susy." She turned from the windows and faced him, hands on her hips. "Did you send round your carriage for us when you were still in your cups? It seems like the kind of joke you'd play."

He licked his lips and took a deep breath. "No. I did it before."

"This is absurd." Susannah crossed the floor, her boot heels hammering a tattoo in his head. She grasped the bellpull and rang it. "You simply cannot go to church in this condition."

Daniel grasped his pounding head. "Do be quiet," he croaked.

"Oh, I am sorry, Mr. Hale." She gave him a mocking curtsy. "Shall I play a polka on the pianoforte? Something good and loud to awaken you?"

"No." The saliva churned in his mouth. He couldn't be sick in front of Susannah. He grasped the nearby wastebasket and breathed deeply. He was too far gone to even be ashamed.

Behind him, a gentle hand patted his back. "There, there. Keep breathing, that's the way." Susannah passed her handkerchief over his forehead. The clean scent of orange blossom soothed his roiling stomach and he closed his eyes, allowing its medicinal scent to calm him down.

The study door opened, and Susannah turned from Daniel, addressing a shocked Baxter. "Mr. Hale is sick," she informed him. "Draw his bath and have Cook make a tray of crackers and strong tea. Send them up to his bedroom when he is done bathing. And show my sisters into the parlor. We shall be here rather longer than I thought."

Daniel marveled at the speed with which she dispatched Baxter. With those commandeering ways, she could have been a ship's captain. "How did you know?" he croaked. It was all he could manage. He wanted to ask a million questions, but they would have to come later, when he felt better.

"My uncle used to come in from faro in much worse shape," she said with a shrug. "And I watched the whole household cater to him."

The vile uncle. The one who spent her inheritance and who tried to force her into an unwanted marriage. This was the uncle that had driven her to come to Daniel for help, and then he'd failed her. To be cast in the same group as him was as low as a fellow could sink. Daniel burned with shame. "I am sorry."

"Come now, don't be maudlin. Let's see if you can stand." She held out her hand and helped to draw him to his feet. He swayed unsteadily, and Susannah wrapped his arm around her shoulder. She was at least a head shorter than him, but her strength flowed through his body and his trembling eased. "Good. Let us walk forward. I shall try to get you upstairs so that Baxter may help you."

They took a step together. It was like dancing. He hadn't danced with Susannah in ever so long. He'd partnered her often in the little country gatherings that were held in the village hall, but never in those merry dances had he felt as close to her as he did at this moment. She knew all his terrible secrets now. And despite that, she was helping him.

As they made their way around his desk, he allowed his head to droop—just a bit—as he breathed in deeply. Susannah smelled so good. Her orange blossom scent was curative in its potency today. And if he leaned a bit closer, he could just catch the scent of her magnificent auburn hair, twisted and looped on top of her head. Would her hair smell like orange blossoms, too?

His mind flashed back to the day they'd sat on her back porch, the length of her hair unbound and flowing to her waist. Why hadn't he tried to touch a lock of her hair as it had floated in the late-afternoon breeze? The thought of how lovely she'd looked as the setting sun gilded her red hair to gold caught in his throat and he coughed painfully.

Why was he always reminiscing about Susannah and how she had been, how she had looked, how she had spoken?

Why did she linger in his mind so persistently?

"There now, we're almost to the banister," she murmured in her quiet voice as they crossed the threshold. "Can you make it up the stairs alone? Or shall I call Baxter?"

"Can't you help me?" he asked. If he kept her with him a little bit longer, maybe he could solve the mystery. 'Twas rather like a Gothic novel. *The Mystery of the Captivating Auburn-Haired Lady.*

"Don't be daft," she muttered. "'Tis scandalous enough that you sent your carriage for me. And even more scandalous that I am here, now, helping you, as it is. I can't very well assist you to your room." She paused at the foot of the stairs and gazed up at him. "Can you make it on your own?"

He looked at the staircase. It shifted strangely from side to side, and he blinked a few times before forcing himself to focus. "Yes, I think I can."

"Very good." She took his arm from around her shoulder and placed his hand on the banister. "Go slowly. I shall watch your progress from here. I don't want you to fall and hurt yourself."

He took a careful step. All was going better than he thought. He might actually make it up the stairs under his own power. And all this thanks to his fiancée. He owed her a debt of gratitude. "Susannah, please stay for luncheon. 'Tis the least I can do to thank you, after all your help this morning."

She tilted her chin, as though considering his offer and preparing to give him a sharp no. Then, inexplicably, her features changed, and she nodded. "Very well. My sisters are here with me. Do you object to them staying, as well?"

"No, indeed." He liked Nan and Becky. They were both sweet, good-tempered girls. Having them here would chase off the hours of monotony and make the day speed by faster. "I should like to have you all as my guests this afternoon. I shall be down as soon as I can."

"Don't rush yourself," she cautioned dryly. "Do take your time."

Daniel chuckled and ascended the stairs slowly, one at a time. Above him, Baxter awaited, drawing his bathwater. Below, Susannah patiently watched his progress, her gloved hand clutching the balustrade.

He was a fortunate fellow indeed to have people to take care of him.

If only he'd taken care of others half as well.

Chapter Eight

Baxter knocked discreetly on the parlor door before showing himself in. "Miss Siddons, Mr. Hale has asked if you would make your own selections for luncheon. You may have anything you wish, according to the master."

Susannah glanced up in surprise. Usually these fine houses had menus planned out well in advance. "I wouldn't dream of changing whatever Cook has chosen for today's menu."

Baxter gave a slight cough. "There was no menu set for today, Miss Siddons. You may choose anything you wish, and Cook will be only too glad to make it for you."

Susannah's confusion grew, and she drew her eyebrows together. "But surely Mr. Hale wanted lunch?"

"Mr. Hale will usually have a slice of bread or some bacon. When he remembers to eat." Baxter shifted his weight uneasily and looked down as though he found his shoes suddenly quite interesting.

The bachelor lifestyle. How very provoking. Here Daniel had an entire estate at his command, servants aplenty, and he would gnaw at a crust of bread for luncheon. Oh, what she could do with just one servant to help her! She paused for a moment, allowing her mind to drift. Someone to help with the cooking and the cleaning…to run errands…

She snapped back to reality and gave herself a little shake. "Then I think we shall have a roast chicken. Have the cook rub it in rosemary—that will give it a nice flavor. A few vegetables—haricots verts, perhaps? And new potatoes. Bread with butter, of course. And for dessert, perhaps a fool or a trifle."

Beside her, Nan and Becky smiled appreciatively, and Baxter bowed with respect. "Of course, Miss Siddons. Anything else?"

"Yes, Baxter." She drew herself up and looked him straight in the eye. "Absolutely no wine with our meal."

A smile hovered over the butler's reserved features. "As you wish, Miss Siddons."

Both girls waited until Baxter closed the door, and then Becky leaped from the settee. "Oh, Susannah, you thought of a menu just like that. Just like a lady of the manor. Imagine having all this to call your very own. Are you so certain that you wouldn't be happy as Mrs. Daniel Hale?"

"Hush." Heat rushed to Susannah's cheeks. What if Daniel overheard her sister's babbling? "Don't be absurd. There was never a thought in his mind or in mine that I would be mistress of Goodwin Hall."

"But, Sue," Nan implored, her dark eyes sparkling. "Imagine. Servants to do your bidding. A grand home. And acres and acres of beautiful land." She indicated the view through the window of the rolling moors stretching out as far as the eye could see, framed by damask curtains.

"Yes, Daniel has been blessed. But the only reason we

are here—and not in church—is because Daniel was—" how to say this delicately? "—quite sick when we arrived. I want to make certain that he is well before we leave. We shall dine with him and then go home to say our prayers. And there is to be no more talk about life here at Goodwin. We should be quite satisfied with the life we have." She shot her sisters her best "eldest sister" look. "Understand?"

"Yes, Susannah."

"Yes, Sue."

Even though her siblings promised to stop their reminiscing, Susannah found it difficult not to allow her thoughts to wander the same path. How would her life be different now, had her engagement to Daniel run its course? What if they had wed, after all? Would she, even now, be planning the week's menu with Cook in the kitchen? Would she be waiting for her husband to escort her to church, his green eyes dancing with mischief and a dimple creasing his angular cheek?

She suppressed a snort. Very unlikely. He'd have run away or found some way to disappoint her, for this kind of life—the responsibilities, the duties—was his idea of a nightmare. She trailed her finger along the smooth mahogany table, relishing the satiny feel of the wood. Imagine anyone hating this house. Or this life. Everything at Goodwin spoke of tradition, of safety. She could throw herself into this home and it wouldn't just catch her— it would support her and nurture her for years to come. Daniel had no idea what he was tossing aside.

The door to the parlor opened, and Daniel came in. His pallor remained somewhat ashen, and the dark circles beneath his eyes spoke of his all-too-recent illness, but he smiled warmly at them all as he surveyed the room.

"How refreshing it is to have three lovely ladies with whom to dine," he proclaimed with a gallant air, causing Nan and Becky to giggle. "Surely Prince George himself isn't half as fortunate as I."

"Thank you for inviting us," Becky replied. "Susannah ordered a lovely repast for us. What a treat, to be dining in such a wonderful home."

"What did you request, Susannah?" He turned his full attention to her, as though she were the only woman in the world, and her heart skipped a beat.

Ridiculous nonsense. Daniel had always been a charmer, and at his best when surrounded by ladies. He wasn't really admiring her. It was just the role he chose to play. "Roast chicken and vegetables. Nothing too fancy. I did want to make sure it was a meal you could stomach after your…illness…this morning."

"Thank you." Frank admiration shone through his gaze. "I declare that your sister can handle any situation with grace and charm," he informed Nan and Becky.

The girls murmured kind words of support, and Daniel insisted that only Susannah's skills as a nurse had kept him alive. Oh, gracious. It was all getting to be too much—too much flattery, too much niceness, too much of being in Daniel's presence. She must gain control of the situation or risk having her head decidedly turned by his engaging ways—or losing her temper altogether. He didn't mean any of it seriously, so she must learn to keep matters very much on the surface with him.

"Yes, well. We thank you for your luncheon invitation. But afterward, we must return home. We missed services this morning and need to have our own prayer meeting." There. That was a pointed reminder that the whole reason they were here was church—and his insistence from the beginning on conveying them there in his own vehicle.

"Prayer meeting? That sounds interesting. I should like to join you, if I may," Daniel replied easily. As though she had invited him to tea, or to a musical recital.

Wasn't religion one of the things he had shunned all his life? Why, then, the polite feigned interest?

"I shouldn't wish to bore you," she began, her tone brittle even to her own ears. Her own faith was something she kept close to her heart. Uncle Arthur had been an avowed atheist and mocked her and the girls whenever he caught them praying. And he made sure they'd never attended services at any church while under his care.

"Nonsense." He cut her short with a wave of his hand. "'Tis the least I can do, especially after ruining your morning."

She opened her mouth to protest but was interrupted by Baxter's arrival. "Your luncheon is ready, sir."

"Excellent. I am famished. Ladies, after you." With a wave of his hand, Daniel ushered the younger girls out of the room. Then he turned to Susannah, offering her his arm. He said nothing, only gazed at her with an inscrutable expression, the troublemaking glint in his eyes completely extinguished.

She accepted his arm without a word and allowed him to lead her down the hallway to the dining room. How very odd, this feeling of naturalness at Goodwin Hall. She hadn't been here since she was a girl, so it was not an ease borne out of familiarity.

What, then? Why was she so comfortable here? Why had helping Daniel come so easily to her this morning?

She gave herself a small mental shake. It didn't matter

why, or how. She was in danger of becoming too much like Becky, mooning over every common situation.

Funny how a little sister could affect one so much. She must be on her guard against such thoughts.

Who knew that luncheon at Goodwin Hall could be such a delicious and convivial affair? Daniel speared the last of the rosemary-rubbed chicken on his plate. The meal that Susannah had ordered was simple and yet sublime, stabilizing his roiling stomach and clearing his pounding head. The notable lack of wine was rather provoking, but one look at Susannah's stern expression, her eyebrow delicately arched, was enough to dissuade him from asking for the decanter. Dining with the sisters was a warm and joyful experience. No great, earth-shaking conversation was made, and no new philosophies were discovered, but what a change from getting progressively drunker with Paul, or making do with a slice of bread and butter.

If only he could give something to them. Something to express his thanks for lifting his loneliness. And Susannah deserved a gift just for coming to his rescue this morning.

Susannah had mentioned having a prayer meeting. And he had tried to help her go to church this morning. Hang convention—she should be able to ride around in his carriage as much as she wanted, especially if all she wanted to do was attend a Sabbath service. He wasn't much on religion, of course, but if that's what made Susannah happy...

Mother's chapel. That was it. He hadn't been in the little cottage in ages, and surely it was a bit run-down, but why shouldn't Susannah have the use of it?

"Excuse me. I shall return directly." He nodded briefly to his guests and rushed from the room, colliding with dignified old Baxter in the hallway.

"Beg pardon, sir," Baxter huffed. "I did not see you there."

"It does not signify, for I was in search of you. Do you know Mother's old chapel, on the north end of the estate?"

"Yes." Baxter knitted his brows. "I recall it, but I do not think anyone has set foot in it for years."

"I want you to send a couple of men out to make it ready to show my guests." Daniel raked his hand through his hair. "After we finish our meal, I wish to take them out to see the chapel."

"But, really, sir. The chapel hasn't been opened in years. I hardly think it will be in fine enough condition for you to show your guests." Baxter's tone conveyed the kind of mild annoyance he usually reserved for Daniel's drunken orders. What was the use of having servants if none of them paid heed to your needs?

"Yes, yes, I am aware of that. Just have the men open it up and make sure there are no creatures that have taken up permanent residence there. I know it's no palace. I just want Sus—Miss Siddons to see it."

Was that the trace of a grin on Baxter's normally dour face? "Very good."

"Don't be cheeky," Daniel muttered as he turned on his heel. One's servants could be most annoying. He'd never asked for this life. Really, he hadn't.

As he entered the dining room, Susannah rose. "If you want to join us for prayers, Daniel, we should probably do so shortly. I never meant to stay so long. And the girls and I have much to prepare for tomorrow."

"Yes, Nan and Susannah are going to Miss Glaspell's house. She's ordering enough bonnets for a season!" Becky piped up proudly.

Daniel turned to Susannah. Already her shop was becoming a success, and she'd only opened it for a day. His mouth turned downward in a rueful grin and he shook his head. Yes, Susannah should have been captain of a ship. Why, with her determination and her desire for success, she would drive the French out of their own homeland.

"Why am I not surprised? Already you are becoming a success. With gentry clientele, you shall go far, and fast." He held out his hand to Susannah. "Come, there is something I want to show you. All of you," he hastened to add.

Susannah stepped forward, her brows drawn together. "What for?"

"I promise 'tis no joke," he assured her. She drew closer but ignored his outstretched hand.

Perhaps his touch was too personal. He offered his elbow instead. "I haven't seen this in years," he admitted. "I'd like to share it with you."

He led Susannah and her sisters out of the house and across the lawn. He breathed in deeply. The smell of drying moor-grass and Susannah's scent of orange blossom created an exhilarating perfume. The rolling pasture was quite lovely, and as they strolled about it, the old dread of responsibility left him. It was pleasing to share this part of his life with someone else. Someone who might appreciate it and care.

The woods around Goodwin surrounded the Hall in a sort of half-moon shape, and in the clearing, the little chapel stood—a bit run-down with the passing of time, to be sure, but still gleaming like a jewel against the emerald background of trees.

Beside him, Susannah stopped, gasping. "It's lovely. I never knew anything like this was here."

"My mother had it built," he explained. "Crich was so far for her to attend services. And when her health began to fail, she wanted still to be able to worship." Funny, he hadn't spoken of Mother in years, and as he recalled her last few days—her ebbing health, her weakness, her frailty—he found it difficult to swallow.

He must pull himself together. He had been nothing but vulnerable all day. Susannah had helped him walk in his own study, for pity's sake. He must stop this nonsense and be a man. He cleared his throat.

"I can't believe it. What a beautiful little chapel." She pulled away from him and took a step closer. Nan and Becky made twin murmurs of admiration, their hands clasped. "May I go in?"

"Yes, of course. I had the servants open it up and make things presentable enough." He brushed past her and stood on the threshold. The windows were so coated in grime that the afternoon sunlight filtered through in grayish-yellow beams, and cobwebs softened the corners of the ceiling. "It needs a great deal of work, though. If you'd like the use of it, I would be happy to have it cleared out for you."

"I don't know," Susannah murmured. She ran her fingertips over the arched door frame. "Though I should hate for it to simply rot away."

"Then it's settled. When you can't go to prayer meetings in Crich, the Siddons sisters may have their own prayer meeting here, in Goodwin Chapel. I'll have my servants start the heavy cleaning tomorrow." The thought of having a purpose, a goal, filled him with a sense of satisfaction. He had no idea how to run a farm, but he could order his servants to clean this little building.

"I think it's beautiful. Thank you, Daniel." Becky glanced at him over her shoulder, her bonnet dangling by its strings down her back.

"Yes, thank you, Daniel. Uncle never did let us worship, so this is a relief." Nan twisted a long lock of hair around her finger as Susannah cast her a sharp, quelling glance.

So Uncle Arthur had a problem with religion, too? Was there anything that man didn't ruin? He himself was not particularly religious, but just because he didn't choose to worship didn't mean he'd keep others from doing so.

"I think now is as good a time as any—and certainly the best place—for us to have our little prayer meeting." Susannah was back in charge, her voice and demeanor changing from wonderment to practicality in the blink of an eye. "Daniel, join us?"

"I should like to. How does one do it?" He was fearfully ignorant of any matter relating to God, but surely Susannah would lead the way.

She gave an embarrassed laugh. "Let us join hands."

They stood together in the old chapel, hands joined, heads bowed, as Susannah offered her prayer. "Dear Lord, thank You for all You have given us. Words cannot express how grateful we are to You—for friends, for family and for Your bounty."

"And for Your grace and Your goodness," Becky chimed in.

"And for good food," Nan supplied. Daniel suppressed a chuckle as Susannah glowered at her younger sister from under her bonnet.

"And for the kindness and solicitude of a dear friend,"

Daniel added. He kept his eyes stubbornly fixed on his boots. 'Twas the only way he could properly thank Susannah, and he'd be hanged if he'd allow her to fix him with one of her baleful glares.

As they said their amens, Daniel took the opportunity to squeeze Susannah's hand briefly before he let go.

He was grateful for her help. If only she would ever allow him to show it.

Chapter Nine

The crunch of wheels on the gravel drive outside the shop heralded the arrival of Miss Glaspell's carriage. She was as good as her word. Susannah flicked a glance at the mantel clock—one o'clock to the second.

"Nan," she called up the stairs. "Do hurry. We must go. The carriage has arrived."

"I'm coming," Nan called, her footsteps thumping across the floor, echoing above Susannah's head.

"Now, do I have everything?" Susannah combed through her parcels. "Ribbons, lace, sketches. Paper and pencils to take notes and make drawings." She glanced up as Nan rushed into the room. "Here, you take these." She piled paper-wrapped packages into Nan's outstretched arms. "Becky, we are going. Will you be all right here?"

"Of course I shall." Becky glanced up from her work with a dreamy smile. "Embroidering my cherry blossoms in reality, while strolling through fields of summer flowers in imagination."

Susannah gave an exasperated shake of her head. "As long as you are happy. But do be careful. I worry about leaving you alone."

"Don't be. I am perfectly capable of managing a store without you for a few hours."

Susannah hesitated. Becky, at eighteen, was a grown woman in her own right. But so romantic and so dreamy. Surely leaving her alone, in the charge of a business, would be all right for a little while? Unless, of course, a knight rode up on a stately steed to sweep her off her feet...

Laughter and worry struggled within her, and she had to force herself to walk over to the door. "Very well," she answered lightly. "We shall return from Miss Glaspell's as soon as we can."

They stepped over the threshold, and the bright sunlight dazzled Susannah's eyes. She put her hand up to block the sun's piercing rays. Bother. Half her parcels slid from her grasp, collecting in a pile at her feet. A servant rushed forward to help her, and the footman beckoned both girls to climb in. As he closed the door, Nan lolled against the cushions. "More comfortable than our beds! Oh, to have a carriage this fine," she murmured.

Susannah settled in, her back resting comfortably against the squabs. The carriage was quite nice, beautifully appointed with cunning little gold lanterns, and so well-sprung she could hardly feel the bumps as they drove through the village and turned on the main road out across the moors.

"Susannah, how far is it to Kelwedge Hall?" Nan asked, fingering the lace curtain at the carriage window.

"Oh, I don't know. My memories of Tansley are vague, more so than they should be. I suppose the manor houses are a good distance from here. Let us just enjoy the ride, shall we?"

"I'm a little nervous," Nan admitted, looking over at Susannah, her bright blue eyes abashed. "Are you?"

She could pronounce her usual "stuff and nonsense" and give a bracing talk about the need to be brave in the face of new changes, but all the fire was extinguished within her. She was nervous. Terrified, in fact. If this visit went well, then her little shop just might take flight. But if it didn't, there was no telling how long it would take them to get a solid business going.

"I'm a little nervous, too," she admitted, her voice quiet and subdued. "But we must have faith that this is the right path to follow."

Nan fell silent for a moment. Nan's silences were different from Becky's. Becky might be close beside you in person, but her mind would be a hundred miles away. Nan's silences were little pauses, during which she refreshed herself with new questions or observations. More questions were coming. Susannah could feel it in her bones.

"Sue—Daniel certainly has a nice home."

And there it was. How best to respond? She had no wish to revisit the past—it had no bearing on her present goals. Not now, not when so much was riding on her future.

"Yes, Goodwin Hall has always been quite nice. A grand old house." There, noncommittal but pleasant. Perhaps Nan's curiosity would be satisfied and she could turn her mind toward Miss Glaspell and her bonnets.

"I was thinking that Daniel seems like such a nice fellow. So funny. And generous, too. Sharing his mother's chapel with us is a very kind thing to do. He doesn't have to, you know." Nan stared out the window as though she found the cows and the sheep dotting the moors quite fascinating, only the curve of her cheek and a waterfall of mahogany-colored curls visible.

"I agree. Daniel has always been generous." A surge of her old anger and frustration welled within. "But then, he's always had so much. It's easy for him to share. It wouldn't mean anything to him."

"I think this did mean something to him." Nan turned from the window, her blue eyes shadowed. She looked older than her sixteen years and more like Mama than Susannah had ever noticed before. "The expression on his face when we entered the chapel—well, he looked stunned. As though someone had slapped him. And he stopped joking about."

Susannah considered this in silence. What Nan said had a bit of truth to it. She hadn't spent much time studying Daniel's face yesterday. Doing so seemed to invite that grin of his, that sly, humorous grin as though they both shared a secret. And watching him when he didn't see her—well, that was difficult, too. It was hard not to imagine him as the young lad who'd kissed her cheek and told her not to cry—that he would take care of everything—as he tied a string around her finger in lieu of a proper ring.

She must stop this foolishness now. Reliving that moment in time would lead to nothing but heartbreak and frustration.

"He shared the chapel with us and prayed with us for a reason. I don't know why. I'm not a romantic, like Becky." Nan played with her long curls, twisting one around and around her forefinger. "But I do think he's trying to make amends for the way he lived."

"What do you know about the way he lived?" Susannah's voice sharpened. What she and Becky had talked about was shared in confidence. Nan was too young to understand what a wastrel like Daniel could do when given free rein. Though Becky had a provoking tendency to think of real life in terms of the latest novel or poem she'd read, she did have a good two years on Nan.

"No one's told me much. But I could tell, this morning, that he'd probably had too much to drink. He had the same look about him, like when Uncle Arthur would come in from gambling."

Susannah sank back against the seat, defeated. Her baby sister was growing up and making her own observations about the world. Susannah would not be able to shelter her much longer. "He had been drinking and was quite sick. But I don't wish to talk about it." The gates of Kelwedge Hall flashed by the carriage window. "Look. We've arrived. And we must be calm and collected if we are to gain Miss Glaspell's trust—and her business. I can't be reminiscing about the past as we walk up to the door. We'll be too—" she cast about for the right word "—emotional."

"Very well." Nan dusted off her apron with the flat of her palms. "But I do think you're being rather hard on Daniel, Sue. He seems a sincere sort of person. I do wish, no matter what harm he did you, that you could find it in your heart to forgive him."

Being lectured by her baby sister was the very last straw. Susannah stiffened her spine and smoothed her coiffure with a hand that trembled only slightly. "That's quite enough, Nan. What happened between Daniel and myself is a private matter, and as much as I love you, I shan't talk about it anymore."

Nan turned her lips down, in a frown or in a pout. 'Twas difficult to tell, for her sister turned at once to the window, as though Kelwedge Hall's façade was the most fascinating thing she'd ever seen.

And it was. Susannah caught her breath as they drew to a halt. Kelwedge was an impressive manor home, built of dark gray stone, its solid front faced with at least two dozen windows. Ivy crept over the sides and wound its way up to the second story; a formal clipped hedge formed a complicated knot before the front steps.

And this was her new client's home? Even Goodwin, as fine as it was, wasn't as large a home as this. She'd felt comfortable at Goodwin, but here? She was as insignificant as a dormouse.

The carriage passed by the front of the house and curved around behind, drawing to a stop near the back porch. Ah, yes, of course. They couldn't go in through the front. Funny, but this moment made manifest the path she'd chosen in life. In opening her own shop, she'd become part of a different class.

The class of women who went in the back door.

"I must say, it's a marvel to find such a brilliantly talented milliner in poky old Tansley," Miss Glaspell said, glancing over Susannah's sketches. "How ever did you wind up in a country village? You should have a shop in Town, you know."

"Tansley was our home for most of our childhood," Susannah replied with a modest air. "When my uncle passed, we came back here. I think it's a lovely place to live."

"It is, but with a talent like yours, you could be making a sizable fortune running your own shop in the Burlington Arcade." Miss Glaspell cast the drawings aside. "Oh, well. London's loss is my gain. Now, we have several gowns planned for the autumn and winter months. Anne, do show her the fabrics."

Anne, Miss Glaspell's seamstress, nodded and pulled several swatches out of an embroidered bag. "We have been looking at the fashion plates and trying to decide which ones would work to Miss Glaspell's best advantage. I think this worsted would look quite fetching for a riding habit."

Susannah peered at the scrap of dark gray wool, rubbing its roughness between her fingers. "Yes. I should think a black silk top hat would set this off beautifully."

Nan leaned forward, staring at the wool intently. "But have the top hat swathed in black netting, or a veil. To soften the severity, wouldn't you think?"

Miss Glaspell clapped her hands merrily. "Perfect. I do love the idea of a severe riding costume, rather tailored, but with a slightly more feminine topper."

Susannah glanced over at Nan with approval. That would look quite stunning. How smart of Nan to think of it. The style wasn't anything like what country ladies would wear to go out riding, and so it would set Miss Glaspell apart from the rest. When and how had Nan come to possess such a strong sense of fashion?

"And this silk—I think it would do quite well as a walking dress. With a spencer made from a darker shade of velvet." Anne passed over two swatches of fabric, one lavender silk and another of plum velvet so soft that Susannah's mouth watered a little as she rubbed her fingers over the nap. Oh, what she could do with fine velvet like that! 'Twas as soft as a kitten.

"I should think a poke bonnet, covered in the silk but lined in the velvet, should do quite well," Susannah pronounced, reluctantly surrendering the swatches to

Nan. "Would you not agree, Nan? The darker color would shade the brim and set off the color of Miss Glaspell's eyes to perfection."

"Yes," Nan agreed. "And I could create some fabric flowers to rest on the crown of the bonnet, just to one side. Two violets would look quite fine, I should think."

And so they spent the afternoon, Susannah making quick sketches and notes on her scraps of foolscap while Nan contributed her own thoughts to the process—giving smart little details to each piece that turned it from a mundane hat to a small masterpiece. They would have their work cut out for them in the coming weeks—but what work! Beautiful bonnets, toppers, tams, hats—all of them made from the finest materials.

Susannah's fingers fairly itched to get started.

When at length the last sketch had been finished, the last fashion plate pored over and the last bits of fabric exclaimed over, Miss Glaspell sat back with a satisfied grin. "Splendid. This shall be my most fashionable winter wardrobe yet. I cannot wait to see the fruits of your labors. And I do want to claim you well in advance for the start of the Season next year."

Susannah smiled warmly. "Of course, Miss Glaspell. With the three of us working, we should have your order ready within the next two months. I can send them one by one, or have them all sent at the same time, when every last one is completed."

"Oh, I cannot bear to wait for them all at once. I was never any good at waiting for a gift, you know. I would always sneak a peek inside, even as a child." She rose and walked over to the elaborately embroidered bellpull. "Would you like some refreshment before you take your leave?"

Susannah darted a quick glance at the mantel clock. They had been working for nearly two hours. The time, so pleasantly spent, had simply flown by. "Oh, dear, no. We left Becky in charge of the shop while we were gone. The poor thing must think we've abandoned her."

Miss Glaspell gave Susannah a sweet smile. "Of course—and you both must be tired yourselves. I shall order the carriage for you, then."

Her butler arrived, and as Miss Glaspell gave him his orders, Nan and Susannah began tying their parcels together. They had so much work to do—and interesting, stimulating work it was, too—but she hadn't dared to broach the subject of payment yet. How was one to handle such a delicate topic? Uncle Arthur had always been late with his bills, to the point that the duns would come pounding on the door at least once a fortnight.

Miss Glaspell didn't strike one as that kind of a person and yet—Susannah's usual common sense failed her. Though she rummaged about in her mind for the right manner in which to say it, she had no idea of how to say it.

And yet, one's dinner did rest on the matter.

Whatever should she say?

Miss Glaspell dismissed her butler and turned to them both. "Oh, don't bother with those parcels. I shall have my servants bring them to you when I have them bring your payment. You don't mind if I send everything to you tomorrow, do you?"

At least she had mentioned making a payment. And 'twould be a relief indeed not to have to carry all those parcels again.

"That would be quite fine," Susannah agreed. Then

she gathered all her courage. "We do ask for you to pay half of the balance when the orders are placed."

"Of course," Miss Glaspell replied, nodding. She strolled over to the pile of sketches. "There's about a dozen hats here. What do you charge for each?"

Susannah hesitated. The sisters had agreed, in advance, that the price per bonnet would be at least six shillings. Would Miss Glaspell agree to such an amount?

She cleared her throat. "Each bonnet costs…six shillings, Miss Glaspell."

Miss Glaspell smiled. "For the beautiful work I know you will do, that shall be a bargain indeed. I shall send my servants by tomorrow, then?"

She hadn't said no. She didn't seem angered by the price at all. In fact, she seemed quite delighted.

"That will do quite well. Thank you." Susannah bobbed a curtsy.

They couldn't give vent to their delight. Not then, not when Miss Glaspell and her seamstress paid them their goodbyes. Not later, as the butler marched them solemnly out the hall and to the waiting carriage drawn up alongside the back porch. Not even as they rolled out across the countryside, for who knew whether the driver would hear their raised voices and ecstatic laughter?

No. They sat on their glee as though it were a cushion on a settee, giving each other excited glances as they endured the fifteen-minute ride back to the shop. A polite goodbye to the driver, and Susannah and Nan rushed inside the shop, knocking against each other in their haste.

Becky rose from her seat, her needlework falling to the floor. "And?" Her eyes grew larger as she surveyed her sisters. Susannah felt the heat rising in her cheeks and could suppress her mirth no more.

She let out a loud whoop that echoed throughout the tiny shop. "A dozen bonnets at six shillings apiece!" She spun around, flinging her own bonnet onto the floor. "This means a warm winter for us, sisters! Upon my word, I never expected this."

Independence was drawing ever closer. If she reached out her fingertips ever so slowly, she might grasp it, as gossamer as the muslin curtains at the shop when they were fanned by the late-autumn breeze. Once she attained her freedom, she would never have to ask anyone for help again.

Not even Daniel.

Chapter Ten

Working on Mother's chapel was the only thing vaguely interesting about the estate. There was much satisfaction in supervising the cleaning and repair of the tumbledown little building. Why, Daniel spent most of the morning working on repairing the archway over the door, which had become cracked and worn with age. His skills in repairing the ship's decking, acquired over the course of many voyages over many seas, was actually standing him in good stead now. One could hardly see the join where the repair mended the split wood.

He ran his palm over the oak panels, testing for other telltale cracks. No, it was good enough for now. The maids would be out this afternoon to give the place a proper scrubbing, floor to ceiling. And then after they'd finished, he'd see about the pew bench and the altar. Those items seemed a bit wobbly, but perhaps the floor had just settled beneath them.

He had never spent as much time in the tiny chapel as he had over the past few days. After Mother died, Father had given up all interest in maintaining the little building, and David was far too staid to care about something that brought absolutely no value to the estate. In fact, it was rather difficult to think of the last time anyone actually prayed here. Susannah's simple prayer was the first in ages.

Daniel sank onto a pew, setting his rough leather gloves aside. His hands flexed together and a momentary urge to bow his head surged through his being. And then, quick as a flash, the moment passed. How ridiculous to think of asking the Lord for anything. He'd never needed faith of any kind before, not even when he was buffeted around on the seas by a massive typhoon.

He must be hungry. That was all.

He'd take a break, have a little lunch, and then get back to work.

He entered Goodwin by the side entrance, the one that led past the kitchens toward the back of the Hall. He paused in the side entry. Time to remove these mucky boots. If he left a trail of dirt down the back hallway, he'd be sure to hear about it from Baxter. And a scolding from the butler was never a pleasant—or wanted—thing.

Daniel removed one boot and then the other with a satisfying thump, leaving them beside the threshold. Then he strolled over to the basin and pitcher to wash his hands. Mother had set the washbasin back here a long time ago so that she could wash up and tidy herself after working in the gardens or being out at her chapel. He gave a lopsided grin as he soaped his hands. How many times had she emerged from the back of the house to receive guests, looking as fresh as a rose? And she'd been mucking about in the garden for hours, though you'd never know it.

Funny, he hadn't thought about Mother for years now. After all, she'd died when he was just a lad. So young he could only remember bits and pieces about her life—like keeping the basin by the side door. Strange that working in her chapel was, in a way, bringing him closer to her once more. Even though he'd been in Goodwin Hall for all these months, he'd never felt a kinship with it until now.

Daniel flung the towel on the floor—a servant would be by to pick it up later. Whistling, he headed down the back passage to the study. He could have a little drink—just one—before time for his meal.

Rounding the corner, he ran smack into his butler. "Dash it all, man, I didn't see you," he muttered, taking a step back. "You're as silent as a footpad, you know."

Baxter straightened his jacket and resumed his usual air of dignity. "A rider delivered this message while you were working in the chapel, sir." He held an envelope out to Daniel. "Since it was a hasty delivery, I thought I should give it to you now."

"Yes, of course." Daniel took the envelope and scanned the handwriting. It had to be Paul's. No one else had such untidy penmanship, all loops and scrawls. He tore it open and headed for his study. No telling what kind of mischief Paul had been up to that required a messenger to break the news to Daniel.

"I'll have my lunch on a tray," he said over his shoulder. "Bring it in about half an hour."

"Very good, sir." Daniel just caught Baxter's reply before shutting the door.

So what kind of scrape had Paul gotten himself into? A week's debauchery in London certainly afforded many opportunities for disaster....

Daniel unfolded the foolscap and sought the comfort of the worn velvet chair, resting his feet—clad only in his socks—on the hearth.

My dear old chap—
I do fear there's been rather a dustup. I was in my cups at the club, and made a wager that you and Susannah Siddons would be wed within a year.

Daniel paused, his mouth going dry. He never suspected that Paul's trouble had anything to do with him. And certainly nothing at all to do with Susannah.

If it was a wager, perhaps no one would think anything of it.

One could hope it would pass over, ignored. After all, he and Susannah were hardly of the *ton.* Now that everyone had settled in the countryside, there was very little chance anyone would care what they did.

The thing of it is, I was playing faro and you know how that loosens my tongue. That, of course, and the liquor. At any rate, I told everyone about your secret engagement to Susannah. Since it happened so long ago, I suppose I thought it more amusing than anything.

Daniel scrubbed his palm across his face. Paul had told everyone about Susannah. The tender secret between them—the source of hurt and the source of misunderstanding—was now laid bare for the entire world to comment on and to gossip about.

How on earth could he break the news to Susannah? She would be furious.

Come to think of it, so was he. He should never have told Paul about the secret engagement. Paul was notorious for sharing confidences when drunk, and he should have foreseen that Paul would announce it to the world at some point.

I thought at first my mention of it would blow over—after all, not everything that is mentioned in a club becomes common knowledge. But I do fear that this has become quite a little scandal among our peers and I feel I should warn you—and offer my apologies. Everyone is abuzz with the story of a boy who ran to sea and the girl he jilted.

He hadn't jilted Susannah. Not really.

Had he?

Daniel flung the letter aside and headed straight for the decanter of scotch. His hands shook with fury, but he could not honestly tell if the anger was for Paul or for himself.

Liquor sloshed over the glass, forming a pool on the satiny finish of the mahogany table. He swiped the mess with his cuff and drank deeply, polishing it off in a few burning swallows. Then he poured another.

Susannah had always been the strong one. She was a lass who always knew what she wanted and how to get what she desired. Her will was strong as iron. Where Daniel concealed and hid, Susannah flung open the windows and let the sunshine stream in. There was never a doubt in his mind that she would find a way out of her uncle's home.

It had been a shock indeed when he met her that fateful day. Susannah had never asked for help for anything. Once he'd held a door for her and oh, she'd given him the sharp edge of her tongue. 'Twas unusual for a girl to be so very independent, but that was Susannah. They'd met at the edge of the park, and Susannah had pleaded with him to help her get away from her uncle.

There were dark circles under her eyes, and her beautiful hair hung limply down her back. She was so defeated. Susannah—defeated. Somehow, the words simply never went together. And he promised to help her. But he went to sea—

He took another long drink. He went to sea—

To escape. He went to sea to escape.

Why didn't he take Susannah with him? 'Twas a pertinent question. He took the decanter from the table beside him and poured another stout glass. Might as well leave it close by. He'd keep drinking until his thoughts turned off. Once he stopped feeling what a despicable rogue he must be for leaving Susannah and everyone who depended on him and needed his help.

He didn't take Susannah with him because, well, because he'd cared a little too much. How could he doom Susannah to the same sort of marriage his parents had endured? His mother, so merry and lovely, and his father, so cheerless and dour. That was what came of responsibilities and duties—they changed a man. He must avoid them forever to prevent the fundamental changing of his character.

He needed to calm her down, though. And so he'd promised all he could give. Susannah would find a way out—she always did. And perhaps someday, he could find her again—

Baxter knocked on the door, but the sound was muffled by the buzzing in Daniel's ears. The butler came in bearing Daniel's lunch on a tray and averted his eyes from the sight of the decanter, now half-empty, resting on the hearth.

"Bad news, sir?" His voice was respectful, but he bent and retrieved Paul's letter, which was still crumpled on the floor.

"Very bad." Daniel managed to get the words out without slurring. "I need to talk to Sus—to Miss Siddons. Can't go there myself. Take the carriage."

"I think you'd better wait until you've had a bite to eat," Baxter replied. He smoothed the sheets of foolscap and placed them on Daniel's desk. "The company of ladies and scotch rarely mix well, especially in the afternoon."

"No. I need her now. Go get her." He had to make things right. He'd made such a mess of things for so long.

"I shall send one of the maids down in the carriage, if you agree to try eating some of your food. Do you want to send a message to Miss Siddons? Perhaps that would be for the best."

"I am not in the mood for a lecture." The words tumbled out, slipping and sliding as though they were sledding down a hillside. "I need Miss Siddons here now. I don't care who gets her, or how, but I want it to happen without any more prevaricating. I am master here now." He drew himself up, lurching forward at an accelerated rate. "And if I want my scotch at noon or at midnight it's no one's concern."

Baxter bowed and withdrew without another word. Daniel raked his hands through his hair, straining for a sense of self-control amid the whirling chaos. Anger gnawed at him like a rabid dog. He'd made Susannah's life miserable, he'd failed in everything he'd tried and he was incapable of either leaving Goodwin or assuming the reins as master with ease. He dithered back and forth like a leaf buffeted by a breeze. Oh, and he was becoming the kind of master who yelled at his servants. Just like Father.

Choking on rage and disappointment, he flung his

glass against the mantel. It shattered with a most satisfying crash, sending droplets of liquor and shards of crystal spraying across the floor.

What a sniveling mess he was. What a failure.

Susannah glanced up from her chair by the window. Daniel's carriage. What on earth was he doing now? 'Twas nearly time to have a bite to eat, and then she had a full afternoon of bonnet making before her. She really had no more time for his games.

The footman opened the carriage door and a maid rushed out. How very odd. Why had Daniel sent a maid instead of coming himself?

Honestly, he would drive her to distraction.

She cast her work—a woolen tam-o'-shanter in a captivating shade of green—aside and rose. Nothing to do now but see what Daniel required.

The maid paused on the threshold and clasped her hands over her heart as she scanned the room. Spying Susannah, she bobbed a brief curtsy. "If you please, Miss Siddons," she panted, "Mr. Hale has asked for you to come see him. At once."

"You can go back to Goodwin and inform Mr. Hale that I am quite busy all afternoon." She gave the maid a pleasant but brief smile. "Some of us have to work for a living," she added under her breath.

"Beg pardon, miss, but I can't do that. Mr. Hale gave strict instructions that I was to bring you to Goodwin without delay." The maid cast a pleading look at Susannah. Poor girl. Obviously she was just following orders. And if she didn't follow them—surely Daniel wouldn't sack her, but there'd be a to-do.

"Is there some sort of emergency?" This haste was

strange. Even for Daniel and his mercurial ways. Perhaps there really was something wrong.

"I don't know any of the particulars. I was just told to come and fetch you." The maid looked as if she might say something more but then hesitated and fell silent.

Susannah sighed. This girl was simply following orders, the orders of a mischievous and quick-tempered master. She wouldn't leave without Susannah, so there was no sense in continuing to quiz her. Susannah acquiesced with a slight incline of her head. "Very well. Let me tell my sisters where I am going."

"Oh, thank you." The maid looked so relieved. Surely the poor dear wasn't about to embrace her. No—she turned on her heel and scurried out the door to the waiting carriage.

"Becky? Nan?" Susannah called as she strode out to the back porch. Her sisters had pulled their chairs outside and were using the full, bright sunlight to their advantage, Becky embroidering while Nan tatted lace. "I must go to Goodwin Hall for a bit. Daniel's in a mood and sent a servant for me."

"Is he ill again?" Nan squinted, holding her work up closer as she concentrated on a stitch. "Surely you've done all you can as his nursemaid."

"Perhaps he has wonderful news," Becky volunteered, her needle flashing in the sunlight. "News of a lost fortune found, perhaps?"

"Whatever it is, he'd better have a very good reason for interrupting my workday." Susannah untied her apron and hung it on the hook just inside the doorway. "Will you be all right whilst I am gone?"

"Of course," her sisters replied in unison, bending their heads back down to focus on their sewing. Gracious, only a few weeks back in Tansley, and already they were becoming so independent. Almost as if they didn't need her help at all.

Well, obviously someone needed her. Daniel Hale. 'Twould be interesting indeed to see what was so blessed important that he felt the need to send a carriage and a maid to interrupt her workday. She blew a kiss to her sisters and walked round the front of the building, where the coachman waited respectfully to hand her into the carriage.

She hadn't expected the maid to volunteer more information, and that was a good thing. For the girl said not another word, but sat silent and pale in her corner of the carriage, biting her lip. Even the ride on the mail wagon from Matlock was livelier than this. And less exasperating.

They rounded the curve of the driveway at Goodwin Hall after a quarter hour of silence, with nothing but the swaying of the carriage to break up the monotony. As she alit, Baxter rushed down the steps, his expression a strange mixture of sadness and fear. Despite her recent annoyance, Susannah's heart fluttered a bit in her chest. Surely nothing was really wrong—was it?

"Thank you for coming, Miss Siddons," he muttered, assisting her up the steps. As they paused on the porch, he spoke again. "I would not usually ask a lady to come and see a gentleman in this manner. But you see, the circumstances are quite strange, and Mr. Hale will not be dissuaded."

Susannah turned, looking the butler squarely in the eye. "What has happened?"

"He received a letter from his friend Mr. Paul, which made him quite upset. It must be the letter, for he spent the morning working on the chapel and seemed in good spirits until I gave him the letter to read. After that— he must have imbibed quite a bit of scotch. And then he ordered me to get you. I'm so sorry, Miss Siddons. I do know it's vastly improper, and I wouldn't have followed his orders—only there's something else happening. He does need your help. I just don't know why."

What a kind man Baxter was. To put up with Daniel's drunkenness. She placed a gentle hand on his arm. "You made the right decision," she replied in a soothing voice. "Whatever has upset him has upset the whole household. And if I can make it right, I will. Where is he?"

"In his study. I sent the maid down to fetch you so I could stay nearby. Shall I go in with you, miss?"

"No, thank you, Baxter. If I need assistance, I will let you know. And I do appreciate your help, as I am sure Mr. Hale does." She gave him as much of a smile as she could muster, but 'twas difficult. Even the normally un-flappable Baxter was decidedly shaken. And not by the upheaval in the household, but by the changes wrought in Daniel. This was, perhaps, the most troubling thing of all. That the butler, who'd known Daniel since he was a child, was truly taken aback by whatever had transpired this afternoon.

She entered Goodwin Hall— It was ominously si-lent. The usual hubbub of servants coming and going was hushed. They must be in the kitchen, waiting for the storm to blow over. Her boot heels rang out across the wooden floor as she made her way over to the study.

Should she knock? Or just let herself in? There was no sound from within. He might not even be there, judg-ing by the silence.

Well, he expected her. So, gathering her courage, she

pulled the latch and let herself in. Sarcasm might work best in smoothing the way. This strange new fear and silence was simply too overwhelming. She must seize control of the moment.

"Well, Daniel, here I am. To what do I owe the pleasure of this midday interruption?"

Chapter Eleven

Daniel raised his head, forcing his eyes to focus. Susannah was here. He'd sent for her, and she'd come. He rubbed his hand over his eyes. Perhaps it could clear his vision. Right now he saw several Susannahs, all pretty and proud, lips drawn down in a pout of disapproval.

"This is the second time I've caught you in your cups. Is this a habit of yours?" All the Susannahs blurred into one as she sank onto the settee opposite him. "And why in the middle of the day? And alone? From what I understood from watching my uncle, gentlemen always drink whilst gambling or socializing."

"Susannah." The single word came out as a croak. He cleared his throat and gave another mighty effort. Her name was so difficult to say when one had been drinking—how difficult it was not to slur the word. "Susy."

She stiffened, drawing her spine up straight, and the soft lines of her cheek hardened. Was she really going to fuss about him calling her that now? When they were on the brink of potential disaster?

"Don't." He pronounced the word sharply. "I know what you're going to say."

She lowered her gaze to the floor as if in acquiescence, and that was enough of a sign for him to continue. "I got a letter."

"So Baxter told me. From Paul." She traced a design in the nap of the rug, using the toe of her boot.

He watched in fascination for a moment. Susannah had such small feet. All of her was small, except for the strength of her will...the thought of which snapped him back to the matter at hand.

"It seems he told a lot of people. About us." There, it was out. Now that she knew, they could plan out what to do. And he wouldn't be alone, trying to fix this mess.

She looked up, the color draining from her face. "What do you mean?"

He seized the letter from where it had fallen beside him on the floor. "Read it."

She took the letter and read through it. 'Twas only a few paragraphs, but she took an eternity about it. When she finally raised her eyes to his face, he had to avert his gaze from the pain he glimpsed in their shadowy depths.

"Susy, I am so sorry." The best way to begin was with an apology. Because he meant it. Paul sounded such a cad in that letter, and Daniel had never meant to hurt her. What a dashed mess he'd made of things. "So sorry. How can I make it better?"

She folded the foolscap back into place and settled back on the settee. He hadn't seen her look this cowed—well, not since the afternoon she'd asked him for help. She was meant for decision, action and movement—not for resting on a settee in the face of social suicide.

"I don't know. You can't reverse what's already been

done." She waved a listless hand through the air. "I don't think we should do anything just now. Wait and see. We're so far out of the way here in Tansley, perhaps no one will find out."

"And if they do?" He turned to her. "Could it hurt your business in any way?"

"I don't know." Her face paled in the dim light. "Oh, Daniel, if only you knew. If only you could understand how very precarious my foothold is right now. I just started this millinery, and I just secured my first large commission. Twelve bonnets for the Honorable Elizabeth Glaspell. And orders from her friends." Her voice sounded warmer now, less weary, and her words tumbled out in a rush. "I am so close to having the kind of security my sisters and I need. So close to finally making a living on my own. What if our broken engagement caused a scandal, and my business suffered? I cannot afford that."

She sighed, rubbing her hands together. Then her expression hardened, and she became brisk and practical once more. "This could cause trouble, but perhaps no one would care. I'm in trade now, and you're a gentleman. The differences in our stations are such that no one would take an engagement between us seriously. At least, I should think not. We can only hope that Tansley is simply too far away for such gossip to matter."

He didn't like that she spoke of the difference in their stations. She was a gentlewoman through and through, no matter that she had to work for a living. And he had hardly earned the title of gentleman. But he knew better than to press his point with the fiercely independent Susannah.

But as to the problem at hand—Tansley was hours away from London, and the gentry families were likely here already, as the Season had ended a few weeks ago. Only bachelors on a bender and a few stragglers likely remained in town. "Perhaps nothing will come of it at all."

"Yes." She smoothed her hair with a hand that trembled perceptibly. "Just don't say anything more. And… don't talk to Paul about us again. Please."

"I won't," he promised. "He just found out about the engagement the day I met you again. The day we were walking in the village and came upon you and your sisters. I was surprised to see you, and I couldn't conceal my amazement from Paul, I am afraid." 'Twas astounding how quickly he was sobering up. The weight of what they faced—the enormity of it—was sobering in and of itself. "I never meant to cause you harm."

"I know you didn't. But—you'll forgive me—that's the trouble with you, Daniel. You never think. And you never mean what you say." Her voice sounded faded and shaky, as though she were speaking from a long distance away. And her words, well, they were an unexpected knife in his gut.

"That's horrible." It was all he could think of to say.

"I just mean—you're so charming. You say things to please others…" She trailed off, her cheeks turning a delicate shade of pink.

He nodded slowly. She had a right to feel that way. "I understand. You don't have to say more."

"And it hurts, a bit, to be referred to in such terms." Susannah glanced up, her large, gray-green eyes sparkling with unshed tears. "The boy who ran to sea. The girl he left behind. As though…as though we were characters in a play, and not real people at all."

"I agree. It's despicable." He raked his hand through his hair. "I thought Paul had more sense, or at least more compassion. I've known him forever. Never thought he'd do this." He glanced over at Susannah, allowing the full frustration and self-loathing he felt to show through his expression. No more masks with Susannah. No more joking about. She deserved better. "If I had, I would never have said anything."

"I believe you." Susannah gave him a half smile. "You're a good person at heart, Daniel. I've always known it in my heart. That's why I came to you…" She paused, as though unsure if she should continue. When she did resume, her words were more even and fiercer. "My anger is directed mostly at myself, you know. Anger that I can't do better than I've done. Anger that my foothold on stability is so shaky. It shouldn't be. I should be a better provider than this."

Daniel chuckled. The sound startled Susannah, who arched one eyebrow as though expecting a sarcastic comment in response. But Daniel shook his head. She was being ridiculous. "You're too hard on yourself. You've done an amazing job, Susy. I am so astonished by all you've accomplished."

She dropped her gaze to the floor. "Thank you." Then, in true Susannah style, she added, "But I could do better."

He grinned ruefully, and an expectant silence settled between them. Would either of them bridge that gap? Say what never had been said? Susannah was the one who usually took command of any situation, charging in where others feared to tread. But as the silence wore on, Daniel's impatience rose. Blame it on the scotch—perhaps it was giving him Dutch courage.

"You never wrote to me, Susy." It was a statement. Not a question. He was merely stating a fact.

"I did, a few times." She looked over at him evenly.

"You never responded. So I assumed you didn't want to speak to me."

"I never got any letters. I suppose it was too difficult, with me being at sea all the time. Letters get misdirected. Misplaced. I would have written back, you know. I wouldn't have left you without a word. But I thought that you had found another solution." He'd been certain that Susannah would find a way out of her terrible situation. She always did. "It wasn't fair of me to assume that, I suppose. But you were always so strong, so certain of yourself. I was sure that if anyone could find a way, you could. And marriage, in my experience, can be a dreadful thing—"

"I know you grew up in a rather unpleasant environment," she interrupted. "I thought you regretted our engagement. After I didn't hear back from you, I was certain you did. And so rather than tie you to a reckless promise, I decided to drop the matter and find my own way."

"I can see why you'd do that." It made perfect sense now. It was laughable, really. It belonged in a book. One long convoluted misunderstanding. But they were both shying away from the heart of the matter. The real truth of it. And somehow, her answer to this question mattered more than anything. "Would you have married me, anyway, Susannah?"

She wouldn't look him in the eye, and it was maddening. If only she would look at him, with those clear gray-green eyes, and tell him the truth. Susannah always told the truth, and it was one of her noblest qualities. And he wanted to know. Why was she taking forever to respond?

'Twas a bold question, to be sure. It fairly took her breath away. When Becky had asked her the same thing, she was able to give a crisp and even response. But now? Daniel sat just a few feet away, gazing at her with such intensity in his green eyes that her heart pounded against her rib cage. Surely he could hear it. She couldn't bear to look up at him. His glance was scorching her skin and she had to maintain some sense of self—some pride, some dignity.

'Twas all she had.

"Yes. I suppose so." It was all she could say, really. Her mouth was so dry that speech was nearly impossible.

"Why?"

"Why not?" She wasn't being flippant. Not at all. But what more could she say? He hadn't professed any kind of love or affection for her. Just admiration, and that was not the same thing. And she wasn't sure she loved him either. His drinking…his jokiness…and his complete lack of faith…he was not precisely the man of her dreams.

"There has to be a reason. You didn't just come to me that day out of the blue. You came to me, Susy. Why? And why did you say yes?"

He was using her pet name, the one he had called her from childhood, and which had infuriated her since her return. But now the sound of it took her back to sunny afternoons spent wandering the pastures of Tansley. A boy and a girl who were friends. Different as night and day in personality, but still—good friends. And she could almost feel the warmth of his hand as he helped her climb over some rocks—daring her to climb to new heights, teasing her when she was afraid, but still warm and tender as he helped her up.

But this was the same boy who had taken her hand and told her he'd help her escape from Uncle Arthur. The same boy who then ran away to sea and left her, cold and bereft, at the hands of her greedy, grasping relatives. And she'd never heard from him again, until years later. She'd hated being so vulnerable and she'd toughened her shell, promising never to allow herself that sense of weakness again.

"Because…you always seemed to know all the answers. We were friends. And I trusted you to know the answer to my problem." It was the best she could manage. Tears pricked her eyes, and she blinked them back rapidly. It would never do to cry in front of Daniel. Weakness indeed! She bit the inside of her cheek so she could focus on a different kind of pain.

"Don't cry, Susy." Daniel crossed the settee and sat beside her, taking her hand. "Don't cry. I am so sorry. You can't imagine. All that I have done. And now Paul."

"I shan't cry." She withdrew her hand from his, for the moment he took her hand she was running with him over the fields of Tansley and she could not allow herself to feel that kind of wondrous freedom ever again. She took a shaky breath. If he was going to keep asking her questions, then she could very well fire them back at him, couldn't she? She was tired of being quizzed. "So what about you? Why did you offer to marry me if you hate marriage so much?"

She stole a glance at his handsome profile and was rewarded with his abashed expression, his jawline squaring as he seemed to wrestle with the answer. "I don't know— it was the best I could offer. I didn't have any independence back then. Nothing to call my own. I couldn't give you money to get away—I had none. Becoming engaged, running away to sea—I felt it was my only choice."

Now she had every opportunity to ask the next question. Would he have married her? But somehow, the words just wouldn't come out. She was afraid of the answer. If he said yes—that would be strange indeed. She would have no idea how to react. And if he said no—a cold feeling settled in the pit of her stomach. No. She never wanted to know the answer to that particular question.

But something else had been bothering her—the glib way that Paul referred to them both. Was that how Daniel saw their relationship, too?

"Did you think of me as the girl you left behind? And yourself as the boy who ran away to sea?"

He shook his head. "No. I thought of you as I still do. As Susannah, strong and beautiful and proud. And myself as the fellow who was your…friend. And I wanted to set myself far apart from Goodwin, and make my fortune, before I came back."

So he had planned to come back. But he could still only call himself her friend. Not her fiancé. And that was her answer. Somehow, that disappointed her more than she'd expected. It hurt more than she cared to admit, even to herself. She sank against the settee, allowing the cushions to hold her up. All the energy flowed out of her being, and she was exhausted. So drained.

But their talk seemed to have had the opposite effect on Daniel. He no longer slurred his words, and the haggard expression had vanished from his face. "You're tired, aren't you?" He patted her hand with a tender gesture. "Poor Susannah. What a day it's been. You can have some luncheon here and rest in one of the upstairs rooms. I'll see to it that you aren't disturbed."

"No, thank you. I really must get back to the shop. I've got a bonnet to finish this afternoon, and the girls will wonder what's taking me so long, as it is."

"I insist. It's the least I can do after all I've put you through today. I'll have one of the maids take you upstairs, and they can send up a meal to you. You can rest as long as you want, and then I'll have the carriage take you home." He leaped up from the settee and strode over to the bellpull.

She couldn't stay. Not when there was so much work to be done at the shop. And a driving need to put a mile or so of good road between herself and Daniel. 'Twas easy to find oneself succumbing to his charm. Already she was softening. He couldn't help being a charmer, for so he had always been. But how much of his charm was honest?

On the other hand, a soft feather bed and a hot meal would be such luxury....

Baxter appeared, and Daniel gave him a few short orders. Susannah rested her head on the settee. She was weary to the bone. And somehow, the thought of surrendering control was appealing, even if just for the afternoon.

"The maid will come to take you to your room." Daniel grasped both her hands in his and pulled her to her feet. "And I'll send your sisters a message so they won't worry. And when you feel better, you can go home."

"Thank you." She gave him a small smile and withdrew her hands from his grasp. "I can't stop thinking of Paul and the rumors."

"It's best to let matters blow over. I had a nanny who used to say 'Less said, soonest mended.' Perhaps we should apply that philosophy to this situation. Say nothing and continue about our business." Daniel put his hand on her back and helped her over to the study door. His handprint still burned through the fabric of her gown after he pulled away.

'Twas a sensible solution. Really, stirring the pot by confronting gossip would do no good. The door opened, and the same maid who'd come to fetch her in the carriage bobbed a brief curtsy.

"This is—" Daniel paused, a confused look creeping over his face.

"Bets," the maid supplied in a helpful, tentative tone.

"And she'll take care of you, Susannah." He gave her a lopsided grin. "Take a rest. I worry you are working yourself to death. And before you leave, I would say goodbye."

Susannah nodded, too fatigued to say anything. A rest would help. She'd be more like herself afterward, and she'd limit herself to half an hour at the most. She followed Bets through the doorway and up the stairs of the home that—had circumstances been different—might have been hers.

Chapter Twelve

And yet, despite their long conversation, which had been akin to a flood breaking through a dam, nothing remarkable happened. Not for a week, at least. In fact, it was all rather a blur when Susannah reflected upon it. She'd rested in the luxurious guest room at Goodwin, said her goodbyes to a sober and contrite Daniel and relied upon his carriage to take her home. She'd waved off her sisters' questions and settled right back into the routine of her new life.

And she'd met with Annabella and Evangeline, Miss Glaspell's friends, with Nan in tow. Their orders had turned a pleasantly occupied autumn into a busy, driven and almost frenetic few weeks. As Susannah carefully wrapped a bonnet frame with rust-colored velvet, her heart beat a little strangely at the thought of all the work that was left to be done. She and her sisters worked fast, to be sure, but they never thought they'd open a business with three large orders from the gentry. Maybe she could hire someone from the village to come help. As it was, they were burning their lamps until late into the night.

She threaded her needle with a quick jab and set to work stitching the fabric in place.

"Sue?" Nan called from upstairs.

"Yes, what is it?" Susannah squinted in the rapidly dimming light as she focused on a tiny stitch. Oh, her neck hurt. For a moment her mind flashed back to the comforts of Goodwin…the feather pillows and cozy quilted bolster…

"We don't have much food left in the larder. Becky and I were thinking perhaps we could go down to the bakery."

Susannah straightened in a vain attempt to work some of the kinks out of her back. What they said was true—there was nothing but a crust of bread left. But if she sent her sisters, they'd dawdle about the business, chattering away to each other like magpies. No, 'twould be better to go alone. At least they could then chatter while working on some new bonnets.

"I'll go." She stood and cast the bonnet aside. "Any requests?"

"Scones."

"Muffins."

"I'll see what Bess has left," Susannah agreed. The cinnamon bread had become her favorite, but she certainly wouldn't turn up her nose at scones or muffins. In fact, anything Bess made was quite good.

She quit the shop and turned down the path that marched along the main part of the village. The street was deserted; not a soul in sight. Everyone must be going home to get their own suppers. Why, the bakery might even be closed. Perhaps they'd waited too long. She'd gotten so busy on that velvet bonnet that she lost all track of time. Only her sisters, with their insistent stomachs, would keep her mindful of when mealtime was.

Oh, good. A lamplight still shone through the window. Bess was there, likely ready to close the store. Perhaps they could get a few extra tasty bites at a discount, if Bess was preparing to throw them out.

She opened the door and the bell chimed its usual cheery tune. Bess glanced up from the back of the shelves, a smile broadening her round face. "There you are," she said with a hearty chuckle. "Wondered when I'd see you girls today. You must be down to crumbs."

"We are. Do you have anything left? I declare, my sisters are like hungry baby birds, just chirping away in the nest."

Bess laughed heartily. "Well, then. Let them chirp no more. I have some lovely lemon scones and a few buns left. I'll wrap everything up for you. And no charge for the buns. I was going to make them into bread pudding tomorrow if they didn't sell, as it was."

"Thank you." Susannah crossed her arms over her chest, relishing the cozy atmosphere of the bakery. 'Twas such a delight to come here and bask in the warmth of the oven and Bess's good cheer. It alleviated her loneliness just the tiniest bit.

Bess handed the wrapped bundle over the counter. "So for the scones, let's say a shilling and call it even."

"Here you go," Susannah replied, handing the coin over and accepting the bundle, breathing in deeply. "Oh, those scones smell delicious. Perfect for the last bit of summer."

"You've been here a few weeks, then. And already doing well, from what I hear." Bess began wiping down the counters with a dampened rag. "You're already making a name for yourself in Tansley."

"Do you think so?" Susannah clasped the bundle to

her chest. "I'd hoped I was doing well. I feel more hopeful than when I arrived, that is for certain."

Bess nodded, and her expression changed. She eyed Susannah carefully, as though taking stock of her. She started to speak and then hesitated. After a heartbeat, she began again. "You might want to avoid Goodwin Hall, though."

Susannah looked up at Bess. How did she know about her trips to Goodwin?

"Mr. Hale's servants have been talking. They come to the village, and they gossip. From what I've heard, just here in my little bakery, you've been to his house a few times, and even stayed there for a few hours one afternoon to rest." She shook her head. "As a working girl, you must guard your reputation, Susannah. Even if those trips were innocent—and I believe they were—others may not feel the same way. You could be compromised. And not only that, but because of it, your business might suffer, as well."

This was the most she'd spoken to Bess since the day of her arrival. Most of the time, they engaged in pleasant but brief chatter. And now Bess was warning her against folly in the same way she might warn a sister or a dear friend. "The visits were innocent," she protested. "But probably foolish. I didn't think."

"If your families were close as children, then it does help. And from what I've gathered, you were. But his carriage has been seen outside your shop a few times, and his servants are talking. I worry that, as your little shop begins to grow, you could find yourself at the mercy of the gossips."

Susannah's knees trembled and a wave of nausea hit her, full force. "Yes. Of course." She sounded idiotic, but it was all she could think of to say. She'd worried about this very thing. But then she'd convinced herself little by little that matters were well in hand, that no one would think a thing of it. She'd convinced herself that she was invisible to the censure of the village.

How imbecilic.

"Here, sit down." Bess bustled around the counter, pulling a chair behind her. "Upon my word, you look pale." She took the bundle of baked goods away from Susannah and pressed her into the chair. "Are you quite all right? You look like you might faint."

"Yes. No. I don't know." Bess's concerned face floated before Susannah, and drops of perspiration beaded her brow. "Oh, Bess. What an addle brain I've been. Here I thought I had done so well at—well, not concealing my friendship with Mr. Hale, but keeping everything proper."

"No harm's been done." Bess patted her back with a soothing gesture, calming her ruffled nerves. "But I did want to advise you. Have you give a thought to it a bit more. You see, it's different when you start to work for yourself. You get to be independent, but you have to be mighty circumspect about how you behave."

"I understand. Thank you." Susannah placed her elbows on her knees and rested her chin in her hands. If only the room would stop spinning. She could gather her food and the shreds of her self-respect and go home.

"Don't take it so hard, my dear. Chin up. You're building a lovely business, and I want to see it continue to thrive. Just—be careful around young men. Especially young men who have a lot of money. I know." Bess pulled up a chair beside Susannah and sat as the chair made a groan of protest. "My sister almost eloped with a wild young buck when she was just a slip of a thing. And it could have ruined our family. They loved each other, but he never would have married her. Not in truth."

"Did your sister fare well? Even afterward?" She turned to look at Bess.

"Bless you, yes. She married a nice young man—a butcher. And they have three children now, and one more on the way. Had she continued down the other path, I know she wouldn't have been so happy. Or so secure."

Security. Safety. Independence. She valued these above anything else. If she could only be secure—and know that no one could harm her family, or make them do things against their will—then she would be happy.

"I appreciate you sharing this with me." Susannah straightened. She must be going home. 'Twas ridiculous to take on so about something that could easily be fixed. And as Bess said, no harm had been done. "I shall be more careful in the future. And if you hear anything more—please do tell me. It's so…lonely out here, and I feel so isolated…" Oh, drat. She sounded just like the heroine in a Gothic novel. At any moment, she'd begin blubbering about strange presentiments she felt in her marrow bones.

"Of course I shall." Bess rose and gathered the bundle of scones. "Are you quite well enough to walk home? You looked so stricken a moment ago that I didn't feel it right to let you leave here. Not until you had a bit of a rest."

"Oh, I am fine." Susannah managed a little laugh and rose, accepting the scones from Bess. "Funny. I just never realized anything was amiss, and I was rather taken aback. But I feel much better now."

"Good." Bess gave her a quick hug, tight enough to feel warmth and friendship but without causing undue harm to the parcel that held dinner. "Off with you now.

And don't brood about this. It will all come out right in the end."

Susannah nodded, mumbled her thanks once more and managed to make it out to the dirt path that rang alongside the store. She had just a few yards to cross, and then she would be home. But with that would come the duties and responsibilities of being the eldest sister—a meal to make, work to put aside until the morning and evening prayer. And no one to confide in. No way to ease the sudden anxiety her conversation with Bess had provoked. She paused for a moment. She had to clear her muddled mind—to rest for a moment before she went home.

She would have to speak with Daniel again. Even though they had successfully avoided one another for a week, she couldn't do so forever. If she stopped speaking to him forever, without explaining why, then it might hurt him. And she had no desire to hurt Daniel. But she couldn't very well lose everything she'd gained over their acquaintance.

She'd go to him tomorrow and tell him the truth. No, if she did that, someone might see her. His servants might gossip or overhear their conversation. Perhaps a letter would be best. She would write a quick explanation tomorrow, when she was fresh, and then she would send it by regular post. Perhaps that would be enough to set them both free.

Funny, it hurt to make that final resolution. It didn't matter to her that much, did it? Surely whether she saw Daniel again or not wouldn't change her life. After all, she'd done without him for quite a long time. There was no need to feel sad or melancholy about this decision. What she wanted was a stable future for herself and her sisters. And to keep that dream alive, she'd have to re-linquish Daniel.

It was as simple as that.

But strange how very much her heart ached as she contemplated a future without Daniel.

Daniel paused before the Siddons Sisters Millinery door. A nice evening walk to visit the girls was just the thing to ward off his burgeoning loneliness. For if he stayed at Goodwin, he'd start drinking. And since his last devastating encounter with Susannah, he'd tried to stay away from liquor. He had a glass or two of wine with his meals, but that was to be expected of a gentleman. As long as he stayed away from his scotch, he would avoid the possibility of another embarrassing situation.

So the only thing to do was to distract himself. And yet, there were few distractions, even on an estate as grand as Goodwin. He could go over the accounts, or work on the chapel a bit more, or see to one of the other hundreds of pressing matters that he was now required to care about. But, in truth, the thought of trying to stay at Goodwin tonight, and trying to be a good lord of the manor, was too much to bear.

So he'd had the brilliant notion of seeing Susannah and her sisters again.

He'd avoided her since that afternoon. But something pulled him back tonight. The Siddons girls worked like a tonic on a man's nerves. They were simple, and good, and hardworking. Being near them was enough to make one feel as if one was good, too. As though the purity of their characters could rub off on a fellow.

And here he was. Funny, the sign wasn't hanging

above the door, as it should. It leaned, propped against the bottom of their display window. How very odd.

He raised his hand to knock, but the door flew open. Nan stuck her head around the edge with a giggle. "Well? Are you coming in or not?"

"I will if you'll have me." He took off his hat and ducked inside. A fire crackled brightly in the grate, warding off the evening's autumnal chill. Lamps glowed softly, and a pretty embroidered cloth was spread invitingly over the oaken dinner table. "Everything's cozy. Are you girls expecting dinner? I didn't mean to interrupt."

"Don't be silly." Nan took his hat and waved him over to a chair. "Of course you'll stay and dine with us. Sue's just gone to get a few things."

"And I am preparing a little soup to go with whatever she brings," Becky piped up from her position by the stove. "Do stay. I know Susannah would want you to."

He grinned. Perhaps she would, and perhaps she wouldn't. He stretched his booted feet out to the crackling blaze. "Smells wonderful. How are you ladies faring?"

"Very well, but quite busy." Nan set a spoon at each place. "You are fortunate that we have just enough utensils for all of us. Otherwise, you would be drinking your soup out of a teacup."

"Oh, Nan." Becky glanced up from stirring a pot. "Don't be rude. You know even if we didn't have a spoon for everyone, we would make Mr. Hale welcome just the same. He could use mine."

Becky and her sweet dreaminess, Nan with her practical and bustling ways. Already they were becoming as familiar to him as his own family. 'Twas a pity that he'd always considered his own family to be more of a burden or an obligation than a source of comfort and even joy. But he had a very different sort of family than the Siddons. Father's dour and domineering ways stretched to the very end of his life. David was dull on his best days and sullen on his worst. And Mother, of course, died so young that his memories of her were tinged with forgetfulness. This coziness and easy banter between siblings was entirely foreign, and yet it wrapped around him like a soft, warming blanket.

The door burst open, snapping him out of his reverie. Susannah stepped briskly over the threshold, calling out "Hello, chickens!" in a cheerful tone of voice he hardly associated with her. Spying him sitting in the most comfortable chair in the cottage, Susannah broke off her good cheer abruptly, her face turning a shade paler in the firelight. He rose. Best to breeze through this as though nothing had happened between them.

"Here, let me help you with that." He took the parcel from her arms and laid it on the table. "Smells jolly good. Bess makes excellent scones, doesn't she?"

Susannah murmured a noncommittal reply and turned to her sisters. "How soon will dinner be ready?"

Becky glanced into her soup pot. "About five minutes more should do the trick."

"Good." She grasped his elbow and guided him toward the door. Funny how strong she was for such a small lass. He gave a half smile and allowed himself to be propelled closer to the threshold. "I need to have a word with Mr. Hale."

He glanced over his shoulder at her sisters as she opened the door. "I have a feeling this is good night, ladies. I hope to see you both soon."

Susannah groaned and shoved him over the threshold.

A Rumored Engagement

Then, after closing the door behind them both with a decided snap, she strode past him. "Follow me."

How curiously she was behaving. He turned, and with a few quick strides drew up beside her. "What is the matter?"

"We can't talk here. We might be seen." She motioned him into a small clearing at the edge of the moor, where the rocky hillside blocked the view of the village. "This should help. No one could spy us here unless they really meant to."

"Whatever are you talking about?" He grasped both her shoulders and turned her to face him. Her brow furrowed, and the expression in her eyes shifted from caution to something like regret. He was losing her, somehow. That closeness they had hesitantly shared over the past few weeks was slipping away.

She paused, as though gathering her wits to continue. Then—

"We cannot be friends any longer."

Chapter Thirteen

The stricken look in Daniel's eyes was rather surprising; surely his friendship meant more to her than the other way round. Here was a man who, after all, had everything. A fine home, plenty of money, servants to do his every bidding. The friendship of a little milliner whom he'd played with when they were both children should mean nothing to him. And yet—he compressed his lips into a thin line and dropped his hands from her shoulders. They'd warmed her through the thin wool of her gown and shawl, and once he removed them from her person, a cold chill shivered down her spine.

"What do you mean? Don't you want to be friends any longer? Or has my drinking disgusted you enough?" His tone was even, but a thread of anger laced through it. She drew her shawl closer.

"It doesn't matter what I want, or what you want. The problem is that your servants have been gossiping, and the villagers have seen your carriage at the shop one too many times. We're being talked about, Daniel. Bess warned me this afternoon when I went to get something for dinner." Surely if she laid everything out logically, he would understand. They would strip the matter of any emotional overtones, and then they could make sense of it together.

"Surely you don't care about what a lot of gossips say." He cocked his head to one side and glanced at her with the same mischievous light in his eyes that would glow when he would dare her to climb a tree or wade through a brook when they were children. "You are made of stronger stuff than that, I daresay."

"I am. But my little shop is not." She straightened her spine and looked him squarely in the eye. "You might not know this—indeed, you haven't had the opportunity to gather it for yourself—but when you are trying to run a business, your reputation can affect how successful you are. This shop is all I have. If I lose it, my sisters and I will be destitute. We've started building it up, and we have a few gentry orders that are helping to ensure that we will make it through the winter."

"But our friendship is innocent. There is nothing to this gossip. And if we bow to it and stop being friends, then we will validate everything they have thought about us." He shoved his hands in his coat pockets and paced a few feet away from her. "This situation is miles apart from the one we faced thanks to Paul's drunken boasting. If it looks as though we were engaged but never wed, we face a different kind of censure. But this? Susy, why allow the gossips to ruin something good and true?"

Anger bubbled under the surface, and Susannah struggled to keep ahold on her temper. He was treating this as though she had a real choice, and as though she was a coward for suggesting that they call an end to their friendship. He had no inkling of the disaster she faced. None at all. "The gossips are going to ruin something,

Daniel. I would rather them ruin our friendship than my business."

He ceased his pacing and his head snapped back as though she'd slapped him. "Do you really?"

Oh, bother. She hadn't meant for that to sound quite so cutting. If only he could understand how very precarious her position was—if only he knew how one slip would cause her to lose her foothold forever. "Daniel, don't look so," she pleaded. "You must understand how difficult this is for me."

"I understand completely, Susannah."

'Twas the first time in ages he'd used her full name instead of her nickname, and from his lips at this moment it sounded cold and forbidding. She clasped her arms together to keep from shivering. This was dreadful. If only she could find a way to break things more gently, to make him see and feel the looming catastrophe she faced.

"I think," he added, "that my reputation as the master of Goodwin Hall is enough to protect both of us in the event of any kind of village gossip. Talk from town—that could be different. Let the villagers think what they want, but if the gentry does start to talk, then surely we could stand together..."

He wasn't making sense. And he was sounding rather a snob. She cut him short with a wave of her hand. "It doesn't matter. Villagers, gentry or anyone else. Gossip is gossip. And when people begin talking about a woman, 'tis as damaging as—oh, I don't know—'tis as damaging as a ship taking on water at sea. A man may be talked about, and his mystique only grows. But if a woman is talked about, she suffers. And since I am a shop owner, so, too, would my business." If only she could bridge the gap between them. She reached out and touched his arm. "You must know that this is difficult for me, too."

"It can't be." He stared down at her, his anger palpable. Beneath her hand, his forearm tensed. "You always know what you desire to achieve, and you do so every time, Susannah Siddons. You don't need anyone or anything else, do you?" He shook off her touch and strode across the moor toward Goodwin.

"Daniel—do wait," she called, but the echo of her voice off the moors brought her up short. Someone could hear her, and then all this heartache would be for naught. She wrapped her shawl tighter and ducked around the corner of the hillside. The path leading back to the shop was empty of any creatures, human or otherwise. She must be safe.

Susannah dared one last glance over her shoulder at Daniel. Gracious, he was walking fast. Striding away from her with the same curiously loping stride that a farmer might use to step off rows of maize. What would he do once he reached Goodwin? Would he dive right back into a bottle of scotch to drown his anger? Even if he did, 'twas no concern of hers. He could send round carriage after carriage stuffed with worried servants, and she would have to turn them all away.

Her heart ached, and she rubbed a weary hand over her brow. The rapidly gathering twilight darkened the road, and the welcome glow of the lamp in the shop window spilled out onto the path. She would feel better when she was warm and had something to eat. That's all this was. Fatigue and hunger. She had made the right decision, and in time, Daniel would come to see it that way, too.

She let herself into the shop, breathing deeply of the wonderfully subtle, rich scent of soup Becky had made.

Nan and Becky, seated together at the table, looked up with twin glances of concern as she came in. Susannah scanned the table and gave a halfhearted smile. Ever true to their upbringing, even in times of crisis, none of the girls had started to eat until she returned home.

"Fill your bowls. You must be famished." She removed her wrap and tossed it lightly in a chair. Then she crossed the room and held her hands out to the blazing fire in the grate. "I took a bit of a chill on my walk. Must warm up a bit." Yes, and compose her nerves before facing their questions.

"Is everything quite all right?" Of course, Becky, the most emotionally astute member of the family, ventured to speak first.

Susannah sighed. She must tell her sisters the truth. After all, the shop was not hers alone. 'Twas a family venture, and the more her sisters knew about how difficult circumstances could be the better. They would all have to begin conducting themselves in a more circumspect manner. She was not the only one who had to mind her own behavior.

"Let us give thanks first. And then, let's eat. I am famished." She strode over to the stove and ladled out three steaming bowls of soup, whilst Nan tucked the scones into a bread basket. After a brief blessing, the three sisters sat, eating in silence for just a moment.

Susannah gathered her courage. Why was this so difficult? She was the eldest; it fell to her to lead the family after Mama's death. Bess's advice was eminently practical and sound, and she had already broken matters off with Daniel. Why was it so terribly hard to tell her sisters that he wouldn't be coming around any longer?

The only way to begin...was to begin.

"I've had to break off my friendship with Daniel," she ventured.

Nan and Becky gasped. "Why?" Nan demanded, setting her spoon down with a clank.

"I know this is difficult to grasp at first, but do try to hear what I am saying." Susannah assumed her "eldest sister" expression and kept her tone even but stern. The more in command she sounded, the less likely 'twas that her sisters would question her. "Our friendship with Daniel is being talked about in the village. And Bess warned me that it could hurt our shop."

"Could it really?" Becky opened her lovely violet eyes wider. "But surely if people knew—"

"There's more." Better to tell them everything. Make a clean slate of it. "Daniel told his friend Paul about our engagement. And though it has been a long time since Daniel and I were betrothed, and we've released each other from our engagement, Paul told half of London society about the matter."

"How dare he?" Nan bit into a scone with vehemence, as though she could bite through Paul and his meddling ways. "What made him do such a thing?"

"He was drinking," Susannah stated flatly. "I am sure that you have gathered that drinking oneself into oblivion is a popular pastime among these young men. It loosened Paul's tongue enough that he spilled all of Daniel's confidences to most of the *ton*."

"That's dreadful." Becky propped her elbows on the table and sipped slowly at her tea. "But are you sure that we must break off all contact with Daniel? I agree that greater discretion is necessary—but do we really need to stop talking to the poor boy altogether?"

"We are in a very precarious position." Susannah

helped herself to a lemon scone and broke it in half. "If we only had to worry about the townspeople gossiping or the *ton* knowing about the engagement, then I might not be as concerned. But with both…" She paused a moment so she could take a bite of the scone—how delightful, it fairly melted in one's mouth. "I don't know. It's just too much. If we err on the side of being too cautious, then we could very well slip by without the gossip harming us in any way."

"But it could cause harm to Daniel." Becky set her teacup down with a clink. "And to us. His friendship was good for you, Susannah. And I know you worked on his nerves like a tonic. I feel sorry for him, alone at Goodwin. Do you think he'll be all right?"

"He'll probably turn to drinking again," Nan pronounced calmly, as though trying to predict the weather.

He might. But that was Daniel's decision. She couldn't continue jeopardizing her livelihood to help him. 'Twas terrible and selfish to think so, but there it was. She had to think of her family first. Though her heart constricted at the thought of Daniel alone at Goodwin, drowning his loneliness in a decanter of scotch, she must always protect her sisters and herself.

After all, 'twas what Mother made her promise. "Take care of your sisters," she had begged Susannah from her deathbed. Mama had lingered longer than Papa after the fever. 'Twas Mama who'd tried to arrange things just so, had made her take a vow to care for everyone, even while dying. And she had to continue to fulfill that promise.

Even if it hurt, deep inside, to do so.

To drink or not to drink? Somehow, the scotch decanter had lost its allure. He could drink, and would probably to excess, later that night. But right now, Daniel needed something more.

As he strode up the moor and came into sight of Goodwin, he paused. He was a man with a burning thirst—a long cool draft of water would quench it. And yet he always reached for the champagne. Or, better still—he was a man who was dying of hunger. But rather than bread, he sampled rare exotic cuisine that did nothing to abate his hunger pains.

Susannah's friendship was bread and water. Simple. Uncomplicated. Nourishing. Fulfilling. With her, he never felt a failure or alone. And now, she was gone. And he would be back to a diet of lobster bisque and champagne.

He had no desire to see Goodwin now. He skirted the side of the house and delved back into the clearing. Mother's chapel. He needed the peace and the simplicity of the chapel.

He found his way in, fumbling with the tinderbox until he lit the candle, sparking the little room with light. He surveyed it with a critical and jaded eye. It still needed a lot of work, but at least one could sit in contemplation without worrying about spiders and without sneezing from the thick layer of dust.

Daniel sank into a pew. A future without Susannah. Funny, he'd never really thought of that. Not that he'd ever thought about how he could keep Susannah in his life. After all, they weren't wed, and as far as either of them felt, not really betrothed, either. So why was he so upset? He'd never done anything to ensure that she would stay with him forever. Never done anything beyond reach out in friendship. What had he expected would happen?

He rested his elbows on his knees and cradled his

head in his hands. He couldn't go on like this. This existence was meaningless. Purposeless. Goodwin had no meaning for him beyond this little chapel that somehow brought him closer to what he was seeking.

"Dear God…" he muttered aloud. If only Susannah were here. She could help him pray. At least help him begin. His very being ached for understanding, for peace. And yet grace of any kind was as distant as a star.

"My Father…" The words rang hollowly through the rafters of the chapel.

'Twas no use. He was not a praying man. The life that he could have led as master of Goodwin Hall, bolstered by his friendship with Susannah, was a mere farce. He would never measure up to it. Never.

If he had no use for Goodwin, why stay? He could very well cut his losses. He could simply renege on his inheritance and pass it to some distant cousin. Or he could lease Goodwin out to someone else—some rich bloke from London seeking a country seat to add that gentry polish.

He raised his head slowly. This had to be the answer. It was best for Goodwin to have a master who could care for it. And it would be best for him if he could go. It didn't matter where—he could sign on with a merchant vessel or sail to America to seek a new adventure. And it would be best for Susannah, for she could carry on with her business without fear of censure by any of their neighbors.

This was the answer.

He would write to Paul directly to get his help in making the arrangements. Paul knew all sorts of people in London—card players who might be looking for a new home. At last, Paul's loose tongue and wide variety of acquaintance would come in handy. And if no one showed an interest, he'd board the place up and go adventuring just the same. Goodwin had been there for decades. It would continue to do well for decades more, even without a master.

He leaped up from the pew. A curious longing tore at him as he looked around at the chapel. Poor little building had just started coming together after years of neglect. 'Twas sad to leave it again, just as he'd begun to take care of it. If only he could bridge the gap that separated him from Goodwin. If only he could fill this emptiness in his life. But there was nothing for it. His friendship could only cause harm to Susannah and he was a dreadfully bad master, so 'twas better to face the fact of his deficiencies full force than to continue playing at a farce.

One couldn't devote one's life to a silly chapel. He'd see to it that this little building was kept up and that it never fell into disrepair again. Everyone could surely see the wisdom of his decision. Better to return to a life at which he excelled, rather than persist in one at which he kept failing.

Chapter Fourteen

Susannah adjusted the willow basket on her arm so that the handle no longer bit into her skin. She would try to finish all their weekly marketing here in the village and return to the shop as quickly as possible. 'Twas still quite strange to leave Becky and Nan in charge of matters. Funny, curious townspeople didn't even look in the display window any longer.

Perhaps they needed to change the bonnets out—give the place a fresh look. After all, there were only so many people in the village—perhaps everyone had already caught a glimpse of their display. Maybe something more autumnal would look nice. Some oak branches with orange-and-red leaves, velvets and dark taffetas—her fingers fairly itched to do the work. But then, someone had to do the shopping. And since business was slow, she could leave the girls behind without having to worry that they could not handle matters well enough on their own—even on a Saturday.

As she neared the main path that led to the other village shops, a trio of villagers glanced up at her. The two women in the group turned away without a smile or a nod. The man who accompanied them simply cocked his hat back on his forehead and stared at her. Susannah gave a cautious nod and continued on her path.

She passed by two other men—each who eyed her with a frankly assessing look, as though sizing her up like a mare in a livery stable. Susannah gave a brief nod and swallowed. Good gracious, what was the matter? Surely nothing had come of her friendship with Daniel. She hadn't seen or spoken to him in well over a fortnight—not since that dreadful day on the moor when she'd broken off their friendship. She must reach Bess's bakery without delay. Bess would tell her if something was dreadfully wrong.

Gathering her skirts along with the shreds of her dignity, Susannah quickened her pace. She passed the smithy just as a lanky young lad with spots over his face stepped into her path. He gave her a carefree grin and caught her shoulders to halt her progress.

"In a hurry, lass?" He gave her shoulders a squeeze. "Never mind. Such a rush on a Saturday! Come and spend a little time with me, then."

Susannah wrenched free of his grasp and broke into a run, holding her bonnet on with her free hand. He was still staring at her. She could feel his eyes burning into her back—well, her posterior—as she ran away. "Come back," he called, and she quickened her pace. She grasped the latch of Bess's front door and wrenched it, sending the door rebounding against the wall with a crash. As she stood panting on the threshold, bonnet askew, Bess glanced up in startled surprise. Her only customer, an elderly woman who was so bent over she was almost double, shuffled out of the shop. "Ought to be ashamed," the old lady muttered as she passed Susannah.

"What is it? What has happened? Do tell me, Bess." Susannah slammed the door shut and tossed her basket aside. "They must know. Everyone in the village is treating me as though I am a hussy."

"Calm yourself." Bess came around from behind the counter and enfolded her in a comforting embrace. "Here. Come to the back. We can chat without being seen." She guided Susannah around the corner of the counter and into the backroom. A large oven gave a pleasant heat to the room; it warmed her bones, but, strangely, did nothing to stop her shaking.

She sank onto a chair and looked up at Bess. "Please tell me," she croaked.

Bess placed her hands on her ample hips. "There is a rumor going around the village that you and Mr. Hale were engaged to be wed. The talk is that he either abandoned you and went to sea or you led him a merry dance and refused to marry him. It rather depends on who is telling the story."

Susannah's palms began to sweat, and she rubbed them briskly against her apron. "But why is everyone treating me like a light skirt? Or a woman with no reputation left to lose?"

"This was what I warned you about." Bess shook her head and turned away. She began fiddling with the oven, catching the top of the stove with an iron hook so she could lift it and stir the fire up higher. "You kept your engagement a secret—that was the first indiscretion. Then, when you began seeing each other again, you did so frequently and without any kind of chaperone. If the gossip is to be believed, you even slept in his home."

Susannah opened her mouth to protest, but Bess shushed her with a wave of her hand.

"I don't believe the gossip, myself. But you must see that it will affect the way you can conduct your business. Has your trade slacked off?"

Of course it had. That would account for the exceptionally slow Saturday they were experiencing. And of course, the lack of villagers peeking in the window at their display. Susannah nodded, closing her eyes. Everything slowed down, as though she were sleepwalking. If only someone would pinch her and awaken her. Then the nightmare would be over. She opened her eyes and heaved a deep sigh. Of course not.

"You must find a way to preserve your reputation." Bess stoked the fire once more and put the iron poker aside. "When my sister almost eloped, we found her a suitable beau as quickly as possible. She married him and had her first baby within the year. The talk died out. It will with you, too. You just need to find a way out."

"A way out," Susannah echoed. There was no way out. She had no family willing to force her into matrimony to spare her reputation. Aunt and Uncle were gone, and if they'd had their way, she'd be married to a pugnacious country squire by now. Scandal averted before it ever began. She shivered. 'Twas as though the heat emanating from the oven wasn't even touching her chilled skin. "This is innocent, you know. Maybe if I explained matters—"

"I don't know that anyone would listen." Bess raised her hands in defeat. "And folks like nothing better than a good gossip. Especially in this village. Precious little happens here, so when people get hold of a juicy bit of gossip, they're like dogs with a bone. If you talk about it, they'll ask more questions. They'll question your actions. They'll wonder why you did things one way instead of the other. If you never answer the rumors and divert their attention because you have nothing of interest to provoke them, the talk'll die down."

"I don't know that I have a way out," Susannah admitted. "I honestly thought the rumors would go away if I stopped being friends with Daniel. How on earth did they get started again?"

"Miss Prestwidge's servant was the one who told me. She came in to buy some special treats for a tea they were going to have, and she mentioned your engagement to Mr. Hale." Bess shrugged. "I pretended like I didn't know anything and she prattled on for a while and then moved on. If gentry servants gossip, then the villagers listen."

Susannah closed her eyes, willing her heart to resume its usual beat. There had to be a way out of this. She had worked too hard, made too many sacrifices for everything to end now. And it was not fair, not fair in the least, for her sisters. "I need to go home." The marketing would just have to wait. She could not endure the stares and the leers from the villagers. She must go home and think of a plan.

"Of course. You'll feel better once you've had a moment to yourself." Bess helped her to her feet and patted her back. "Mind you, if there's anything I can do to help, do tell me. I tried to keep the rumors quiet here in my store by refusing to act interested."

Susannah murmured her thanks. Bess was being as kindhearted as she could—after all, they barely knew each other. For her to ignore the rumors rather than add fuel to the fire was a tremendous help to Susannah's cause.

Bess retrieved the willow basket from the front room of the shop and tucked it under Susannah's arm. "Here.

Go out the back way." Bess led her to a door in the rear
of the kitchen, one that opened on a grassy alley. "Fewer
people out here this time of day. Everyone's either inside attending to their business or out front talking with
each other. Can you make it home all right? You look
awful peaked."

"I'll be fine." Susannah tugged her bonnet down over
her forehead. Perhaps if she ducked her head and ran
along the back path, no one would notice her. And Bess
was right. The alleyway was deserted. Nary a soul in
sight. If she hurried, she could make it home without
encountering another human being. "Thank you, Bess."

"Not at all, dear. Let me know if I can do anything
to help." Bess gave her shoulder a final, comforting pat
before ducking back indoors.

Susannah picked up her skirts and walked as briskly
as she could without breaking into a run. Though every
nerve in her being begged her to run, she would not give
in to panic. As long as she made it home quickly, and
with a minimum of interaction with others, she would
be fine. She would make a brisk cup of tea. They would
close the shop—after all, 'twas unlikely anyone would
come in today. And then she and her sisters could try to
think of a plan.

The little tumbledown cottage looked charming from
a distance—amazing what a bit of care could do for a
building. And right now, it was all the prettier for being
her hermitage. She would have peace and privacy here
until she could find a way to face the village. She dropped
her willow basket on the back steps and burst through
the doorway in the rear.

Nan and Becky scurried in to greet her. "Why are you

coming in this way?" Nan demanded, flicking a long, dark curl over one shoulder. "You startled us."

"I need a moment to compose myself. Then I can explain." Susannah removed her shawl and hung it on the wooden peg by the doorway. "Becky, can you put the kettle on? I need a bracing cup of tea. Strong enough to melt paint."

"Of course." Becky led her into the front room and beckoned her to a chair. "Poor thing. You look drained."

"Nan, close the door. Lock it." Should she order her sister to draw the curtains, too? No. That would be too much. Better to have a modicum of privacy rather than to seal oneself in so tightly that they were sure to invite further comment.

"Is this about Miss Prestwidge?" Nan asked as she brought down the latch to lock up.

"What do you mean, is this about Miss Prestwidge?" A fresh feeling of dread flooded Susannah's soul. Had Miss Prestwidge's servant come here to gossip, too? Mercy—this day could not get any worse.

"Her servant came by today. Just after you left." Becky set the teakettle on to boil, her usually gentle voice quivering a little. "She canceled her order for the Season, Susannah. All her bonnets. She asked us to return half her money."

And there it was. The final blow to her security. Even the gentry were turning their backs on her. And in a particularly cutting fashion, too. That money was meant to see them through the winter. Materials had already been ordered based on the design of those very bonnets that Miss Prestwidge had so carelessly turned away.

She hadn't cried. Not since childhood, at least. She was the eldest sister, the stalwart one. A regular tower of strength. But every soul has its breaking point, doesn't it? And though she could steel herself against the stares of the townspeople, she could not bear the loss of the very bread from their table.

There was nothing for it.

All was lost.

Susannah pillowed her head on her arms and broke into sobs.

Daniel surveyed the drawing room with a critical eye. The dustcovers the servants had put out shrouded the furniture completely. The entire room looked as though it were covered with cotton wool. Only the Aubusson carpet lent a splash of subdued color, and the prisms of the chandelier sparkled in the late-afternoon sunlight. The chandelier. Of course—someone must cover it up, as well.

He rang the bell to summon Baxter. The sooner these preparations were done the better. He could be on his way to London within a day or so. Paul awaited him there, and impatience mounted within Daniel's very being at the tedium of readying Goodwin for his long absence. Only a day or so more, and he could leave. He could bear it that long, surely.

Baxter opened the drawing room door. Even in the midst of upheaval, dustcovers and packing, Baxter remained unflappably clad, even down to his jacket. Daniel gave his head a rueful shake. Goodwin was in good hands—he had no reason to show a moment's concern for the Hall.

"Yes, sir?" Baxter bowed.

"See that someone covers the chandelier. There's about a hundred different prisms on that thing. It will be a nightmare to clean if we don't shroud it like we've done with everything else in the room."

"Of course, sir. I was waiting to cover it until the last moment." Baxter's tone reflected wounded dignity. "All of the lights are being saved until just before you leave."

"Very good. Should have known you'd have a plan." Daniel cast one final glance around the room. "Well, then. I think this room is done. Guess I'll go have a look round the parlor."

Baxter cleared his throat. "Before you go, sir, I think there is something you should know."

Daniel sighed. What would it be this time? A lecture about family responsibilities? A pointed reminder about one more thing on the endless list of repairs for the estate? "What is it? And be quick about it, man." He had no more time to waste.

Baxter turned and shut the door. How very odd. Usually Baxter didn't seem to care whether the staff could hear their discussions or not. Whatever had happened, his butler needed privacy to tell him. "Out with it, then."

"Well, sir, there is a rumor running rampant in the village that you and Miss Siddons were engaged to be wed, and that you jilted her, or that she cried off. And our own servants—without my knowledge until this very day—were gossiping about Miss Siddons's frequent visits to Goodwin."

So there it was. The worst had happened. Paul's story—which was, in fact, the truth—had finally reached the ears of their small town. Daniel tightened his grip on the back of the chair and prepared himself for the worst. "Is that so?"

"Yes. Of course I had a sit-down with the servants in the kitchen and told them in no uncertain terms that if there was any more gossiping about Goodwin, the offender would be sent packing. I have no use for rumor-mongering in my household, sir. All that does is stir up trouble and discontent."

True words. He glanced over at Baxter, his heart hammering painfully against his rib cage. "Has any word of this reached Miss Siddons?"

Baxter shook his head. "I don't know. All I know is that our servants played a role in it, for which I am terribly sorry. We can express our regret to Miss Siddons personally, if you wish."

"That won't be necessary." Daniel straightened and released his grip on the chair. "I appreciate you handling this so swiftly, Baxter. You're a good man." And he meant every word. Baxter might be meddlesome and could nag better than anyone's mother, but his heart and his loyalty were for Goodwin. For some reason, that had never really mattered much until now.

Baxter bowed. "Is there anything else I can do?"

"Not at the moment. I leave on the morrow, so if between now and then you hear more about the rumors regarding Miss Siddons, please let me know without delay." If Susannah hadn't heard anything yet—and there was a possibility that she still didn't know—he would hate for her to be distressed by him poking around and bringing the subject up.

Baxter quit the room, closing the door quietly behind him. Daniel stole a look around the room, lingering on the shrouded furniture. Once before, he'd left Goodwin and his family and Susannah behind. Was he merely repeating his own past mistakes?

No. Susannah told him that she didn't want his friendship—that her business meant more. If he stayed, he would be jeopardizing what she loved most. And if he left, perhaps the rumors in the village would all die down before they had a chance to harm her little shop. Susannah was strong. She would be able to face any difficulty that came her way. And if he stayed, he'd be nothing but an obstacle in her path.

He tugged the shroud over the chair a little tighter and turned it slightly askew. There it was. Better to let things go. He would join Paul in London and Susannah would have her shop, and their paths need never cross again.

With that last jarring thought, he turned and drew the curtains, blocking out the last of the autumn sunshine, cloaking the room in darkness.

Chapter Fifteen

The warmth of a woolen blanket enveloped Susannah. "Come, now. Let's get you upstairs." Becky tugged on Susannah's shoulders, using the strength of her small body to move her sister out of her position of misery, draped as she was over the wooden table.

"I can't." Susannah sniffled. "I've some work left to do."

"You can't stay down here in your condition." Nan, always the practical one, brought Susannah crashing back to earth. "Assuming we do have a customer—which I doubt, as we haven't had a soul peep in here the whole morning—then you will drive them away if you're sitting there crying."

"Nan is right," Becky averred in her gentle tone of voice. "You've been working too hard, Susannah. All this fuss over losing a customer. It's not like you to take on so. You need a rest."

Her sisters didn't know the whole truth. They thought she was waxing hysterical over losing Miss Prestwidge's trade, when really the loss was just the one last thing to utterly ruin an already ruined day. "It's not just that."

She raised her face, daring herself to look her sisters in the eye. Why was this so hard to tell them? They already knew what had transpired between her and Daniel. But she'd never had to tell them something this vastly unpleasant. They'd all been together when Papa and Mama died. And when they got the news about Aunt's and Uncle's deaths, well, that wasn't terribly awful to face.

But this? This matter went beyond embarrassment. It ate at her very soul.

She wiped her eyes with the corner of the blanket and took a deep, shaky breath. "It's not just Miss Prestwidge. No—not just about her order." This was difficult. "The townspeople—all of them—are talking about me. They all know about my secret engagement to Daniel, and as we know, they've already been talking about the improper amount of time Daniel spent at the store."

"Who cares what a lot of people think?" Nan shrugged. "Everything you've done is perfectly innocent."

Susannah gave a bitter little laugh. Oh, to be sixteen again and so sure of oneself. "It's not just what they're saying. It's how they are treating me. And how they will treat all of us. I was shunned by people just as I was walking into town. And a cheeky lad accosted me. Bess helped me by telling me what had happened, and she showed me the back alley so I could get home without being seen by anyone else."

"You were accosted?" Becky sank onto the chair beside her, grasping Susannah's arm. "Are you quite all right? Did he hurt you?"

"No, he just wounded my pride." Susannah dabbed at her eyes once more and straightened her posture. "But Miss Prestwidge canceling her order is another matter entirely. If we are going to be laughed at and gossiped about, and we won't be able to earn a living, what shall we do?"

"We could sell the building and move to another village. One where no one knows us or our family," Nan volunteered. She sat down on Susannah's other side and planted her elbows on the table. "We started from nothing here. We could do so again."

"But that could take time. And would we be all right to stay here in the meantime? Oh, I wish we had someone we could go to—someone who lived far enough away that we could close the shop and stay with them until the talk died down." That was the problem with her family. It was small, and when available—thoroughly unhelpful. Well, except for her sisters.

"Have you spoken to Daniel about this?" Becky's voice was quiet and subdued.

"Of course not, silly. She just got back from the village," Nan snapped.

Susannah glanced at both her sisters from under dampened lashes. They were snapping at each other—they who had grown so close of late. She must gather her self-control and resume her position as head of the family before the entire day devolved into a welter of crying and confusion. "Nan. Do not be unkind. Becky was only trying to help." Perhaps if she did have a lie down, she could take control and master this situation before it mastered them.

She rose stiffly from the table and wrapped the woolen blanket more tightly about her person. "I am going upstairs for a rest. I need to calm myself so I can think clearly. In the meantime—" she eyed both of her sisters and treated them to her sternest "elder sister" expression

"—I want no bickering. If you want to close the shop and simply work quietly, then that will be fine."

"I notice you did not do any marketing." Becky eyed the empty willow basket, where it lay abandoned in the hallway. "Shall we do the marketing for you?"

"I don't know. I don't think that's a good idea. People might be as rude to you as they were to me." The staircase squeaked in protest as Susannah began her ascent. "Perhaps we'd better stay home."

"No indeed. Let us do the marketing," Nan pronounced firmly, tossing a long, dark curl over one shoulder. A flicker of something—understanding?—passed through her sisters. Perhaps they would feel more united again if they took on a difficult task together. "We shall take the back route. We'll go straight to Bess's. Then we'll be home."

"Very well." Susannah passed a weary hand over her brow. "But mind you—be careful. If anyone says anything to you that isn't pleasant or polite, I want you to return home immediately."

Her sisters murmured their agreement and ducked out the back door as though hounds were baying at their heels. Probably they were hungry. Hungry for Bess's scones, and perhaps a little hungry for the excitement of gossip. They had no inkling, as she had, of just how dreadful this entire scandal was.

Susannah sat on her bed and removed her boots, then tucked the blanket around her just as she was—dress, shawl and stockings. She had no desire and no energy for making herself comfortable. Just wrapping herself up like a broken china doll in a handkerchief so she could rest without causing further damage.

She burrowed her head in her old feather pillow for

warmth. The sweet, musty smell of the feathers was oddly comforting, for it reminded her of home. She would breathe deeply of it every night before bed and think of Mama and Papa and the carefree days when one could walk through the village of Tansley without being an object of fun.

As her eyes drifted closed, her thoughts turned to Daniel. Where was he? What was he doing now? And did he know of her troubles?

Probably not. Daniel was sheltered from so many unpleasant things through the power and wealth of his position.

But…for some reason, she couldn't stop thinking that it would be nice if she could share this burden with him.

Daniel opened his trunk one last time. Everything was in order—Baxter saw to that. There was really no reason to check, except a strange, nagging feeling that he'd left something behind. But no, that would be ridiculous. His butler was efficient and thoughtful, always prepared for any contingency. Well, then. There was nothing he'd left behind, and there was not one more thing that could be done to prepare for his journey to London. A good night's sleep, and they'd start at first light.

A loud knock sounded on his bedchamber door. Daniel straightened and let the trunk lid fall shut. "Enter."

Baxter poked his head around the door frame, his expression reflecting confusion and caution. "Sir, the two youngest Siddons sisters are here to see you. Shall I show them into the parlor? I have them in the front hall. I hated to put them anywhere, seeing as how the dustcovers will make the furniture uncomfortable."

Nan and Becky? What on earth was going on? "No,

don't show them into the parlor. The dust sheets are depressing. I'll meet them in the hall, and I shall take them for a walk around the estate." Besides, if they were outdoors, there was less likelihood that their conversation would be overheard by any prying servants. 'Twas quite likely they came to him about Susannah, and if something was indeed the matter, he should hate for it to be bandied about the village, making the situation worse for her.

He followed on Baxter's heels and overcame his butler, going down the staircase two at a time. "Hello, ladies," he called as he neared the bottom of the stairs. "I daresay you've come to say goodbye."

Nan opened her mouth, her brows drawn together as though to protest, but he shushed her with a wave of his hand. "Come on, then. Let's take a tour of the grounds before I leave it all behind for the glories of Town." He offered each sister an elbow and propelled them out the front door.

"Let's get a distance from the house before we talk," he muttered, pitching his voice just loudly enough that they both could hear him. "My servants have been gossiping."

The girls nodded their assent, and he led them off toward the clearing in the woods, where Mother's chapel stood. The windows had been covered with shutters, lending the small building a strange look of blindness. His heart hitched for a moment in his chest, and he drew them to a stop. Foreboding washed over him as he turned to face the two girls.

"What has happened?" he demanded. No time for pleasantries or formalities. He must know what had transpired to give both of the sisters such a pallor and such widened eyes.

"The news of your engagement to Sue is all over the village," Nan panted. She straightened her bonnet, which had been knocked askew in the rush. "And Miss Prestwidge canceled her bonnet order."

"She's demanding half her money back," Becky added. She grasped his arm with a pleading gesture. "We had counted on that order, along with the other ones from the gentry, to see us through the winter."

So there it was. The worst had happened, after all. And it was his fault.

All of it.

He could blame no one else. He'd left Susannah behind when they were engaged. And then, later, drink had loosened his tongue. And then Paul had aired their secret to London. Had he been more circumspect—more of a gentleman—more of a man, in fact—none of this would have happened.

"There's more. Today, Sue tried to go into town to do our weekly marketing. And the villagers shunned her. And one boy was cheeky to her. She ran home by a back alley so as not to be seen by anyone else." Unshed tears sparkled in Becky's eyes, and her lips trembled. "Susannah is strong enough to muddle through anything. And yet—I fear for her now. I don't see how we can extricate ourselves from this mess."

Daniel clenched his jaw. Someone had been cheeky to his Susannah? "Who was it?" He would thrash the blackguard within an inch of his life.

"We don't know. Sue didn't recognize him." Nan twisted her hands in her apron, as though the movement would keep her still and calm. "We had to come to you,

Daniel. This is more than we can bear. We know you are leaving for London on the morrow, but—"

"I am not leaving." All at once, 'twas crystal clear. He must stay here, at Goodwin, and become the man he should have been when he was just a lad. He needed to set things to rights with Susannah, and he needed to protect her from the village. And from any other scoundrel who suggested she had done anything wrong. And as for Miss Prestwidge—well, he would see to it that her order was reinstated.

"I must get my horse." He turned and beckoned the girls to follow him. He walked as fast as he could without breaking into a run. He must go to Susannah. He must convince her that he and he alone could help her. That he wanted to help her. That her happiness was paramount in his life. If he repaired this damage, then 'twas as if he had never been a villain or a coward.

"You girls go into the house. I am headed to the stable. I need to speak with your sister." He motioned for them to go inside. "Baxter will attend to your needs until I return."

"But—" Becky gasped from behind him "—Susannah is resting. And if the villagers see you—"

He stopped in his tracks and turned to face them both. "I no longer care what the villagers say or do or think about the matter. 'Tis a private affair, between the two of us."

"But what shall you do?" Nan put her hand over her heart and breathed in sharply. "Gracious, you walk fast."

Well, he didn't precisely know what to do. But he wasn't going to let Susannah suffer for all his stupidity and cowardice. "When I planned to leave for London, I thought I would be doing what was best for your sister.

But now I see how wrong that is. If people are canceling their orders and being cheeky to her in the street—" he clenched his hand into a fist, allowing his nails to bite into his palm "—then I must set matters straight. I want your sister to be happy. She cannot be happy if her business fails on account of our broken engagement."

Becky gave him a gentle smile. "Daniel, I have always liked you. And I like that you are putting Susannah's happiness before your escape to London."

He faced both sisters. Getting their good opinion meant more to him, more than anything he'd wanted before. More even than his freedom. For freedom, once gained, had a certain hollow feeling to it that never abated. His liberty from Goodwin brought years of rambling, and drinking, and carousing—not things he was proud to admit.

"I like you both, too. And I admire your sister too much to let her suffer. I shall go and talk to her without delay. No matter what the village says or thinks about it. And both of you stay here. I shall have my carriage bring you home in a few hours." He gave them both what he hoped was a reassuring smile.

"You haven't told us what you plan to do about the matter," Nan demanded, her hands on her hips. She gave a defiant lift to her chin. "All heroes have a plan, you know. If you want to be Susannah's rescuer, you must know what to do."

"I don't know." Dash it all, Nan was right. He couldn't go storming into their home without knowing at least what he planned to say. "I just want to make amends. Make her happy."

"But why do you care?" Nan took a step closer. By Jove, she was strong as iron and as practical as a geom-

etry figure. Unlike Becky, she cared naught that he liked
them and that his intentions were pure. She wanted a map,
drawn out like a general waging a campaign.

"It's as I said. I admire her—" If he were wearing a
cravat, he'd loosen it.

"Admiration isn't the same as love." Nan dismissed
him with a wave of her hand. "And if you offer Susannah charity, you know as well as I do that she will box
your ears."

That was true. He raked his hand through his hair.
What could he possibly say or do that wouldn't insult
Susannah?

Becky laid a hand on Nan's shoulder. "Nan, you
shouldn't take on so. You shouldn't force Daniel to say
anything about what he plans to do. Nor should you criti-
cize the manner in which he does it."

"But what Nan says is true. If I barge in there and try
to bend her to my will because it's what I feel is right,
then she will drive me away from pride. There is nothing I can do or say to make the matter acceptable to her.
To make her understand…" He trailed off, for the words
would no longer come. If only he wasn't such an inar-
ticulate fool.

"What would you like her to understand?" Becky's
sweet voice was cajoling him, lifting the veil that stood
between himself and his actions, his words.

He closed his eyes. The autumn wind sang through
the trees, rattling the leaves as they began to fall. He
breathed in deeply. Smoke drifted on the air and stung his
nostrils. The sounds and smells of Goodwin comforted
him—wrapping around him as securely as a blanket. At
that moment, and at that time, Goodwin gave him courage as nothing else had. For the first time in his life, his

house was his home, enveloping him and strengthening him in the way his family never could.

He opened his eyes to find the Siddons girls staring at him. No, not the Siddons girls. The Siddons sisters. His sisters, if they wanted to claim the kinship.

"I want Susannah to understand that I want her to marry me. In truth, this time. No false engagements, no wishes to evade anything or anyone."

"Because?" Nan prompted, and Becky followed the single word with a quick jab to her sister's right side. "Ouch."

"No. No more. What needs to be said, I must say to your sister. Now, go inside, the pair of you."

He strode off, leaving them behind. He was, at last, a hero with a purpose and a strategy.

Now, to get the damsel in distress to agree to his plan.

Chapter Sixteen

Whatever was that noise? Susannah sat up in bed, her hair tumbling down her back, her heart racing. Had she drifted asleep, and this was just a dream?

No, there it was again. A decided pounding at the door. She shoved her hair out of the way and fumbled with her slippers. Perhaps it was a customer or perhaps—more likely—someone else had come to cancel their order. Well, jolly good, then. It wouldn't matter if she looked a sight or not. And according to her reflection in the looking glass, she most certainly did look a disaster.

She scurried down the staircase. "Wait a moment," she called.

A deep, familiar voice answered. "Do hurry, Susy."

Daniel. What on earth was he doing here? She scrambled over to the door and unlatched it, shoving it open. "Daniel," she seethed. "Make haste. You might be seen."

He stepped over the threshold and latched the door behind him. "I really don't care if I am, Susy. I've come here with no bad intentions, and everything that has transpired between us since you set foot in Tansley has been quite proper."

"You don't understand." Gracious. She surveyed him as he crossed the room, her brain still addled from being awoken so abruptly from her rest. Here, just an hour before, she had wished for him to be near so she could confide all her troubles in him. And now he sat before her, his hat in his hands, bereft of cravat and quite wind-blown. Surely she was dreaming. "Everyone knows—"

"I know, too." He tossed his hat onto the hearth and leaned forward, clasping his hands. "Your sisters told me everything."

"Nan and Becky?" They told her they were going to do the marketing. A strange mixture of anger, pride and gratitude began to swell within her chest. "To go behind my back…to…to…" she sputtered. Really, there were no words for the emotions that swirled within her, but whatever it was certainly made her dizzy. She touched her temple gingerly.

"Don't be angry at your sisters. What they did was right. I know your formidable pride, Susy. And I know how very willful you can be. But didn't it ever occur to you that I might want to know the truth? After all, I have a right to know. My behavior has put you at risk of losing everything. I've come to make matters right." He took her hands in his and drew her down beside him on the settee.

This was quite strange. Susannah swallowed and tried to pull her hands free, but they remained trapped within his warm grasp. She fought hard to look him in the eye, but 'twas difficult, her heart fluttered so. And there was a thread of anger running through the flutters, as if she despised herself for being so affected by him to begin with.

"I've come to ask you to marry me, Susannah. In truth this time. Not an extended farce with a decidedly bad ending." He gave her a crooked grin.

Was this his attempt at making things right? Or was it merely a joke in poor taste? She gave her hands a final wrench and set them free. "You are talking nonsense. And I wish you would stop. It's bad form. And moreover, if anyone sees that you are here, I might as well lock up my shop forever and wander the moors as a beggar."

"I don't care what other people think." Daniel lowered his brows and fixed her with his piercing green gaze. "I only care about—" He broke off abruptly, his expression clouded.

Susannah's heart pounded in her chest. "Of course you don't care about other people, Daniel! You've never had to." Oh, this selfishness. His cocoon of wealth and privilege. When would he ever learn? "I don't know how to stem the tide of disaster myself, but I know that your being here and exposing us both to further scandal shan't help matters." She rose and turned toward the door. "You should go."

"No." He rose, too, towering over her. She gulped. She had forgotten how very tall he was. She had to crane her neck backward just a bit to look him in the face. "I'm not going anywhere. Susy, you must see how this is as much my disaster as yours. And I want to help you."

"You offer marriage out of pity and nothing more." 'Twas difficult to say, and, judging by the way his expression hardened, not terribly pleasant for him to hear. She didn't mean to hurt him, but she couldn't bear pity. Not from him. Not when he'd hurt her so many years before. She softened a bit. "I know you mean well…"

"Why must you look at things in terms only of value, of repayment?" Daniel yelled, striding across the room. "You think only of my offer as a manner of charity for you. Do you have any idea what it means to me?"

He'd never raised his voice to her before. Always, their moments had been joking, or anxious, or even tender. But now—his expression was wounded. His voice was raw. Daniel's proposal was serious, and it must mean something to him beyond an offering of kindness.

She took a deep, steadying breath. "Go on," she murmured.

Daniel's head snapped up and he fixed her with such a powerful stare that it quite took her breath away. "What I did was wrong, so many years ago. And I apologized, yet I feel that apologies were not enough. And I want to make amends for it because my behavior has jeopardized all you hold dear."

Yes. That was understandable. But marriage? She would need more justification than simple regret to start a successful marriage.

"I want to protect you. When I heard that some rogue was cheeky with you today, Susy, I was ready to kill him. And the townspeople turning their backs on you? Why, you are more pure, more innocent than anyone I know. And I admire you."

"Thank you." She exhaled slowly. It was not an admission of love, yet—'twas good to have someone want to kill a scoundrel for being flirtatious with her. No one had cared enough about her to stand up for her before. It was nice to have someone recognize and cherish her. And the burden of loneliness somehow abated when Daniel spoke to her thus.

"When I propose marriage, it is in some ways to right that wrong I committed a long while ago. And it is also a plea because I don't want to leave. I don't want to be the fellow who dodges and ducks and weaves any longer. I want life at Goodwin, and I want you there with me."

Never any words of love, not yet. Words of admiration, of friendship, of wanting to make amends. Could that be enough? Would she be happy with him? And could she make him happy enough in return?

On the other hand, that burden of loneliness—it eased when he was around.

But—could she leave the shop behind? The shop was akin to a living thing, something she was nurturing and developing into a healthy, resilient being. She couldn't abandon it. Not now. Not when there was so much trouble that could kill it.

"Could I keep the shop?" It was an incongruous answer to the question he'd posed, but she couldn't bite the words back any longer.

He raised his eyebrows. "I suppose," he replied in a surprised tone. "If that's what you wish."

"It is." Well, it seemed to be, anyway. Though it felt odd to ask, she couldn't let go of her only means of independence. Not yet.

"So…is that a yes?" He was looking at her in such a strange fashion. As though the well-being of the entire world depended upon her answer.

"I suppose it is." It wasn't entirely an ungracious response. Just hesitant.

Daniel nodded and squared his jaw. "We should think of the wedding, then. I can procure a special license, or we can have a traditional wedding in St. Mary's. Reading of the banns, and all that."

"Yes. Of course. The wedding." Like that. They were engaged again just like that. The years of sorrow and anger neatly swept away, and a future as mistress of Goodwin Hall before her.

"I don't have a ring." Daniel looked abashed, as though

he'd read her thoughts and her blank astonishment. "But I shall get one. A string won't do this time. We shall handle matters properly."

She nodded. He was right—everything must be formal and decorous between them, and that meant having a ring. "Thank you."

They stood for a moment, facing each other across the room, but Susannah found it hard to meet his gaze. She snatched for ideas of what to say next, as though they were stray bits of hay floating by on the breeze. Daniel's wife. She was going to marry Daniel. There was a solemnity to that thought, one that was both sobering and strangely right.

"Shall I get a special license? The sooner we are married, the sooner the talk in the village will die down." Daniel took a step to close the gap between them, and Susannah dared herself to look him in the eye. Should she marry quickly, then? Daniel was wealthy and powerful enough to secure a license somehow, and that would end village speculation that much sooner.

And yet—the thought of becoming his wife would take getting used to. Perhaps village talk would die down once the banns were read the first time. And she could adjust to the idea of marrying Daniel and settling in to life at the Hall. And his drinking—well, that was a problem, too. She would have to find a way to help stop his reliance on the bottle.

"I need more time," she blurted. "A traditional wedding ceremony at St. Mary's sounds fine."

He nodded. "Very well."

Another silence stretched before them. Her nerves were wearing thin. She needed time to think, to contemplate, to talk to Nan and Becky. And come to that, where were Nan and Becky? "Did my sisters go to the village to finish the marketing after they met you?"

"No. They stayed at the Hall. I instructed Baxter to send them home in my carriage. They should be here in just a few moments."

"Thank you for taking care of them." She managed a smile. Funny, weren't engagements supposed to be joyful? And both times she became engaged to Daniel, 'twas to avert disaster. So a sense of joy pervaded neither— only a feeling of protection and security.

He didn't love her. And she wasn't sure she loved him. He was so charming—could one ever really believe anything he said or did? But she appreciated Daniel for all his kindness, his sense of humor, his frank generosity. Surely that could be enough.

"Well, then. I shall go to St. Mary's and see about the banns," Daniel replied, shifting awkwardly. "And I shall get a ring. I suppose we should be wed as soon as the banns are read?"

"Yes. Please ask Reverend Kirk what we should do." The kindly old reverend would be able to help them muddle through the intricacies of setting the wedding date. What seemed so momentous to them would likely be a minor diversion for the reverend. "And once you know the date, I shall begin to prepare my dress."

He stood there, before the hearth, looking abashed and nervous as a schoolboy. Her heart surged with warmth for him. Dearest Daniel. She strode over to the hearth and picked up his hat, handing it to him. "Off you go, then."

He took his hat, offering the same crooked grin that won her affection when they were children. "Off I go, then."

She followed him across the room, a thousand questions beginning to form in her mind. How would she continue to care for the shop as mistress of the Hall? How was she going to fill that role? And what would be expected of her as his wife?

He grasped the door latch and turned toward her. "Everything will be all right, Susy. You have my word on it."

Again, that surge of warmth and gratitude flooded her soul. For the first time in ages, she couldn't think of a sharp retort or a witty insult to him pledging his word. In fact, she felt no rancor at all. Funny, at this moment it was easy to forget how skillfully he could use his charm. Instead, she stood on tiptoe and kissed his jawline. "I want to believe you."

Daniel looked down at her with an intense expression in his eyes but said nothing. In a moment, he was gone.

She latched the door shut behind him and turned to watch him canter off across the moor on his horse.

She was engaged to Daniel Hale, once more. Only this time, he'd said he would keep his promise. She'd have to try to believe him.

But just in case, she'd hold on to her little shop a bit longer.

"So Baxter sent us home in a carriage," Becky explained to Susannah that night as they brushed out their hair. "And he said Daniel had ordered all the dustcovers be taken away from the furniture. The house was in an uproar when we left."

"I think it's jolly good that you and Daniel are finally getting married," Nan pronounced, unwinding a tangle in one long ringlet. "The talk in the village will die down. And you can finally have your happily-ever-after, Susannah."

"I wouldn't exactly call it that." Susannah tucked her knees up to her chin and wrapped her quilt around her body for more warmth. "But I do think it is the right thing to do."

"What do you mean?" Becky glanced over at Susannah. "Isn't he falling in love with you?"

Susannah's heart skipped a beat. She dropped her hairbrush on the floor, where it landed with a decided clatter. "Don't be silly."

"He can't say it yet, but he's probably head over heels for you, Sue." Nan scooped up the brush and handed it back to her sister.

"Rubbish." She worked the brush through her hair with stubborn strokes. "Daniel doesn't love me. He admires me."

"Yes. And love and admiration are not the same thing, which is what I told him when he said as much to me," Nan said. "But something in his expression made me believe that he was. He may be in love with you and may not even know it yet."

"And you might love him, too, and not know it yet," Becky chimed in. "After all, meeting him again, after all this time—it's not a mere coincidence. And still caring enough about him that you took care of him when he was sick."

Sick with drink, of course, but her younger sisters need not know that. Daniel had simply told her sisters what they wanted to hear; when speaking to her this afternoon, he had been much more practical. As he should be. "I do think fondly of Daniel, and I do like him a lot, but I am not marrying for love. It will be rather a mock marriage, I think. Something to help us both. I enjoy Daniel's company. He says he wants to marry me to protect me and to care for me. That is a good thing. I cannot say no to that."

Her sisters shared a sideways glance, and Susannah sighed. "Stop it, both of you. Nothing will change. I shall even find a way to manage the shop once I become mistress of the Hall. We've agreed to it."

"Don't be absurd." Nan turned to face Susannah, her eyebrows raised. "Your duties will be at the Hall. There are tenants to manage, menus to plan, rooms to furnish. How on earth will you have the time to manage the shop?"

"Not to mention that it simply isn't done," Becky added in a gentler tone than her sister's. "If Daniel agreed to it, then that shows how very eager he is to compromise so that you will marry him. But as mistress of the Hall, your days will be full. You'll have very little time to manage anything but your obligations on the estate."

Susannah fought a rising tide of panic and licked her lips so she could respond. "But if I don't manage the store, who will?"

"We will, of course." Nan reached over and patted her on the shoulder. "Never mind about us. If we have questions, 'tis but a short buggy ride to the Hall. We can ask for assistance and even discuss matters with you every week."

"Or every day, if need be." Becky rose and walked over to Susannah's cot. "Come, now. We have been trained by the very best shopkeeper there is. Susannah Siddons. We shall be able to manage beautifully."

Susannah gave her sisters a halfhearted smile. Of course they might. But they were so young. For as long as she could remember, they had been her sole responsibility. Everything she had done, she had done to protect them and secure their independence. And now—could she really leave them and her beloved shop behind? They had been everything to her—her reason for being, in fact.

"You should go round to the Hall tomorrow. Take a look at the tenants' homes, and see what must be done about the place. Daniel hasn't been very thorough keeping the place up. There is bound to be much to do." Nan helped Susannah lie down, and Becky tucked the quilt about her. Susannah rolled her eyes. Lovely. Now they were treating her as though she were old and decrepit, unable to see to herself.

Nan blew out the candle, and the room faded into darkness. Very well. She wouldn't give up her shop completely, and just to appease everyone, she'd go and have a look at the Hall tomorrow.

But the shop would always be hers. No matter what her sisters said, it was her creation, the reason she'd uprooted her family and come back to Tansley. 'Twas the only thing that separated her from the wolf at the door. Her shop meant she never had to do another man's bidding and that she was earning her own way in the world. Could she give it all up for a charming young man who often drank to excess?

The shop was her only freedom.

It was her only security.

How could she simply relinquish both for marriage?

Chapter Seventeen

'Twas a fine, crisp autumn day to ride out to Crich. Daniel brushed aside Baxter's suggestion of a carriage and ordered that a horse be saddled instead. A ride would do him good. The miles of open country and the fresh cold air would give him the clear head he needed to think. For despite Susannah's acceptance yesterday, a fellow felt vaguely unsettled. Susannah had agreed to be his bride. In truth, and not in artifice. 'Twas a thought that was both exciting and sobering. One had to grasp the mantle of master of Goodwin Hall so that he could provide a good home for its mistress. And that, too, was a sobering thought.

So it was with a muddled head and an urgent need to sort through matters that Daniel rode out to St. Mary's to meet Reverend Kirk and see to the reading of the banns. He hadn't visited the little church in ages, not since he was a boy. And even then, his visits had been under extreme protest. He didn't bow to the obligation and will of his father; much less would he bow to the will of his Lord. So, why go? If he was truly the master of his own destiny, he had no need of a higher power.

Somehow, he would have to neatly sweep that affirmation under the rug when speaking to Reverend Kirk. Marrying Susannah meant bowing to society's whims in at least this small regard—a church wedding. And the pastor, whom Daniel remembered from childhood as a kindly, gentle man, would probably not care to hear the truth about Daniel's views on religion.

The ride was short, for his horse was brisk and the roads quite fine; autumnal rains and winter snow had not yet carved deep ruts across his path. As he drew nearer, the spire of St. Mary's rose majestically on the crest of the moor. Daniel swallowed. He wasn't nervous, not really. But a fellow did feel a twinge of the old desire to run in the face of so much tradition.

And once he was done here, he would be free to go back to being himself. This would be one mere sacrifice to gentility, having a traditional church wedding. It didn't mean he was changing who he was. He wasn't going to give in to all forms of duties and obligation.

Just this once. For Susannah's sake. It was what she wished, after all.

He turned his horse into the churchyard and stopped, considering the little parsonage off to one side, and then the stone facade of the church. Where would he more likely find the reverend?

He'd try the parsonage. He nudged the horse forward, over to the block, and dismounted. As he tied the reins to the post, he willed his hands to cease their shaking. He hadn't brought anything to drink with him, and that was too bad. 'Twould give a fellow Dutch courage when facing the shadows of his childhood.

"Hello, there," a cheerful voice called from behind him. Daniel whirled around. "Reverend Kirk?" He was grayer and rounder than he had been in Daniel's youth, but his face still reflected the same kindly light.

"Yes, indeed. And who might you be?" The reverend stepped forward, his hand outstretched. "Forgive my appearance, my lad. I was tying up the rosebushes on the opposite side of the chapel. We're in for a bit of a windy afternoon and evening, I predict. If this old leg of mine is a proper barometer."

Daniel grasped the reverend's hand cordially, as one might a distant uncle. "I'm Daniel Hale. I believe you knew my family—we're of Goodwin Hall, in Tansley."

"Of course," the reverend exclaimed warmly. "I do remember the Hales. You can't possibly be Daniel. Why, you're far too grown-up. The lad I remember preferred climbing trees, bare feet and all, than church services. And didn't you go abroad? How extraordinary." Reverend Kirk released Daniel's hand and gestured toward the parsonage. "Would you like to come in for some tea? I was just headed that way myself."

Something about this chapel and Reverend Kirk's warm and friendly demeanor was grating on Daniel's nerves. He had the strangest urge, just as he had as a child, to run off—to bolt to the safety of the nearest tree, or to lose himself on the moor. But that was ridiculous. The chapel at Crich and its reverend might be a part of his childhood, but they asked no more than that of him. Why, the old fellow merely asked him in for tea—not to take up the whole mantle of Goodwin and the Hale family.

All the same, he had no desire to linger.

"No, thank you," he responded evenly. "I've actually come to ask…" What would this be called? A favor? His blessing? A helping hand? This was ridiculous. Even in the most dire circumstances, be it a typhoon on board ship or a row with drunken shipmates, he could hold his own. Why was this particular task so hard? He cleared his throat and tried once more. "Banns. I need to see about the reading of the banns."

"Ah, my dear lad, how delightful." Reverend Kirk clapped him heartily on the shoulder. "Of course, we shall set about it this very Sunday. And the young lady…?"

"Miss Susannah Siddons." Saying it aloud did nothing to make it seem more real.

"Ah, yes. I remember the Siddons family well. They came here often when the girls were little. A tragic story, that. Death, the breakage of a family. I was glad to hear the young girls were doing well." The reverend bestowed a benevolent smile on Daniel. "You are a fortunate young fellow. I shall see to the details at once. When shall the wedding be, then?"

"When the last bann is read, I suppose?" He was completely out of his depth here. He shifted from one foot to another.

"Of course. That would be the first Sunday in October. Shall we have the ceremony the week after?"

"Yes, that would be fine." He burned that thought into his brain—by the second week in October, Susannah would become Mrs. Daniel Hale. And he—would become a husband. His old panic began to rise to the surface, and he tamped it down with an inward promise of a good stout drink when they were done here.

"Well, then. I'll set about the planning." The reverend looked at him with a curious expression, his grizzled eyebrows lifted. "Are you quite all right? You look a bit peaked. The offer for tea still stands, you know. 'Tis a long ride back to Tansley."

"No. No, thank you. It's just—" The fresh air and the

reverend's friendly ways must be conspiring to loosen his tongue. He'd never felt such a surge to confess, not in all his years of rambling. "I want to make Susannah happy. I've made a dreadful hash of it so far." He paused. "I try and try to do the right thing, but I feel as though I come up short. Even though I outwardly appear to be doing well, I don't feel as though I am inside."

"So it sounds as though your dilemma is that you feel there is a division between yourself as you are alone versus how you appear to others? That you are somehow lacking?"

"Precisely so," Daniel admitted. Reverend Kirk had, in his gentle way, uncovered the problem. "I feel as blank as an unwritten page."

"Well, then." Reverend Kirk chuckled. "You must endeavor to fill that page."

"But how? With what?" Daniel raked his hand through his hair. "Always in the past I embraced the void. I drank to feel the emptiness, to allow that emptiness to wash over my wretchedness. But now—what shall I do? I have entertained the possibility of giving up liquor entirely for Susannah. And it's terrifying, Reverend. So frightening to know that I am asking so much of Susannah, and she is asking so much of me— And I have been such a failure in the past—"

"But you are making amends now," Reverend Kirk interrupted, holding up one hand to stem the flood of Daniel's confession. "Marriage is meant to be a partnership. 'Tis a symbol of the relationship we have with our Lord. He asks much of us, but He gives in return. This is what happens in a true marriage, my son. There is a give-and-take from both parties."

Well, that was true. Daniel pondered the pastor's

words for a moment. "But how—how do I fill the void? So that I can come to Susannah as a whole person, not as a doll made out of straw?"

"What you are undertaking is no small feat, Daniel. When a man comes to rely upon drink, it becomes the center of his world. And when a man gives it up entirely, it is not uncommon for him to feel as though he is drifting, without anchor. Know that you have an anchor, Daniel. The Lord loves you and watches over you. And He will give you the strength to see this through."

"He will?" Daniel murmured the words like a prayer under his breath. His shoulders relaxed and his breathing eased. "All my life I have avoided the trappings of family and duty. How can I, in good faith, pledge to love and protect Susannah when I have avoided those very things in my life?"

"Many young men feel the same way," Reverend Kirk replied in a gentle tone. "Many see family and obligations as a kind of prison. But I would think that deepening this part of your life now, with Susannah by your side, perhaps you won't find these things as difficult or as challenging."

With Susannah by his side. The words had a certain ring to them. The thought of Susannah walking with him about the estate, or reading beside him in the study as a storm raged across the moor—why, it would be a delight just to have her close by.

But—would she be happy with him, as he hoped to be with her?

"I've disappointed her in the past. I want to make amends for it. I just don't know how. And she seems reluctant to—I don't know—somehow become a part of my life. She wants to keep her millinery shop, but there is so much work I need help with at the Hall. I need a helpmeet in so many ways, Reverend. How can I make certain that she is happy enough with me?"

"You must show her that your marriage is a partnership. Obviously, Susannah has a great deal of independence and spirit. It has served her well over the years, I am certain. She may be so used to fighting alone that she doesn't realize that a marriage to you can be a wonderful partnership between the pair of you. You need her, Daniel. And I think she needs you. Both more than you think, I am fairly certain." The reverend patted his shoulder with a gentle touch. "And now—about that tea?"

Daniel stepped back with a regretful smile. "I've kept you from it far too long. Enjoy, Reverend."

"Goodbye, Daniel. Remember, allow your faith to grow and deepen with Susannah as your helpmeet."

Daniel replied with a carefree nod as he turned back to his horse.

But he felt anything but easy inside as he led his horse across the moor. Funny—he had weathered so many storms as a sailor, but nothing seemed as daunting as this. A partnership with Susannah. One that would last for life.

He kicked his horse into a canter.

Susannah had pondered her sisters' words all night, which naturally resulted in only fitful sleep. Could she simply hand over the shop to the pair of them? No. Surely not. There must be a way that she could handle everything. Goodwin Hall was a manor house, and every big home required a kind of maintenance. But likely Daniel's servants had seen to those matters themselves over the years. So she might be able to simply step in and make decisions where her advice or opinion was needed. And that would give her ample time to watch over her sisters and the shop—guarding them all as closely as she ever had.

But—purely for appearances' sake, of course—one had to make one's sisters believe that she took their words to heart. So Susannah struck out for Goodwin the next morning with a feeling of certainty in her heart. She would take a cursory stroll about the grounds and be home in time for luncheon.

Should she ask for Daniel at the main house? Ordinarily she would try to avoid him, but after all, he was her fiancé in truth now. And this was his home. So, no matter what the servants said, she should make the attempt to see him and offer to tour the grounds with him. It didn't matter now that gossip would link their names. Since they were engaged, this was to be expected.

Funny, no matter how many times she explained it to herself, the matter still felt like a dream—as though it never really happened.

She gathered her skirts, which had become dampened from her lengthy stroll across the frosted moor, and mounted the front steps to the Hall. Baxter opened the door as she climbed the final step, a smile of welcome on his distinguished face.

"Miss Siddons, how good of you to come. Mr. Hale is in Crich this morning, but I am sure he will be happy for you to stay in the study until he returns."

Crich? Oh, yes. The reading of the banns. Well, he'd certainly wasted no time about it, and that was a good thing. The sooner their engagement became public knowledge, the better. "Oh, no, thank you, Baxter. I came to take a stroll about the grounds. To see the tenants, and the fields, and…" She trailed off with a shrug. He must think her awfully presumptuous, coming over to assess the lay of the land the day after she became betrothed to his master.

But to her relief, he nodded emphatically and closed the door behind him as he stepped onto the porch. "Yes, please do," he replied in a confidential undertone. "Mr. Hale has been reluctant, shall we say, to handle these matters. And I am afraid things are in a bit of a fix. Shall I order a carriage for you? Or a horse? You might cover more ground if you can move faster."

Gracious—just how large was the Hall, and just how badly had the situation declined? She quirked an eyebrow at him. "Would you really recommend a carriage? Are matters that bad?"

The butler nodded gravely. "I am afraid so, Miss Siddons."

"Then yes, please do." She straightened and looked him squarely in the eye. "I appreciate your help, Baxter."

"Not at all, Miss Siddons. I'll just go round to the stable myself."

Susannah watched the butler cross the yard and head off to the stables. For a man who was born and bred to tradition, he was certainly not relying on either. Going to the stables himself rather than sending word round by one of the other servants? Yes, things must be in a fix, indeed.

What on earth had she gotten herself into?

She didn't have long to wonder, for a carriage arrived within the next few moments. She ordered the driver to take her to the tenants first. These were the people who, other than the servants, depended on her husband-to-be the most. If they were suffering, 'twas likely the entire estate was not doing well at all. And perhaps Baxter was exaggerating. After all, he was the sort of fellow to raise a fuss if everything wasn't in perfect order. Likely he was just affronted by the laissez-faire way in which his master chose to run Goodwin.

They took the winding road past the chapel in the clearing, over the moor. As they rolled slowly over the hillside, she breathed in deeply. In just a few weeks' time, this would be her home. An unfamiliar feeling of warmth and acceptance settled over her like a cloak. The moor was as much a part of her childhood as her own family. 'Twas good indeed to be returning to it.

The carriage swayed sharply left, and they veered onto a flattened part of the hill, where a cluster of thatched cottages huddled close together. Columns of smoke drifted through the chimneys, rising lazily toward the clouds. A cluster of ragtag children played, barefoot despite the frost on the ground, watched over by a gray-haired woman who was wrapped, head to foot, in a quilt.

Why, 'twas as if they'd traveled backward nearly two centuries in coming up the moor. Thatched roofs? Barefoot children? Surely Goodwin could do better than this. She rapped on the window to signal the driver to stop.

Before the footman could even open the door, Susannah alit from the carriage. What more was there to see? She stepped over the ruts in the dried mud and approached the old woman, keeping her expression humble and open. 'Twould never do to start playing Lady Bountiful, lording it over the tenants. To help them, she must earn their trust.

"How do you do?" she called as the children squealed past her. "I'm Susannah Siddons."

"Are you to be the new mistress here?" The old woman

kept her countenance, peering at her from under grizzled brows. "We heard the master was getting married."

"Yes." Gracious, the news had spread fast about the estate. Well, at least they knew who she was. No need to try to explain why she felt the need to poke around the grounds in a fancy carriage. "I've come to help. Seems as though some parts of Goodwin are in need of repair."

"Aye, true that. Though we are better off here than in some places round about. I am glad to meet you. My name is Ann Tucker. Been living here all my life."

"Mrs. Tucker, I am so glad to make your acquaintance. Since you've lived here for so long, I value your opinion above all others. Tell me, what could be done to improve the lives of the tenants on this estate?" She settled on a fallen log nearby, spreading her skirts out, heedless of her finery.

"Well, that could take some time. And I am just one woman. What I have to say may not be all that everyone would wish to see done on this place." Mrs. Tucker settled back on her seat and folded her quilt more securely about herself.

The sooner she could get started the better. A sense of purpose flooded her soul. "If you like, we could call on some of your friends and acquaintances. Meet inside someone's home, perhaps?" Susannah nodded at the tumbledown shacks and drew her shawl tighter. "I have dedicated my whole day to this task alone. Making Goodwin a better home for everyone is the most urgent of my duties." She had not felt this revitalized since she made her plans to move to Tansley after Uncle Arthur's death. And yet, there was something more underlying this sense of worth. She wasn't merely helping herself. She was helping others, people who had come to rely on her fiancé's graces for the better part of their lives.

How could she possibly answer this call fully? Could she really give up her shop and devote herself entirely to the needs of the estate? In doing so, she would give up the very thing that she'd worked so hard for, that she'd driven herself to achieve.

Was she really ready to let that independence go and turn her full devotion to Daniel and his estate?

Chapter Eighteen

Daniel swirled the brandy in its sparkling glass. The diamond pattern of the vessel pressed his palm and he gripped it more tightly. The feel of the rough edges was something.

He stretched his booted feet closer to the hearth. Was he ready for all the changes that lay before him? If not, surely his existence would continue this way forever. Susannah would be out of his life—forever this time. For if he acted the coward a second time, there would be no forgiveness. Indeed, he was a fortunate fellow to even warrant a second try with Susannah. If he was too afraid of committing to Goodwin, to Susannah and to change, she would leave him. He would be a failure in truth. And he would drink. There would be no companionship, no warmth of feeling in his life.

And no children. He'd never given real thought to having a family of his own. Somehow, the idea of family had stifled him as a young man—they were burdens, mere weights to hold him down. But now—he glanced out the window at the moors, the yellow grass bitten with frost. Now, the thought of a little girl with Susannah's auburn hair and freckles scattered across her nose wasn't a weight at all.

He couldn't bring himself to drink the brandy, not yet. Even though he needed to stop feeling anything at all. Somehow, it was as though drinking it was admitting to his own weakness. That he could never, ever change. Was he ready to make that admission, despite Susannah?

Daniel rose and strolled over to the mahogany table beneath the window. An array of cut-glass decanters winked alluringly in the late-afternoon sunshine. He traced the stoppers with his fingertips. He wasn't ready to make the trip back to his chair just yet. Propped nicely against this sturdy ledge, he could study the moor-grass and feel—for a brief moment—that all this land was really his, that he was a good and gracious and steady lord of the manor.

A flash of gray caught his eye. Susannah. She was half walking, half running across the field, her cloak billowing behind her. Her bonnet dangled from its strings down her back and her bright hair tossed carelessly in the wind. He straightened and set his glass down. His mind, muddy as it was, could not reconcile the image of his betrothed—his decorous, proud fiancée—and this apparition who fairly skimmed the frozen ground. He pressed the heels of his palms against his eyes, and when he removed them, Susannah was gone.

It must have been a dream. It couldn't be the drink. He hadn't swallowed a mouthful yet.

The study door banged open, a sound sharp as a musket shot. He jumped and turned toward it.

"And there he is, drunk as a lord. I am not surprised, but I vow, Daniel, I had hoped to speak with you in a sober state of mind."

Susannah stood in the doorway, panting, her cheeks

rosy from the cold. He strode over to her, taking her hands in his. "I vow I haven't had anything to drink yet. What's the matter? Are you unwell?"

She withdrew her hands from his and crossed her arms over her chest. "No. I am not unwell. But I fear many of your tenants are."

"Oh. The tenants." He quirked his eyebrow and shook his head. Why was Susannah rattling on so about the tenants?

"Yes." The single word cut through his unsettled emotions sharply as a knife blade. "Your tenants. I've just come from there, and did you know that they live in dreadful conditions? Were you aware of this? Can you imagine such poverty exists? The hovel my sisters and I purchased in the village is a palace compared to most of the huts your tenants call home."

"Yes. Well." He cast around for something sensible to say. "The tenants, you know, are always rather poorer than the rest of us. We care for them as we can, of course."

"You do not care for them at all." She spat the words out and strode into the room, slamming the door behind her.

"Susannah, stop this." He struggled to get a grasp of the situation, to be the master as he should. "We provide our tenants with the basics of care. I do not understand why you are carrying on so. They are as well provided for as any others in the county."

"Oh!" Susannah rounded on him. "I will not stop this. It is time someone told you the truth. Who better than your betrothed?"

"You aren't my wife yet." The words slipped out before he could stop them. Weeks of this dance between them

still to come—conditions she chose, terms she dictated—
his heart pounded painfully in his chest as Susannah's
eyes flashed.

"If I am to bear your name then I vow that I shall ensure that name is respectable and good. What I saw today
was neither." Though her voice had grown quiet, the set
of her shoulders and the haughty tilt of her head betrayed
her fury. "You don't know what it's like to be poor. To
have other people in control of your destiny. Selfish people, who care naught what you suffer. I will not inflict
that misery upon others as it was inflicted upon me."

Something in her voice gave him pause. Susannah was
furious, but she was hurt, too. Wounded. He suppressed
a sudden urge to gather her in his arms and stroke her
hair until she calmed. Would Susannah ever want him
to hold her? 'Twas unlikely.

"I know you think you are doing all you can," Susannah continued, her voice steady and even. "But there is so
much more that can be done to care for your tenants. The
roofs of their cottages are straw—straw, Daniel! 'Twas
like stepping back in time to see them—and they leak
like a sieve. Some of the tenants lack the proper attire
to weather a harsh winter." She sank onto the settee, her
eyes downcast. "We must do more, Daniel. We cannot
allow others to suffer so. Not when we have so much."

Daniel closed his eyes, breathing in deeply. This
was all he'd run away from years ago. Responsibility. Duties. He could continue to shirk any semblance
of accountability—but in doing so, he would live a life
apart. The years stretching before him would remain
bleak and cold. Susannah would remain a stranger to
him. He set his untouched glass aside.

His Susy. Beautiful, brave, determined Susy. He

opened his eyes and looked at his betrothed, but her glance remained stubbornly fixed on the floor.

Passionate words, words that begged for Susannah's forgiveness and kindness, bubbled to the surface, if only he had the courage to say them. He sank down beside her on the settee. He was as close to her as he'd been in the shop when they pledged their troth—and now, as then, he caught her scent of orange blossom. Sweet and innocent. Susannah had shown him that she was no fragile, shrinking miss, but she was deserving of protection and shelter. And what she said had a ring of truth to it. Why should others suffer while he had so much?

"You are right." The words fell heavily from his lips. He turned to look at her, his heart warming, and she lifted her gaze to his. "But I don't know how to start."

"There is much to be done," she agreed, nodding slowly. "Cottages that need mending, children that need warm clothes. But I think the most fundamental change must be wrought today."

"Very well." He rubbed his hand over his brow. "Help me. Where shall we begin?"

She cleared her throat and turned to face him squarely. "You must stop drinking."

The words had to be said. His drinking was the root of his inactivity, his carelessness—every aspect of Daniel that detracted from the man he should be. But in saying them aloud, and in saying them with a purpose beyond mere nagging, she made a commitment. And that thought was terrifying.

How could one commit to a man who'd left her so long ago?

Wouldn't he just leave her again?

Why invest any time, any energy, with this man after he'd crushed her girlish hopes of being rescued?

And Daniel's face, rapidly draining of all color and his clouded expression—certainly she had crossed a boundary with him. He rose from his place on the settee and turned his back on her, facing the hearth.

"Y-you see," she stammered, "when you drink, you lose all sense of perspective, of time. And I am left to run things in your absence, for even if you are still here in the flesh, it's as though you are still out on the high seas, without a care in the world. Even when I came to luncheon that day, and you were drunk, I had to run the household and order the servants to serve luncheon. I don't mind doing so, but I need a helpmeet. You are not a helpmeet when you are drunk."

Daniel looked over his shoulder at her and winced, the corner of his mouth turning downward.

"I'm saying this stupidly. I don't know how to say it right. But I do feel that giving up drink would help you to manage the estate and help your tenants." If only she could phrase things well, if only she had the gift of blarney to gloss over such a difficult and tender issue. Blurting things out as she always did—what good could come of it?

"Our estate. Our tenants. What I have is yours, Susannah." He turned from the hearth and walked with slow, halting steps to the window. The room turned chillier without his warmth beside her, and she moved closer to the blazing hearth.

He always said things like that. Why did he say it? This was not her home. Not in reality. Everything about her life had become a sham in the course of but a few weeks. She'd come to Tansley to start afresh, to build a life of solid strength for herself and for Becky and Nan. And here she was, trapped in an engagement she wasn't sure she wanted, facing the thought of living in a fine home with a drunken husband, caring for tenants whose needs were overwhelming. This was not the life she'd imagined when she climbed on the mail coach bound for Tansley.

"I don't feel that way." She suppressed a shiver and inched closer to the hearth.

"You just said that while you bear my name, you will attend to the tenants," he reminded her with a snap, his back turned toward her. His head bent down, and she could glimpse the bare skin between his collar and the trimmed edge of his dark hair. Funny, she'd always thought of him as she remembered him at sixteen, tall and rangy with long arms and legs and that uniquely loping gait he used when he walked, as though he were a farmer stepping off rows of maize in a field.

But Daniel was a boy no longer. His broad shoulders, the heavy strength of his arms belied the fact that the years had wrought changes in him. And in her, for that matter. She glanced down at her hands, once so pretty and small and white, now work-roughened and decidedly, well, older. She clasped them together in her lap. "Yes, I did," she admitted, her voice hushed.

He glanced at her over one broad shoulder. "Is there no way to bridge this divide between us? Will you not at least admit that we shall share a home, that the problems of Goodwin Hall will be ours to handle together?"

It was a fair enough question. If she was willing to take his name to escape her own troubles in the village, surely she couldn't shirk all the responsibilities. Even if she and Daniel were wed in name only, she would have a duty to maintain the facade and to assume the cares that came with the running of a household. She lifted her chin. "Yes, I will admit that."

"I need you here." The words, a low rumble, caught her off guard. "I can't lose you to the village and to your sisters' millinery shop every day. I know you want to keep the shop, and I shouldn't interfere with that. But I can't help how I feel."

"Yes, of course." He must mean that the duties of running the estate and seeing to the tenants would be too time-consuming. Her sisters had encouraged her to give up the shop, it was true—but to have such a thing requested by Daniel was something else altogether. Could she possibly capitulate? Perhaps she should merely promise him what he wanted and hope in time that the issue of the shop would abate. "I shall visit my sisters on Sundays, but I could spend most of my time here, helping you. I know now that the cares of the tenants will occupy most of our time, as it is."

"No. *I* need you." He turned to face her. His eyes were ringed with fatigue, his broad shoulders slumped. The mischievous glimmer in his expression was quenched. He was a man hounded by troubles, and she rose from her seat and took a step closer before she realized what she had done. Abashed, Susannah stood perfectly still and waited for him to continue.

"I'll give up drinking if you want me to. But I cannot do it alone. I need you, Susy. Please. I won't ask any more than that. I just…need you here. This is hard for me to do. Staying on at Goodwin and giving in to duties and tradition—it goes against everything I wanted as a lad. I don't want to become like my father. You can help me. Please, Susy." He twisted his mouth downward in a grimace and folded his arms across his chest.

Susannah paused. Since their engagement, she'd refrained from using her usual admonishment about her nickname. When he spoke like that, the years fell away. She was as close to him in that moment as she had been at sixteen, and his use of the old, tender Susy drew them ever closer.

"I'll be here. I promise." She said it soothingly, as she would to Nan or Becky if they'd had a nightmare and she'd awakened to care for them. "It won't be as bad as you think, Daniel. In fact, it might be fun. Look at all the work you've done on your mother's chapel. That was your effort, you know. And it's paying off beautifully."

He closed his eyes and breathed deeply, then took his glass, still half-full, from the table beside him. With one swift move, he parted the curtains wider and opened the window latch with a flick of his hand. Then he poured the amber liquid out, spattering the frozen moor-grass.

She gasped, and Daniel smiled at her from the window ledge. "Come help me, Susy." He motioned to one of the decanters on the table. "Let us pour them all out."

Susannah crossed to the window, the bitter and chill wind of October spanking her cheeks as she drew near. She grasped a heavy cut-glass decanter in both hands. "This one?"

"All of them." He grabbed one and lifted out the stopper, pouring the contents out with a mighty splash.

She laughed at the ridiculous sound and removed the cork from her bottle, accidentally spraying the side of the manor house with the liquid. "Oh, dear. I am not a terribly good shot, I must admit."

"Ah, I am certain scotch is good for stone. Probably

helps it set well, or some such nonsense." Daniel chuckled and dumped another decanter out.

She grinned. This was more the way they had been in childhood. The easy banter. The tenderness between them. They'd helped each other then, just as they were doing now. And it felt right. She would have to watch herself and guard her emotions. Daniel was easy to fall in love with when he was so charming. If only he could be so loving and kind and delightful always.

The smell of alcohol wafted in on the bitter north wind, making her eyes water. "What about your father's wine cellar? Certainly we cannot flood the moors with the finest vintage in the county."

"Ah, well. We'll keep a few bottles around for sickness. And I'll send the rest of them to Paul and to our friends throughout the village as a goodwill gesture. And I shall have to learn to enjoy the rather tepid thrills of water and tea, starting now."

"I shall have Baxter bring in some tea directly." She placed her now-empty decanter on the table and drew on the bellpull. "And do close the window, Daniel. You'll catch your death."

There she was, bossing him around again. Just as she had everyone else, for as long as she remembered. But instead of looking perturbed, a shadow of that old playful grin crossed his face. "At least I shall have a wife to nurse me now. You promised, after all. I am your responsibility, you know—utterly and completely."

A wave of exasperation seized her, but at the merry look in his eyes, she broke into a mirthful chuckle and tossed a needlepoint pillow, smacking him square on the shoulder.

"Ah. I see my future bride has excellent aim when it

comes to firing vessels," Daniel teased. "If not as much when pouring out whiskey. I shall have to take you along on a hunt, Susy. You would be a formidable shot."

Her heart lurched as he spoke—the reality of all she'd done flooding her with a mixture of anxiety and hope. This would be her home, and Daniel would be her husband—and somehow, that was all rather daunting.

Chapter Nineteen

Well, Susannah had promised to stay with him during marriage and not try to divide her time between the shop and the estate—which was rather remarkable, Daniel reflected. But he had made a promise to her, as well. His promise to stop drinking was not idly made, for the anger and passion he'd glimpsed in Susannah's eyes had shamed him into giving up the vice. He was asking a lot of her. And in return, he needed to make a commitment, as well.

It scared him—more than any typhoon had, buffeting his ship about on the high seas.

And it was going to be well-nigh impossible to maintain, given that Paul had written, warning Daniel of his impending return to Tansley, with a promise to get the prospective bridegroom well and truly sloshed long before the wedding. Today marked a week after Paul's letter had arrived, so if his friend had traveled at his usual breakneck pace, Daniel could expect to have company for dinner tonight.

Daniel tugged on his jacket before descending the stairs. Bother the cravat, he wasn't going to go that far.

He was meeting with his estate manager, and the fellow could accept a little informality on Daniel's part. Taking the steps two at a time, he rushed downstairs and burst into his study, where Mr. Donaldson was waiting to receive him.

"Mr. Hale. I am so glad to see you." Donaldson rose and executed a brief bow. "And may I congratulate you on your engagement to Miss Siddons."

"Thank you," Daniel replied, bowing slightly in return. "I've no use for formalities today, Donaldson. I hope you can understand. I may seem brusque, but I am trying to get at the heart of what is ailing Goodwin. My fiancée has brought the plight of the tenants to my attention, and I want to help them as much as we can without bringing Goodwin to ruin. You've had some suggestions about how to improve things in the past, and I must admit I was loath to listen. Now you find me with a mind clear and willing to accept suggestions. Please tell me your thoughts."

The estate manager seemed as relieved as Daniel to let go of the usual chatter, for his shoulders relaxed and he nodded briskly. "Well, the mill and the lands are producing adequately."

Daniel sat before the fire and motioned Donaldson to follow suit. "Everything on the estate is at a minimal standard, then?"

He sat and faced Daniel, his countenance open and honest. "Minimal, yes. But it could be much better. The tenants' living conditions could use a definite improvement. And, as I mentioned to you before, the lands around Goodwin could produce better if we followed a more rigorous standard of changing out the crops and even allowing some fields to lie fallow just long enough for the soil to recover. Some of the crops we raise here deplete the soil of valuable nutrients, which can make it difficult for them to produce well season after season."

Well, that suggestion made sense. Why not let some fields rest so that they could produce well the following season? "I like that idea. I'm sorry I never gave much credence to it until now. I wonder why my brother or my father never followed through with it."

Donaldson cleared his throat. "The suggestion was made to them, sir. But it was too radical a notion for them to entertain. Your brother told me quite clearly that allowing a field to lie fallow was a shameful waste."

Daniel gave an inward chuckle. Yes, that did sound like his brother. Hidebound and glued to tradition, just as Father had been.

"Well, you will not find me so recalcitrant. It makes sense, this plan of yours. I should like to go over the plan for the crops, to see which fields will rest and what crops will be used. I intend to be involved in the management of the estate quite closely from now on."

Donaldson nodded, a sigh of something like relief emanating from him. "Very good, sir."

Daniel leaned forward. "And the tenants?" Surely something could be done to assist them. Susannah had been right. Allowing them to skimp by on the very bare necessities was shameful when he had so much.

"Well, as I said, the tenants' lives and homes could be improved. Many estates around Tansley care for their people in a similar manner. But I will say that the happier and healthier your people are, the more they will, in turn, contribute to the estate. Already Goodwin is producing enough to cover its needs—in fact, even without making a single change to our plans, we could rebuild some of the more tumbledown cottages, repair the roofs and the like." He pulled a ledger book out of his leather saddlebag and opened it. "If you care to take a look."

Daniel accepted the book and peered closely through the columns of numbers, all written in his estate manager's meticulous hand. A few months ago, the mere sight of these figures would have sent him on a raging drunk—but now, now they made sense. "I see what you mean. But if we increase the productivity of the fields and the mill, we can improve the lives of everyone at Goodwin—including the tenants'."

"Absolutely. And a few changes could be made to bring the mill more up to date, changes that are again outside the norm of what has been done in the past but which I feel are simple enough to implement. Come, I'll show you." Donaldson walked over to Daniel's desk and withdrew a long scroll from the saddlebag, which he unfurled with a flourish. "You see? Here—" he pointed to a drawing of a machine "—and here." He launched into a brief yet thoughtful explanation of the changes that could be made to make the machines more efficient.

Daniel listened, giving the man his full attention. When he paused to draw breath, Daniel peered over the drawings. "You have obviously given this a great deal of thought. I am impressed. I wonder if you've considered simply rebuilding, rather than repairing, the cottages. When I worked on a merchant vessel, I often worked with wood that had grown rotten with time. Often, 'twas cheaper and better to simply replace a piece of decking than to try to repair it once more."

"I think that rebuilding could be more profitable—certainly with some of the more tumbledown cottages."

Donaldson nodded, adding a few figures to the columns. "I'll draw up some estimates for the work."

"Excellent." Daniel straightened and looked squarely at his estate manager. "I am in awe of your tenacity, my good man. Any other fellow, when confronted with my father's and brother's hidebound ways, and my own indifference, would have given up in despair."

The young man gave a rueful smile and shrugged. "I love this land," he explained simply. "Goodwin has the opportunity to be quite a grand estate. All it needs is a bit of—"

"Care." Daniel sighed. "I've neglected it far too long." He rolled up the parchment scroll and handed it back. "You have my leave to begin working on the crops and the mill. I'll draw up some plans for new cottages if you can provide estimates for the building materials." He paused. Since Goodwin was going to be Susannah's home, too, he must involve her in the decision-making process. She was as much a part of Goodwin as he was. She had, in fact, a better claim on it than he, for she cared about his people when he did not. "As for the tenants themselves, I should like to have my fiancée in on the discussion. I'll have her come over tomorrow afternoon, and we shall talk over the matter together, if that is all right with you."

"Certainly, sir." A dawning light of—what was that? Respect, perhaps?—was kindled in Donaldson's normally serious eyes as he answered. "I shall come over tomorrow around three o'clock, if you wish."

"Yes, fine." Daniel extended his hand. "Until then."

Donaldson grasped his hand and shook it, and showed himself out of the study. As the door closed behind him, Daniel stood quiet for a moment, bowing his head. He leaned his weight against the massive oak desk for support. He had done it at last. Goodwin was finally his. Funny, he hadn't accepted tradition as his own. No—he had bucked tradition, in fact.

He was allowing Goodwin to progress, to grow with the times. Outmoded practices, outdated machinery and the old-fashioned way of caring for one's tenants—they were gone. He had banished them and in doing so, he made the Hall his own. 'Twas no longer a millstone about his neck.

Goodwin and Susannah. He closed his eyes for a moment, allowing thoughts of his fiancée and his home to wash over him. The two things he'd run away from, that he had callously abandoned in his youth, were now the dearest things in the world to him.

"God, make me worthy." He uttered the words aloud. The first time he'd ever prayed by himself in his life. Somehow, saying the words brought comfort. The situation he faced wasn't as daunting—in fact, it was a challenge that, perhaps, he could meet. With help.

He'd begun the process of making things up to Goodwin, starting today. And he would spend the rest of his life trying to make Susannah happy. She deserved happiness. After the years of anxiety and terror she had endured, after the years of hardship and deprivation, he would see to it that she would spend the rest of her days in comfort and peace at Goodwin Hall. With him, of course. And that meant he must radically change who he was. No more running, no more fear, no more indifference.

He would have to face the things he had done and change what he didn't like. 'Twould be a difficult process, and a painful one, but worth it. The empty shell of his life was slowly filling up, with light, love and grace.

He must continue to grow as a man and in faith. He must start now, without delay, for Susannah's sake.

Susannah squinted in the late-afternoon light and carefully sewed another stitch in the pale green silk bunched in her lap. In a few days' time, 'twould evolve in beauty and become her wedding gown. Although the engagement had not been officially announced, word spread fast through the village. And, as the news of her impending nuptials spread like wildfire throughout the countryside, her life was easing somewhat. For one thing, she had gone to see Bess in peace, without any townspeople shunning her or making cheeky remarks. And while business hadn't picked up, at least people dawdled past their shop window now, instead of avoiding them completely.

All in all, she reflected, matters were considerably better, and she had Daniel to thank for it.

Gratitude to Daniel. An odd feeling indeed. And one that she wasn't sure how to return. He hadn't propose to her out of love, of course. He'd proposed to help her. And what was she doing in return? Nagging him about his drinking and his tenants.

She picked up another stitch and shook her head. When would she ever learn to stop bossing people about? Daniel would flee to London the first chance he got rather than face the prospect of being cooped up at Goodwin with a shrewish wife. And she would be alone, and somehow that thought was even more daunting than the thought of marrying Daniel.

"Sue, a carriage has stopped outside," Nan announced from her perch near the window. "It looks like Miss Glaspell's. Do you suppose she's sent a servant to cancel her order, as well?"

Oh, how perfectly perfect. Naturally, once one gentry canceled, she should expect them all to cancel. "Yes, I imagine so." She rose and rolled the fabric she'd been working on into a ball, tucking it in her sewing box. "How far have you progressed on the tweed tam-o'-shanter? Is it ready? I know Becky is still upstairs, working on the feathers for the trim." Might as well take stock of how much money they were about to lose.

"I was going to finish stitching the side, but I'll wait." Nan cast the tam aside and stood. "Should I go and get the door for her ladyship?"

"No, run upstairs and tell Becky to stop working on the feathers. And stay up there until Miss Glaspell's servant is gone. You two have handled enough of this nonsense when you dealt with Miss Prestwidge's servant." She squared her shoulders and clenched her fists, preparing to remain as civil as possible under the circumstances. At least she had Daniel. The family would not be destitute. Daniel wouldn't allow her sisters to starve. Funny, she was coming to rely upon the one thing she'd fought against her whole life. The support of a man. And yet—given all they'd promised each other yesterday, she and Daniel were more of a team, weren't they? He would be her helpmeet in this trouble, just as she would be his as he fought his urge to drink.

"Are you certain?" Nan hesitated, biting her lip. "I should hate to have you be insulted, Sue."

"Nonsense." Susannah gave her a forced smile and smoothed her apron. "I am certain I can handle this matter. I shall be polite, and nothing she says will provoke my temper. Besides, it's probably only a servant she sent— I am sure she wouldn't lower herself by crushing my dreams in person. I shall be fine. Go on." She shooed her sister upstairs with a wave of her hand.

Better to be done. She crossed the room in a flurry of footsteps and wrenched the door open. Perhaps they could just handle the transaction on the threshold, and she wouldn't even have to allow them into her home.

"Oh, mercy," a cultured voice exclaimed, and Miss Glaspell herself fell back a pace on the front step. "You startled me!"

"Miss Glaspell," Susannah gasped. "I didn't think it was you. I figured you had sent a servant."

"No…" Miss Glaspell held her gloved hand over her heart. "May I come in?"

"Yes, of course." She grasped after her manners as she would a straw tossed on the wind. She opened the door and held it for her ladyship.

Miss Glaspell walked over to the hearth and held her hands out to the blaze as Susannah closed the door. "Well, I shall come straight to the point, Miss Siddons. I am not canceling my order. In fact, I would like for the Siddons sisters to be my exclusive milliners from now on."

Had she heard aright? She drew her brows together and glanced over at her ladyship. "Are you quite certain?"

"Quite," Miss Glaspell pronounced briskly. "I thought Annabella was being ridiculous, and told her so myself. Whatever was she thinking, canceling her order because of gossip? I kept my order in with you, as did Evangeline, because we love what you do with bonnets. We do not care about your past or about idle gossip."

Which was, of course, what human decency would demand. But somehow, hearing it from the gentry made it all the more extraordinary. "Thank you." It was all she could muster at the moment. She had been so certain of disaster.

"And now that you are engaged to Daniel Hale, all is forgotten. Annabella has changed her mind and wishes you to reinstate her order. And, of course, Evangeline and I shall continue to order from you exclusively." Miss Glaspell cast her a winning smile. "So, there you have it. Is anything of mine ready?"

A sudden surge of rage and despair welled within Susannah. Miss Glaspell was talking about the matter so casually, as if it hadn't meant a thing to anyone involved. But it had meant the world to herself and to her sisters. It was, after all, the reason she had accepted Daniel's protection.

"I suppose you are saying that, if I hadn't become engaged to Mr. Hale, I would be in danger of losing your business." She struggled to keep her voice even, her tone disinterested and polite. It was the truth. Bess had warned her so.

"No, not at all." Miss Glaspell shook her head. "Annabella, perhaps. She sticks with tradition. And she adheres too much to gossip, I believe. What you do in your own life is your own affair."

"I see." She should be grateful to Miss Glaspell for her rather progressive views, but bitterness and anger still filled her soul. Susannah struggled to remain cool and businesslike; after all, Miss Glaspell was not only keeping her orders but had managed to persuade Miss Prestwidge to do the same. Her sisters would do very well. The shop would see a tidy little profit this year.

And yet, she was still bitter.

"I do understand how you must be feeling right now."

Miss Glaspell removed her wrap and laid it on the hearth. "May I sit down?"

"You may." Susannah drew the worn old velvet chair up to the fire. It was one of the shabbier pieces of furniture they owned, but it was by far the most comfortable. One had to be hospitable, if nothing else.

"Thank you." Miss Glaspell accepted the chair with a smile and sank down. "Upon my word, this little shop works like a tonic on me. The first moment I saw it, I was enchanted." She turned her dimpled grin upon Susannah. "I had hoped only the best for you. And, given your impending marriage, I can see that my wishes are coming true."

If only her ladyship knew how very little she had to congratulate Susannah on. After all, the marriage was a mock one, arranged to save her family's reputation and their livelihood. "Thank you," she murmured.

"You seem unhappy, though, which is why I wanted to stay a little longer, and to be frank with you. You see, your engagement to Mr. Hale is wiping out all the gossip in the village, but I do believe it would have died out in time. Evangeline and I had already decided to support you, and with our patronage 'tis quite likely that all of this ridiculous chatter would cease." She held her gloved hands out to the blaze, tucking herself into the chair more comfortably.

So…what was the Honorable Miss saying? "I don't understand you."

"Well, a twice-broken engagement would be cause for a lot of talk, but I would say that the chin-wagging can die out again. If marrying Mr. Hale is making you unhappy, then don't do it. My papa tried to force me into marriage once. And I gave him the tongue-lashing of a lifetime. We women are pushed about entirely too much for my taste. Do you not agree?" She turned a warm, sympathetic gaze upon Susannah.

"So what you are saying is…" Susannah tried to wrap her mind around her patron's words. "You will continue to support me whether I marry Mr. Hale or not. And with your assistance, my shop is sure to survive."

"That is precisely what I am saying." Miss Glaspell rose and grabbed her wrap from its place on the hearth. "Now, you never answered my original question. Is anything ready for me yet?"

Susannah blinked several times. She must clear her mind. She must remain focused and professional. "Not quite yet, your lady—I mean, Miss Glaspell. We are putting the final details on some of the bonnets now. Next week, perhaps?"

"Oh, bother. I was hoping they would be ready for me to take home." She tugged her shawl over her shoulders and grinned. "Well, I shall be all the happier for seeing them next week. Goodbye, Miss Siddons. And I still wish the best for you."

"As I do for you," Susannah murmured in reply. She showed her ladyship to the door and watched, her head propped up against the cold plate-glass window as the woman's carriage traced a half circle across the moor.

She didn't have to marry Daniel. The shop would be fine. The little life she had struggled so hard to create for herself and her sisters was still hers to take up, at any time she chose.

And yet, somehow, she had no desire to stay in that little life. Daniel needed her, and Goodwin Hall and its tenants called out to her. They had become partners in this new venture—life together. As hard as it was to give up her shop, it had become harder still to think of turning her back on her fiancé and his home.

Chapter Twenty

"So, if I understand you correctly, there is no wine and no liquor in Goodwin to be had." Paul looked at his teacup with a dismal frown. "Have you gone mad, my good fellow?"

"Not at all." Daniel leaned back in his chair and glanced down the length of the dinner table at his friend. "Susannah asked me to stop drinking, and I did so. I want to make her happy. Besides, the management of Goodwin is coming much easier to me now that I'm not in my cups all the time."

"Where is my friend Daniel? Whatever has possessed you? There are plenty of ways to make a lass happy. Gowns. Jewels. I am certain your mother has some bits of sparkle you can give her as a wedding present." Paul pushed the teacup aside with a shudder.

"Susannah would not be easily persuaded or pleased by any of those things," Daniel replied with a snort. "She is not the type of girl whose head is turned by a pretty bauble. She's strong, independent and resourceful—and for some reason, she's decided she can bear to spend the rest of her life with me. If it means I must stop drinking, then I shall."

"What do you mean—she's decided to bear it?" Having given up on his tea entirely, Paul turned his attention to the baked chicken on his plate. "I know your engagement is in part due to my slip of the tongue, but surely she must want this life. What girl wouldn't?"

"Ah, yes." Daniel grinned at his dinner companion. "Of course, any girl would want this. A house in dire need of a mistress after years of neglect. A former drunkard for a husband. And the censure of an entire village because of an incident—quite beyond her control—that occurred when she was too young to think and act sensibly. Yes. Any lass would want this." He toyed with his fork, drawing a spiral pattern in the saffron sauce on his plate.

"You sound maudlin. Are you so bitter at heart?"

Paul was mocking him. That teasing tone of voice would be a welcome invitation to spar at any other time, but not now. What he felt for Susannah was too private, too dear. He couldn't bear to hear anyone speak lightly of her, or of their situation.

"Paul, we do not have scotch here at our disposal to loosen my tongue and assist me in waxing poetic. But Susannah means more to me than anything. I am blessed beyond measure at her acceptance of my hand. And if she told me to journey to Timbuktu and back before winning her hand, I would do so. She merely asked me to give up drinking. And I have."

The corner of Paul's mouth turned downward. "You sound as though you are in love with her."

"I might be at that." Admitting it out loud to someone was both terrifying and liberating. He struggled to keep his countenance even and impassive. Showing the depth of his emotion would only provoke more teasing from Paul, so he would settle for acknowledging the truth.

"Good gracious, man, that is astounding news. I'd offer to stand you a toast, but seeing as how you are a teetotaler, I can't very well do that." Paul raised his teacup instead. "And how does the lady feel?"

Daniel's elation crashed down about his ears. "I don't know how she feels about me," he admitted. In fact, if the truth be told, he was scared to know her true feelings about him. "I know she loves Goodwin. She must, or she wouldn't care what happened to my tenants or to the house."

"And when is the ceremony?" Paul took a careful sip of his tea and grimaced.

"She wants a traditional wedding, rather than a special license, to get used to the idea of marriage. She has to move away from her life as the head of her millinery shop and adjust to life as mistress of Goodwin. But as for how she feels about me…" He trailed off, shaking his head. "I would almost rather not know, to be honest."

"If you have three weeks left until the wedding, then you should woo her," Paul pronounced, pounding his fist on the table until the silverware rattled. "If she's not the kind of lass who likes jewels and flowers, then so be it. Find other ways to enchant her."

"I don't want her to fall in love with me because I buy her presents." How could he make Paul understand? He wanted Susannah to fall in love with him, not with what he could buy her.

"It's not about what you bring her. It's showing love and affection through your actions." Paul shook his head, giving Daniel a crooked smile. "You really don't know anything about women, do you? Take it from a fellow who knows—use these three weeks as an opportunity to show her the depth of your emotion, and you may well be rewarded with her love in return."

Baxter opened the door a crack. "Is there anything the matter, sir? Shall we clear the plates?"

That was Baxter and his sharp ears. Thanks to Paul's pounding fist and meddling ways. "No. Nothing else. We shall retire in a moment to the study."

"Very good, sir." Baxter closed the door with a quiet click.

"In the first place, I'll thank you not to lecture me in my own home and pound on the table. You bring the servants running." Daniel cast a cool glance at his friend. "And do remember that Susannah is not one of your London light skirts. I won't win her over easily, and certainly not in the span of a few weeks' time."

"I was in love once, too." As he spoke, the color drained from Paul's thin cheeks. "If you feel for Susannah what I felt for Ruth Barclay, then I am only begging you to heed the passage of time. Ruth was taken from me by fever. There's not a day that goes by that I don't think of her and wish that I had her back."

Ruth Barclay. Paul had suffered through the loss of his first love; it was not good form to assume Paul knew nothing of love or romance. "My apologies, old fellow. I shouldn't have said that about light skirts, 'twas unfair."

"Apology accepted." Paul gave him a tight smile that cut short any further protestations. "Just heed my words."

"I shall." 'Twas an awkward moment, and one that could not be lightened or easily passed over by pouring more wine or filling a glass to the brim with scotch. In a few moments, they could retire to the study and enjoy brandy and cigars—no, wait. No brandy. Only cigars. This new life was difficult indeed to accustom himself to. He must find some other distraction. "In keeping with your advice, perhaps I could have Susannah and her sisters come by tomorrow. I need to discuss the plans for the tenants with Susannah and my estate manager. Perhaps you could play duenna and take care of her sisters for me. Take them out riding, or some such." It would be good for Paul to be around the Siddons girls—they were both so fresh and lively and sweet. Their companionship might smooth away some of his jaded edges.

And it would be good for the girls to come and spend more time at the estate. It might make the transition from sister to wife easier for Susannah if her siblings were already intimately acquainted with Goodwin.

"Well, never let it be said that I shirked my duty as a friend." Paul sighed. "Very well, I shall play nursemaid on the morrow. As long as you are not shirking your duty as a fiancé."

"No, indeed." He would have to spend the rest of the night thinking of ways to woo Susannah. He didn't desire a loveless marriage with her; that was what he had witnessed as a small child. He would not be dour and cheerless like his father, and he would see to it that Susannah was happy. His desire was to keep her safe and protected. If he could somehow change matters, and cause Susannah to fall in love with him, then that would be the culmination of his dreams.

But how could a fellow woo a girl as strong and independent as Susannah? True, Mother's jewels were in a vault in London—they would be rightfully hers as the new mistress of Goodwin.

But what else could he offer her?

He had nothing she would value, for certain.

"So, what does the message say?" Nan tried to grasp the foolscap away, but Susannah held it out of reach. "Why are you being so missish? After all, 'tis only from Daniel."

"This kind of behavior is precisely why I feel wary of leaving the millinery shop in your care," Susannah chided. Honestly. Sometimes Nan acted as though she were eight instead of nearly seventeen. "Do control yourself."

"Nan, sit down," Becky added, speaking up from her spot near the hearth. "You know that Susannah feels particularly odd at the moment regarding Daniel. She doesn't have to marry him to save the shop. 'Tis natural for her to wish for some privacy."

"Thank you for that, Becky." Susannah stepped past Nan and settled in a chair opposite her sister. Everyone knew everything about her romantic life, it seemed. The village knew of her engagement, her sisters knew that she could break off said engagement at any time. Sometimes it would be nice to have everyone in the world focus on someone else's private affairs. But since her sisters knew the whole of the tale already, she could at least rely upon them for advice. "The message is quite simple. We are bidden to Goodwin Hall tomorrow, if we wish. You girls may go out riding, and Daniel has requested my help with the tenants. We are to meet with his estate manager to discuss the matter."

"A day off? Away from the shop?" Becky sat up straighter in her chair, her eyes glowing. "And riding, too?"

"Yes." A pang of guilt assailed Susannah at Becky's excitement. Poor girls. They never had a moment's peace to enjoy life—they worked so hard, all of them. "If you want, we could close the shop and spend the day at Goodwin."

"Wait a moment." Nan stilled Becky's eager gasp with a wave of her hand. "So, does this mean you've made your decision, then?"

"Decision about what?" Susannah folded up the scrap of foolscap and tossed it into the flames. Honestly, life with Nan was akin to life with a bloodhound at times, so determined was she to root out the absolute truth in every situation.

"Decision about marrying Daniel." Nan flounced over to the hearth and sat between her sisters. "You can't carry on with Daniel, mucking about at Goodwin for a day, if you intend to break off the engagement later."

Susannah watched the scrap of foolscap turn black and crumble to ash. Nan was right. She must make a choice. She would have to break off the engagement right away if she wanted to keep the store under her care. The banns would be read day after tomorrow for the first time. So while village gossip had been contained, there was no official announcement of their engagement yet.

On the other hand, she had promised Daniel she would help him stop drinking. She couldn't demand that of him and then leave him to handle it alone. Not when she'd vowed to support him. If she chose that path, she would never see Daniel again. They couldn't very well be friends after that. Gossip would continue to link them together forever—or until he married someone else. Her heart pounded against her rib cage. Daniel—engaged to some other girl? Why did the mere thought of that possibility cause so much pain?

She pressed her hand against her heart to steady its beat. "I can't make that decision now."

Becky leaned over and swatted Nan's knee. "Stop pestering her so, Nan. One visit to Goodwin would do no lasting harm. As of this moment, they are engaged. And that's all the village cares about."

"Well, I don't mind a respite from all this work. And I do think that riding could be fun. So I shall hold my tongue about it until the morrow, when we return home," Nan promised. "By the by, who will be riding with us when you are working with Daniel? A groom, I suppose."

"Daniel's friend Paul is home again from London. He will be over tomorrow and will ride with you. And, of course, you shall have a groom for propriety's sake." The words flowed out of Susannah, but she gave no thought to them. The idea of Daniel with another girl still occupied her mind.

"Paul? That blackguard? He's the reason you're in this mess," Nan cried. "I shall give him a piece of my mind when I see him tomorrow."

"You'll do no such thing." Susannah tucked the thought of Daniel and this fictional new girl away in the back of her mind and rose. "If you two wish to come with me, you shall be on your best behavior. Both of you. And I shall help Daniel, no matter what happens to our engagement. 'Twas I who pestered him into taking a hand to better the tenants' lives."

She shooed her sisters up to bed, over their groans of protest. And long after they said their prayers and blew out their candles, she lay awake, staring at the ceiling.

What should she do? What was the right thing to do, for both of them?

She was a horrible person for feeling this way, but a dark part of her enjoyed the fact that, at long last, 'twas her decision to make. She could walk away from Daniel, just as he had walked away from her long ago. It was a powerful and intoxicating feeling, much like what Daniel must feel when drinking his liquor.

But…she liked Daniel. She always had. He was a natural part of her and had as much a place in her childhood as the moors that circled Tansley. Being with him was— oh, it was difficult to say. But it was as though he was as much a part of her being as breathing.

Those mischievous green eyes. His careless, easy way of moving, as though he was secure in the knowledge that he was master of all he touched. She could admit to herself here, in the dark, that she found him to be quite a handsome young man. And she could come to him of her own free will now. The barriers that had existed between them, barriers of betrayal and class and money, were swept away. Thanks to Miss Glaspell, she had gained her hard-won independence.

So, the question remained. Did she want to marry Daniel?

She turned on her side, causing the mattress to squeak in protest, and rubbed the pillow against the side of her cheek.

"Are you still awake, Susannah?" Becky whispered from her bed.

"Yes. I can't sleep." Susannah rolled over to face her sister in the darkness.

A scurry of slippered feet sounded across the wooden floor, and Becky sat next to her. "I was worried you might be. Never mind Nan. You know how she is. She wants to know the absolute truth of every situation."

"I know." Susannah scooted closer to the wall to give Becky more room. "But she is right. I can't be friends with Daniel if I am going to break our engagement."

Becky tucked her feet up onto the bed and covered them with a scrap on Susannah's quilt. "I know that you love the shop and that you love us both. No one could have taken better care of us than you have, Susannah. Mother and Father would be proud."

Sudden tears pricked the back of Susannah's eyes, and she blinked rapidly. "Shush. You'll wake Nan."

"You know as well as I do that Nan doesn't waken for anything. An orchestra could march through here playing as loudly as they wished, and she would sleep on." Becky giggled. "I have to tell you this, though. Without Nan's prying and nagging. You can let us go, Susannah."

Susannah's breath caught on a sob. "What do you mean?"

"Just what I said. You've cared for us forever. Let us go. You should be free to enjoy life. I've seen the way you look with Daniel—your face lights up, you laugh—'tis lovely to see. You mean the world to him, too, I think. I've seen the way he looks at you when he thinks no one is watching." Susannah gave a happy sigh. "We shall take care of the shop beautifully. And you—you need to explore this new life with Daniel."

With Daniel. Funny—Becky's words, murmured in the darkness, were releasing a part of her she hadn't realized had been pent up for years. "I don't know if I love him or not," she admitted. It was easier to say it aloud to her sister than to herself, in a way.

"I know." Becky patted her shoulder. "But give yourself time. Don't run away from this new life because you think you still have to provide for us. And don't turn away from Daniel because you worry that you don't love him. Allow yourself the luxury, for once, of allowing things to happen rather than making them happen."

Susannah laughed quietly, for she had no wish to awaken Nan. "You know me too well. And, pray tell, when did you become so wise?"

"I had a good teacher in my eldest sister." Becky gave her shoulder a final pat and rose. "Now, let's sleep. We don't want to arrive at Goodwin with shadows under our eyes—though some poets might find that irresistible."

Susannah grinned and tucked herself farther under her quilt. She was exhausted. So very, very tired. How much of her life had been spent pounding away, like a racehorse on the turf? Becky had opened the gate to turn her out to pasture. And for the first time in her life, she could just enjoy each day.

And she might, just might, enjoy those days with Daniel.

Chapter Twenty-One

"Beg pardon, sir, but you really should hire a valet," Baxter explained, his tone gently reprimanding, as he assisted Daniel with his coat. "I am sure we could find someone to assist you."

"In the past I've had no need for one, especially since I haven't ever worn a cravat. No need of having anyone fuss over me. But, as master of Goodwin, I do foresee the necessity." Daniel flicked a speck of dust off his coat sleeve. "And Susannah will need a lady's maid. After I consult with her about the tenants today, I shall ask her if she wishes to hire someone from the village or from among our tenants."

"Very good, sir. Will there be anything else?" Baxter stepped back, his hands folded behind him.

"You've made sure the carriage was sent round to pick up the Siddonses." He couldn't very well have his future bride traipsing about over the frozen moor.

"Yes, indeed. The carriage left about twenty minutes ago. Anything else?"

"Just make certain that my study is set up in a comfortable manner for our meeting with Donaldson. Make sure there's a roaring fire in the grate, for as you know, that part of the house gets awfully chilly. And bring refreshments in about a quarter of an hour after we've started." He glanced over his shoulder at his butler. "And thank you for coming to assist me in the middle of the day like this. I know how busy you must be, and I will make sure that we make the arrangements to hire a valet who can take up some of these duties."

Baxter blinked, as though he was surprised by his master's gratitude. "Of course."

Daniel kept his composure until his butler quit the room, and then he started to pace. Everyone would be here in a moment's time. Paul. Susannah. Her sisters. Donaldson. He was playing host and trying to woo his fiancée, both at the same time. And what was he using to lure her? Hard work, of course.

Daniel pressed the heel of his hand against his forehead. What could he offer Susannah beyond the myriad responsibilities and hard work that he would pile on her once she became his wife?

He strolled to the window and gazed out over the frost-bitten countryside. He would send for his mother's jewels, for one thing. He had been telling the truth when he said that Susannah would not be impressed by mere baubles. But they were quite elegant, and as they were emeralds, would look stunning against Susannah's fair skin and auburn hair.

He lost himself in thought for a moment, leaning up against the window frame. Susannah's vivid, glorious locks and those bewitching gray-green eyes...

A flash of black caught his eye. That was his carriage. The Siddonses had arrived. And Paul wasn't even here yet. Fashionably late, as usual. He'd have to entertain the entire clan until his friend bothered to show up. Honestly, one could smack Paul sometimes. He was probably at home, asleep even yet though 'twas early afternoon.

He rushed from his room, landing on the bottom step just as Baxter opened the door to admit his guests.

Susannah looked up at him as she stepped over the threshold, the hood of her cloak pushed back, her lovely hair a bright contrast to the pale porcelain planes of her face. There were dark smudges under her eyes. She was tired. Or worried. Or both. An uncertain smile broke across her rosy lips. "Good afternoon, Daniel."

"Susannah." He caught her hands in his, and heedless of her sisters' amused gazes, brushed his lips across her gloved knuckles. Then, even though he had no care beyond his fiancée, he turned to her sisters and bowed. That was respectability kicking in. Even though he wanted nothing more than to bundle Susannah off to the study and find ways to lift her sagging spirits, he must pay some attention to his other guests, as well.

"Can we go riding now?" Becky's face was aglow with excitement. Obviously she was too anxious to remember protocol or her manners.

"As soon as Paul arrives," Daniel promised with a grin. Having sisters around was so much fun. They lightened the mood—even this hallway in Goodwin, so formal and polished—came alive when graced with their presence. "Shall we have tea? My man of affairs should be arriving soon," he added, glancing over at Susannah.

"That sounds nice." Susannah cast a warning glare at her sisters. "And of course, we shall amuse ourselves until Paul arrives."

Nan and Becky nodded, turning their eyes down toward the parquet floor, and started to remove their cloaks.

Baxter stepped forward, clearing his throat. "Beg pardon, ladies, but Mr. Paul is in the stables now. One of the grooms just walked down to tell me so. He will bring the horses here, if you care to wait."

"Must we wait here?" Becky pleaded. "Couldn't we walk up to the stables ourselves?"

"Yes, I agree. After all, we have two good feet apiece," Nan added, her tone dry as paper. "No need to stand about, waiting to be waited upon."

"Oh, very well. Go on." Susannah shooed her sisters out the front door with a wave of her hands. "Baxter, would you please send the groom with them? To show them the way?"

Nan snorted and rolled her eyes. "As if we would get lost. The stables aren't that far from the house."

"For propriety's sake, if nothing else. Baxter—has the groom left?"

"No, Miss Siddons, he has not. I'll send him round to show the ladies the way." Baxter gave a slight bow and quit the threshold.

"Now, mind you, be polite to Paul. He's going out of his way to entertain you both," Susannah hissed as though her tone wouldn't reach Daniel's ears.

He tried to hide the smile that was threatening to break out across his face. Sisters. "And have a lovely time." He pulled Susannah away from the threshold. "Enjoy your day."

The girls nodded, beaming up at him in a way that warmed his heart. Nothing, not in all his years of wandering, made him feel as affectionately welcome as those smiling faces. This must be what family was supposed to be— This was why people had families in the first place.

He gave them a nod and a wink, and closed the door.

They would be well taken care of. The girls would ride about the estate, and Paul would be at his most charming, and then they'd all have dinner together. And that meant he was free to focus all his attention on Susannah.

"Are you all right, Susy? You look pale." He'd never say that she looked tired. He had been around enough women to know that could be taken as an insult. "If this is too much—"

"No, no. Don't be silly. Just a long night." She stifled a yawn.

"Ah, well." What had kept her up all night? Was she reconsidering their engagement? Best not to ask too many questions—he might find answers he'd rather not know. Instead, he would endeavor to show her how very right her decision had been. "Come into the study, my—" Was it too early to call her "dear" or "darling"? Probably so. He didn't want to sound too forward. "My…estate manager will meet us there." There. That was a good cover for his near mistake.

She looked up, gazing at him with those lovely gray-green eyes that changed color depending on her mood. But she said nothing and only tucked her arm under his elbow. 'Twas the first time she had touched him deliberately since childhood. He would merely ignore the time she helped him up the stairs. This touch communicated more than care. It showed…that she was perhaps willing to be his.

He ushered her into the study and closed the door, glancing quickly about as he guided her to the settee. Yes. Everything was in order. The fire crackled on the hearth, and not a speck of dust marred the furniture. Someone—a maid, ordered by Baxter, most like—had created a lovely arrangement of autumn crocuses and placed it on the mantel. This was Goodwin at its most gracious, and for the first time in ages, a feeling of pride filled his soul. Would Susannah like it, too?

His future bride had stripped off her gloves and was holding her hands out to the blaze. "What a cheerful room this is. It must be quite nice for your work."

"Thank you. But it's our work now." Best to go ahead and seize the moment. "I need your help, Susannah. My estate manager has come up with some changes that will greatly increase the productivity of the farm and mill. And with that, I want to improve the lives of everyone on this place. He has some ideas of where to start with the tenants, but I want your input."

"Well, of course. I can share the information I gleaned from the tenants themselves, when I visited the other day." She tossed a smile over her shoulder at him, as she might toss a blossom at his feet.

"Yes, that's precisely why I want your help. But not just because you spoke with the tenants. Because I value your opinion more than anyone's." He crossed the room and sat opposite her, forcing himself to look directly into those lovely eyes of hers. In some ways, this was as difficult to say as a declaration of love. In some ways, it was a declaration of love. "I admire all you've done. Keeping your family together. Starting your own shop. I want your input before I take another step."

She blinked rapidly, her eyelashes fanning out across her cheeks. "Of course, I will help as much as you need."

"I cannot do this without you. Thank you for helping me so. For agreeing to marry me. You have no idea what it means."

The color had risen in her cheeks, and her gaze remained fixed on the floor. "Daniel?" Her voice was soft, hesitant even.

"Yes?" Something profound was happening between them. He held his breath, as though by exhaling he would frighten her.

"I need to tell you something. I—"

At that most inopportune moment, Baxter opened the study door and ushered the estate manager in. Daniel jumped from his position in the chair, and Susannah's head snapped up. The moment had ended. And how much had Baxter and Donaldson seen of that brief, intimate flash betwixt them?

No matter. He was engaged to Susannah now. He could be seen with her and even be espied in a tender moment with her. He had no need of shame.

But 'twas disappointing all the same. He almost had Susannah— She was there, with him, for that second. She was no longer demanding and thorny and disappointed.

She had been warm and uncertain and gentle. His Susy.

'Twas a very good thing Baxter burst in when he had. Susannah had almost confessed—something—to Daniel.

She assumed the mask of civility and graciously made the acquaintance of Daniel's estate manager, all the while inwardly fanning herself. She hadn't made a complete cake of herself.

She hadn't been certain what she was going to say. But her talk with Becky was still fresh in her mind, and she felt the need to make some sort of statement. A commitment, or a pledge, or something. Obviously, he didn't love her and she didn't love him. Funny how it still hurt to admit the truth of that inside. 'Twas like falling from a tree and hitting the ground—all the wind got knocked out of her.

She could not be vulnerable to Daniel again. Nor could she confess her strange feelings to him. He admired her, he had said. Admiration was not the same as love. One admired a beautiful painting, or a statue in a garden. 'Twas a distant emotion, one that set her deliberately apart from him.

She didn't want to be apart from him any longer.

Whatever was she thinking? Susannah stuffed that last honest admission down deep within and sat on it, as she sat on the settee and went over the plans for the tenants. She shut off her rebellious thoughts with a snap and gave her full attention to both men.

"I think we should start with repairing the roofs," Donaldson was saying. "Even though the weather is already turning foul. By winter a strong, sturdy roof will be a blessing to many of these people."

"Susannah, is that what the tenants mentioned when you spoke to them? What were their greatest wants?" Daniel turned his gaze upon her, his dark green eyes so somber and serious that her heart fluttered.

"Y-yes." Gracious, she must get her turbulent emotions well in hand. 'Twould never do for Daniel to see how very flustered she was. Besides, the tenants were depending on her. "Leaky roofs, warmer clothing—preparing for the winter is topmost in their minds."

"You know, if we give the southern field a rest, as we had been saying, we could use the spare farmhands to mend the roofs." Daniel sat back in his seat, nodding. "That would be at least a dozen men. Perhaps more. We would have everything repaired within the course of a few weeks."

"Excellent idea, sir." Donaldson made a few quick notes, his quill scratching across the foolscap. "That will give us enough time and enough labor to make other improvements, as well."

And the women. They needed to take care of the women and children, who would suffer the most from the cold. "I should like to order several bolts of wool and begin the process of making good warm clothing for the tenants, especially the women and the little ones," she interrupted.

"I understand that you want to help them, Miss Siddons, but we must be very careful," Donaldson warned. "We don't want to seem as though we are offering charity."

"I fail to see how offering them winter clothing is inappropriate when we are also repairing the roof over each tenant's head." Susannah straightened her spine and looked directly at the estate manager. "After all, one of the women there told me that, aside from a leaky roof, their biggest hardship was staying warm through the winter while wrapped in rags."

"Susannah is right," Daniel interjected. "We cannot allow our people to suffer through the winter with clothing that won't keep out the weather." He turned again to Susannah, encouragement in his deep voice and in the level gaze of his green eyes. "How do you feel we should go about this, my Susy?"

Her cheeks were growing hotter. He had called her his Susy. And not only that, but he was asking for her opinion, allowing her a say in a matter about which she already took ownership. "I—I don't know," she confessed. She really must stop allowing her emotions to run rampant over her common sense. "But I do believe that if all the women worked together, as the farmhands will to repair the roofs, then we could have everyone clothed well enough for winter, and in a hurry."

"By Jove, I think you're onto something." Daniel beamed. "A kind of sewing bee, perhaps? My mother used to have parties like that. Only, the women would work on quilts."

"Yes, precisely so." She had been too little to remember Daniel's mother, who died when they were both so young. But she was an indelible presence nonetheless. Her own parents always spoke of Daniel's family quite highly, reserving special praise for the mistress of Goodwin.

And in just a few short weeks, Susannah would be stepping into her shoes.

This was all too much. Her head was dancing about in circles. Her muddled feelings for Daniel, his lavish praise for her and thoughts of his parents—why, she would faint if she couldn't leash her own emotions. She, who had never fainted in her life.

"Susy, are you all right?" Daniel's voice echoed in her ears.

"Yes, yes, quite all right." She forced herself to look over at him. If only the world would stop spinning so. "I just had very little sleep last night. I must be tired."

"Donaldson, I think we have at least a path cleared for getting started." Daniel rose, drawing their meeting to an abrupt close. "Let's leave the south field fallow, and start instructing the men on repairing the cottage roofs. In the spring, let us look into rebuilding some of the cottages when the weather is more amenable. And we shall order the woolen cloth for the tenants' garments without delay."

"Yes, sir." The estate manager bowed. "But if I may

say so, it might be better for Miss Siddons to organize the sewing. 'Tis likely to be more readily accepted, and not thought of as an act of charity, if proposed by the lady of the house."

"Of course." Daniel extended his hand to her. She accepted it. So strange, her hand in his. The strength flowed from his body into hers and her dizziness abated. "You will see to it, Susannah?"

"I will." And she would. Goodwin Hall would be her home soon, and the tenants would be her responsibility. She would make sure that everyone could depend upon staying warm and well fed through the harsh winter months ahead.

She stood beside her future husband, his hand, rough and strong, enveloping hers. He stood with her, when others had failed her. He asked for her help, and begged for her support, when others withdrew from her.

The young lad who fled all responsibility and crushed her girlish dreams of rescue was gone. And in his place a man stood, a man who was accepting the responsibility of Goodwin and of marriage with strength and purpose.

And he was asking her to join him.

Chapter Twenty-Two

Once his estate manager left them, there was really nothing or no one to whom Daniel could look for distraction. Susannah was at Goodwin for the afternoon, and she was no mere guest. This would be her home in just a matter of weeks.

How could he spend the afternoon convincing her that she'd made the right choice?

He could show her how well Mother's chapel looked now that it was done. That was one improvement to the place that he had supervised all on his own, and its completion could now be a point of pride. And since she had shared this journey with him, it might be nice to show her how far her encouragement had led.

Daniel offered her his arm. "Would you like to come with me to see Mother's chapel? It's all finished, and I am rather proud of my handiwork."

Susannah placed her hand tentatively in the crook of his elbow. Warmth raced up his arm as she touched him, though the pressure of her fingertips was light as a feather. "Yes, thank you. That sounds lovely."

They strolled thus, Susannah lagging half a pace behind him as he led her through the main house and down the front porch. "I don't know why it became so important to me to finish the job, but it did. All at once, I felt a burning need to make the place beautiful again, as Mother would want it to be." He shrugged. "Perhaps because it was something so small and manageable. Not at all like taking on the entire estate, just a little piece of it."

"Or it could be that there was a deeper reason. Perhaps you needed to find a sort of spiritual center—a calm place you could claim as your own for contemplation and reflection," Susannah added in her soft voice. "I could well understand that."

Funny, he hadn't really regarded it in that light. But the void within him was filling as he finished the chapel and as he worked on the Hall. Perhaps this was what happened when a man finally recognized his home. He said nothing but pulled her arm a little closer to his side.

They fell silent as they reached the clearing in the grove. Reverend Kirk was right. Susannah's faith had sustained her through all her trials and tribulations. It wasn't that he didn't believe in God. He'd never really given the matter much thought before. It was just that God was wrapped up with his dour, domineering father in a sort of traditional, hidebound package that left very little allure. And now, Susannah's gentle friendship had opened his eyes to what faith meant.

He opened the door of the chapel, which had been painted a lovely, rich shade of brown. It swung easily on its hinges, without emitting a rusty squeak. Yes, every detail had been accounted for. The stained-glass windows sparkled, casting jewel-toned patterns over the wooden floor. The cross that adorned the altar had been thoroughly polished and now gleamed in the pale afternoon sunlight. Scents intermingled—the citrus scent of lemon-polished wood, the slightly acrid smell of new velvet and the sharp contrast of new paint. He closed his eyes for a moment, inhaling. Yes. This was good.

Susannah broke free of his elbow and took a few steps forward. "Oh, it is lovely. Well done, Daniel. Your mother would be so very proud of you, and so happy that you've restored this tiny place to such grandeur."

"Do you like it?" And it was no idle question. He desired Susannah's good opinion with every fiber of his being. She was not one to give praise where it was not deserved. He hadn't deferred to her on the matter of the tenants because he wanted to flatter her. Susannah would see through that straightaway. No—he desired her to care as much about Goodwin as he now realized he did.

If only she would think well of him, too. Not love him—he couldn't ask that of her yet. But if only she would feel some measure of affection for him.

"Like it? Oh, *like* is too weak a word." Susannah clasped her hands and spun around.

Daniel laughed, surprising them both. It had been so long since he'd seen Susannah do anything so girlish. Her manner had become so serious, so somber of late. 'Twas a beautiful thing to see her happy and lighthearted.

Susannah joined in his laughter, her eyes sparkling with mirthful tears. "I suppose I looked a right ninny."

"Not at all. You're delightful, Susy." The words tumbled out of his mouth in a rush before he could halt them. How would she react? She prickled so whenever he tried to compliment her.

Her laughter ceased, but she offered him a hesitant smile. "Thank you."

Well, that was something. At least she hadn't flounced

out of the chapel in a huff or hurled insults at him. Nor had she trundled past his compliment without acknowledging it. This was progress, then. And even though they'd seen everything there was to see in the chapel, there was no reason why they couldn't linger a bit longer. Something about the atmosphere there—the quiet, the calm, the richness and beauty of it all—was drawing them closer together.

There was no other explanation for it.

He beckoned her over to Mother's pew and sat. Susannah joined him, turning just a fraction to one side so they could see each other face-to-face. This, too, was a novel experience. Susannah turning toward him, and not away from him.

"Thank you for allowing me to show you this. And thank you for all your efforts on behalf of the tenants," he offered. "I am afraid I am just working you harder than you ever worked in your shop. For when you are mistress here, I shall lean on you for everything."

"I am happy to help. I love…I love Goodwin." Her cheeks grew rosier in the dim sunlight. Or had he just imagined it?

"Do you really?" Susannah never minced words. There was no reason to doubt her. But still—hearing it spoken aloud made his heart swell with pride.

"I do. I am so glad you stayed here. Even if you did so simply to rescue me. Goodwin needs you." She glanced away from him and began drawing circles on the bare wooden floor with the toe of her slipper.

"I didn't merely rescue you," he admitted. "I didn't simply do what was right. I wanted you to marry me. I still do." 'Twas the truth, after all.

She opened her mouth as though to protest but then closed it and kept staring down at the floor.

Should he press the matter? Tell her the complete and utter truth? That his life would be meaningless and purposeless without her by his side? Strange that they were going to be married in a matter of weeks—the most intimate relationship a man could experience—and he still felt as though he must conceal his true feelings from her.

"How are things going…with the change in your drinking habits?" The question came from out of the blue, and Susannah bit her lip after she spoke the words, as though she wished she could take them all back.

Well, 'twas her right to know. It was a condition she asked him to agree to, and difficult though it was, his abstinence would make him a better master for Goodwin. "It's not as simple as I thought it would be," he admitted. "Paul thinks I am insane. But it has made me a better man, and so for that I should be grateful." He sighed. "I actually prayed to be worthy of all this. My first time to pray, Susannah. So much in my life has changed for the better. I want to be worthy of it all."

Susannah nodded slowly, turning her eyes up to his. "I understand. And I am so proud of you, Daniel. You are deepening and growing in so many ways. Accepting God into your life—turning to Him—this is a profound step."

"It's so difficult, though. I must admit, the thought of liquor is as intoxicating at times as the actual taste of it." He admitted this because he needed someone else to hear it. Someone strong, like Susannah. "And it is all I can do not to go down into the cellar and take one of the few remaining bottles. I'd uncork the thing and drink myself into a stupor if I could."

The silence before them stretched into an eternity. He

had gone too far. He had pressed too much, revealed too much, and Susannah was backing away from him, fleeing in spirit as though she were running as fast as she could over the hills back to her shop. What a dunce he'd been. He should have just shown her the chapel and been done.

On the other hand, she had brought up the drinking herself. So she was as much to blame for this sudden awkwardness.

Well, he had to do something. They couldn't just sit in silence forever. He removed his hand from her arm and started to rise.

"Giving up anything you have depended upon is difficult, Daniel." Susannah rose and grasped his elbow. "I know."

He turned to face Susannah. Her eyes, in the dim afternoon sunlight, turned a mysterious shade of gray. And if he squinted just a bit, he could pick out the sprinkling of freckles across the bridge of her nose. Susannah was a natural beauty. How many times in his travels had he seen women who were painted or plucked or stuffed within an inch of their lives? And none of them could hold a candle to her as she stood now, with her small pointed chin turned up and her magnificent eyes gazing into his.

"Yes, but you've always been brave." He was the one holding still now as she reached out to him. Any sudden movement might break this lovely peace. They were walking together through a mist, in a way, and he could see the clearing if only they could walk slowly.

"Not always. In fact, hardly ever. I've spent many nights crying quietly into my pillow, or pacing the floor after the girls have fallen asleep." She gave him a wry smile. "What you are trying is no mean feat, and I am here to help in any way I can."

"I shall depend upon your help." He was holding himself still, as though she were a deer he might startle with any kind of quick movement. "Teach me, by your example, to grow closer to Christ. To invite Him into my heart. That was something that Reverend Kirk and I spoke about. I will need your help every day for the rest of my life, Susy. Will you help me?"

"Of course I will." She gazed at him, her eyes turning a darker shade of green in the dim light. "I should like nothing better." She turned briskly, and the moment of intimacy between them was broken. "I suppose we should be getting back. I have no idea how long it will be until my sisters wear Paul out."

She was right, of course. Even so, he hated to go. "Oh, I am sure that Paul is having the time of his life. He grew up in a large family, you know. Seven sisters and three brothers, and he the eldest of them all. I am certain that squiring Nan and Becky about is merely reminding him of the years he spent playing chaperone to his own sisters."

"Ten siblings! Upon my word, I would have no idea what to do with myself if I had to shepherd that many. As it is, two are enough to keep me hopping." She tucked her hand into his elbow once more, as though it was all quite natural and matter-of-fact, and as though nothing profound was transpiring between them at all.

He must give her time. Even though he knew the truth of his feelings for her, and even though he knew how very vital she was in his life, he could not press his suit. If he did, she would withdraw further and further until she had left him completely.

He must, for once in his life, practice patience. His reward would be worth it in the end.

* * *

"Paul, you are a tease," Nan scolded. "I know very well that the object you're thinking of is a flower, so don't prevaricate any longer, if you please."

Susannah glanced up from her sewing, a stern rebuke for Nan writ plain across her features. An afternoon's acquaintance wasn't nearly long enough for her sister to speak so familiarly to a man. And really, Nan must learn not to be so forthright. Why, here was Paul, entertaining the girls with a silly game as they whiled away the long afternoon at Goodwin, and Nan was already insulting him instead of merely being thankful that someone was willing to play.

"He is a dreadful cheat, Nan." Daniel propped himself up on his elbow. He had been reclining on the floor at Susannah's feet, reading through one of the interminable ledger books that Donaldson had left for him. "Don't let him get away with it."

"Says the young man who once won an entire game of faro with a raised eyebrow," Paul retorted, his hearty laugh filling the room. "Daniel is notorious throughout London for his ability to mask and bluff while playing cards."

Susannah's heart lurched, but she kept her countenance. She stabbed the needle through the fabric with the precision of a machine. Daniel had led a very worldly life—much more so than she. 'Twas unfair to think that he would change once they were married. But still—any mention of faro brought up the memory of Uncle Arthur, and his gaming debts, and his insistence that she, Susannah, must save the family from the ruin he'd caused.

"That was years ago, and it wasn't even that good of a bluff. Some other young buck will have to take my place as the most infamous faro player in Town. I have other, more important business to attend to. I am a farmer now, if you will but recall."

Susannah shifted her gaze from her sewing to Daniel's face. His eyes remained stubbornly fixed on the ledger, but with a slight and gentle gesture, he reached over and tapped the toe of her slipper with his quill pen.

Susannah's shoulders relaxed. She hadn't realized until he touched her that she'd drawn them up to the very tips of her earlobes.

"Ah, how very disappointing. Fine, then. You have me at your mercy, Nan. You've won that round." Paul made an exaggerated half bow to Nan and then turned to Becky. "Your turn, my dear."

They nattered on, playing their silly game. Daniel scratched his pen across the ledger, making notes. The fire crackled in the grate, and the wind—which had started out as a playful fall breeze—began howling in earnest. How nice to be cozy in the parlor together, everyone enjoying each other's company, everything snug and warm. And even the tenants were being seen to, which made the enjoyment of this afternoon together even more joyous because it was not selfishly spent.

She cast another glance over at her sisters. Was everyone behaving themselves? Yes, yes, they were. Becky was speaking to Paul, her wide eyes sparkling as she described some object for him to hazard a guess upon. Very good. With her sisters occupied and not in immediate need of her guiding hand, she could allow her mind to wander.

Some intense change had come over her since their quiet moments in the chapel. They were bound together now. Equal partners in a terrifying yet exhilarating venture. They were both giving up something that symbolized freedom. And Daniel had embraced his faith, and would rely on her to help him, just as she relied on him.

That moment in the chapel—what she'd said to Daniel was true. Giving up something she depended upon was a terrifying thing. Once, she had surrendered control to Daniel. She'd bobbed along in the wake of his plan, convinced that he would make everything right. And when that did not happen, she built up her own tower of strength in the shop. And now that shop would have to be passed on to her sisters. She was relinquishing control of the one thing that kept her safe and secure, certain in her own purpose. The shop was supposed to be her haven over the years, but 'twas time to let it go. She must do so, for there was no other way. There were too many things that needed her attention at Goodwin. The tenants. The household.

Her husband.

She stole a glance down at Daniel. Funny, she always expected to see the boy he had been, but of course, time had wrought its changes. He was taller, and filled out, and more angular than he had been when they were fifteen. The planes of his face were darkening as the day wore on—he'd need a shave in the morning. He was a man now, and a man to whom she would give her life in just a few weeks' time.

Becky's words drifted into her mind. *Let things happen.* What a novel concept.

What if she forgave Daniel for what happened in the past? He had apologized once before, and was working to make things right. And after all, he was a mere boy when everything transpired. How many boys, when confronted by a breathless, sobbing girl, would propose marriage on the spot? He was brave and kind then, as he was now. Only now, he had matured and become the kind of person who followed through on his promises. As he was trying to do with giving up liquor, and how he had stepped in to save her from the rumor mill.

What if she finally let go and let things happen?

What if she admitted to herself that she was falling in love with Daniel?

Chapter Twenty-Three

"I have assembled us all for a very important purpose." Susannah sat at the head of the worn oak table and assumed her most commanding "eldest sister" expression. "We must talk seriously about our future here in Tansley."

"You've been acting exceedingly odd since we met at Daniel's house a week ago," Nan replied dryly. "I rather expected a talking-to. Why did it take you so long?"

"And why are we discussing our future in Tansley?" Becky grasped a lock of her dark hair and began twirling it around her forefinger. "I thought the matter was settled. You're marrying Daniel in a fortnight, and then Nan and I shall keep the shop. Is that not so?"

Susannah felt rather deflated. After all, this was her moment, her grand pronouncement as head of the family. And moreover, she'd kept her roiling emotions well hidden, or so she thought. There was no need for Nan to act so superior, or for Becky to become so agitated.

"A few things have changed since we visited Goodwin last week," she began. 'Twas hard to say the words properly, as she had rehearsed them in her head over the past few days, when her sisters were taking on so. "Important things that I must discuss with you."

"Very well. We are listening." Becky elbowed Nan. Nan scowled and rubbed her upper arm, but she did stop short of interjecting an acerbic comment.

"What's changed is this." Susannah paused and took a deep breath. This was most difficult to say, for it meant putting aside all her reservations and her hesitations. Once said, the words could not be unsaid. "I realize... I know now...that I am...in love with Daniel."

The words tumbled out of her in a rush. She hazarded a quick, darting glance over at her sisters. Nan gaped openly, her mouth forming a perfect little O. Becky smiled, her wide blue eyes sparkling with unshed tears.

"Oh, Susannah," she breathed, clasping her hands. "How wonderful."

"Wonderful and terrifying," Susannah admitted. "I have found that I must relinquish all my earlier prejudices against Daniel, and that has been most difficult."

"But—you have relinquished them?" Becky tilted her head to one side, as though considering the matter.

"Yes." Yes, she had. She could no longer hold her fiancé responsible for the decisions he made as a boy. They had no bearing on the man he had become.

"Hooray!" Becky leaped from her spot at the table and hurtled toward Susannah, enveloping her in a fierce embrace. "Oh, I knew it would be so. What a romantic story you two have shared. True love thwarted...forgiveness... and he your hero, after all!"

"I wouldn't put things in quite so melodramatic a fashion, Becky," Susannah said with a laugh. She squeezed her sister before untangling herself from Becky's embrace. Then she glanced over at Nan, who was still sitting as though dumbstruck. Her heart lurched. Was Nan somehow displeased? "Nan? What say you about this?"

"I say…" Nan shook her head slowly, her eyes downcast. "I say…'tis the first time I've heard my bossy eldest sister own up to a mistake." She raised her eyes to Susannah's and laughed. "I am so happy for you, Sue."

"Stuff and nonsense," Susannah retorted. "I'm always eager to make amends for my mistakes."

Nan and Becky rolled their eyes at each other, a private gesture that—though it was playfully intended—always made it quite clear that Susannah was the mother figure, while they were the daughters and chums together.

When she married Daniel, she might finally have someone with whom she could be best chums, as well as husband and wife. That would be quite nice. Loneliness could be so all-consuming. Perhaps marriage was more about companionship and partnership than capitulation.

"Does Daniel know?" Becky flounced back over to her place at the table and sat. "Have you admitted this to him, as well?"

"I— Uh." No, she hadn't. It took all of her courage and strength to tell the truth of her emotions to her sisters. What on earth would it take for her to own the truth to Daniel? "Not yet."

"Well, you should do so without delay. Aren't you going to Goodwin this afternoon?" Nan smiled. "Perfect opportunity."

"I am. I am supposed to choose a new lady's maid to assist me. But—do you really think Daniel needs to know?" She turned away from both of her sisters and crossed her arms over her chest. Telling Daniel the truth meant leaving herself completely vulnerable once more.

And though she'd forgiven him, was she ready to be that open with him again?

"I think 'tis essential." Becky's soft voice floated over to her. Of course, Becky would say that. She was the romantic one.

"But—what if he doesn't return the feeling?" She kept her tone brisk and impersonal, but even so, there was a catch to it. She cleared her throat. "I'd look a right fool then."

"He does return the feeling," Nan stated in her flat, matter-of-fact tone. "I've seen it in his eyes. And in everything he's done for you. He probably hasn't told you yet for the same reason you haven't told him. You're both scared."

"I'm not scared," Susannah began to protest, but then she paused. Of course she was afraid. This entire leap into a new life with Daniel was quite terrifying.

"I'm not saying that you are a coward," Nan added, her tone a little gentler. "But I think there is a misunderstanding, and fear from both of you. One of you must tell the other. I think it should come from you, Susannah."

"Why from me? Shouldn't the man always declare his intentions?" Gracious, this was maddening. Why should the declaration of love be her sole responsibility?

"Because, of the two, you are the most formidable," Nan teased. "And because you'll say it. I know you will, Sue."

Susannah turned back to face her sisters. They were both leaning across the table, their expressions expectant and encouraging.

"You are certain of his regard for me?"

Becky nodded.

Nan piped up, uttering a single word. *"Yes."*

Of the two, Susannah expected Becky to champion this marriage, for she liked anything that smacked of romance. And even if a situation weren't romantic, she might concoct a dreamy scenario out of thin air.

But…Nan? Nan was the matter-of-fact one. The plain-spoken one. She would never be dreamy or idealistic about anything.

If Nan saw love in Daniel's eyes, then it must be true.

"I don't know if I can actually bring myself to say those words," Susannah admitted. "Perhaps I could just show him I love him, through my actions. And that way, he would feel no pressure from me to say anything about love, either. Wouldn't that be best?"

"Sue, I have never known you to be a coward about anything." Nan faced her squarely, as though issuing a challenge. "Why now?"

"I am not a coward." Why was this so difficult? She shouldn't have said anything. Bother her need to be open and direct about everything, and bother her need to have a nice clean finish to her ownership of the shop. Now she had to face things with her sisters that she could hardly face on her own. "This is an entirely different matter. Always, in the past, I have been able to guard my own feelings. I had to give nothing to this shop but my hard work. But now—what you are telling me I must do is give Daniel my heart. And yes, that surrender is quite hard for me to accomplish. You'll understand it someday, Nan. When you are older."

"Nan, you're being too harsh on poor Susannah." Becky stood and reached her small hand toward Susannah, and she accepted her sister's hand with gratitude. Becky might be entirely too dreamy and romantic for her own good, but at least she was sympathetic. "This would be hard for anyone to do, much less someone as strong and independent as our sister."

"Thank you," Susannah murmured.

"But, Susannah, you have to understand something, as well." Becky clasped her hand tighter and gave her sister a tremulous smile. "Anything worth having in this world involves some sort of difficulty. Some effort. And a strong marriage to the man you love is worth this effort. Just as it took bravery for you to move us to Tansley and start this hat shop, so, too, must you embark on this phase of your life with courage…and honesty."

Susannah sighed. Nan's stubborn persistence and Becky's gentle persuasion had worn her down. She was licked. And even though the thought of confessing her love to Daniel was absolutely terrifying, 'twas also rather exhilarating. As though she were standing on the highest point on the moor, and all the beautiful, rolling vistas were before her, and nothing but the vast sky above her.

She was ready to climb to the precipice.

Daniel squinted at his estate manager's fine handwriting on the ledger before him. Yes, indeed—if he understood what he was reading, then the repairs on the tenants' roofs were progressing nicely already. 'Twas only a week ago that they implemented the plans for changing Goodwin, whisking away the old way of doing business and replacing it with the methods that Susannah, Donaldson and he together decided would work well.

Susannah might be here herself in a little while. She was beginning her work on organizing a sewing bee for the tenants, and the wool she brought from her little shop had already been gladly received in some quarters. Perhaps when she was here, he would have a few moments of her time. Not to press his suit, but just to bask in the warm glow of her company.

That wasn't enough, of course, but it was enough for now. In time, she might come to hold him in the same regard as he held her.

A rapping on the study window startled him out of his reverie. Who on earth could that be? In all likelihood 'twas Paul, playing at some sort of joke. No one else would be foolish enough to traipse about on the moor when the weather was this freezing. He stalked over to the window and prepared to give his friend a good tongue-lashing for behaving like an idiot.

But as he tossed back the curtains, 'twas Susannah standing out in the cold. She wore a long velvet cloak and a matching tam-o'-shanter. Her bright auburn hair stood out in bold relief against her rather severe winter garments, and two pink circles—brought on by the winter chill, no doubt—stained her cheeks.

"Susannah? What on earth are you doing out here? You'll catch your death. Come inside, I've a fire going here in the parlor."

"No," she cried, her cheeks turning pinker. "I was on my way to visit the tenants for the sewing bee, but I need to tell you something. And I have to tell you out here." Her breath came out in little puffs of smoke on the frosty air.

"All right. Is it about the house? Did you see something on the exterior wall as you walked past?" He leaned out the window and scanned the blond stone walls of the Hall for anything unusual.

"No. I just…I just need to say something." She bit her lip and paused.

For a moment, his heart pounded against his rib cage.

Why was she behaving so strangely? Why would she not come inside? She hadn't come to break their engagement, had she? "Proceed, Susannah." He bowed his head. The blow might come at any moment.

"I realize the utter strangeness and stupidity of what I am about to say, especially when you consider that we are already engaged," she blurted, speaking so quickly that he had difficulty understanding all that she said. "But I've been in conference with my sisters, and we all agree that this must be said."

He tightened his hand on the window sash. "Yes?"

It was all over. It must be.

"What I have to tell you is that I realize that I have fallen in love with you. Even though we're engaged to be married, and even though we have been engaged to be married in some form or fashion to each other for many years, I realized the truth of my feelings for you recently."

Had he heard aright? Daniel raised his eyes slowly from where he had been staring at the tips of her little boots, almost buried in the snow, to her lovely warm eyes, now widened with something like apprehension. She clasped her gloved hands together, almost as though she was pleading with him to understand.

"Say that again." He couldn't help it. He must be dreaming. There was no way that he had heard what he thought he heard. 'Twould be all the fulfillment of his dreams if it were so.

She swallowed and sighed. "I said that I love you. I realize how ridiculous I must sound—"

That was all Daniel needed. With one quick leap, he was out the window, and his boots crunched on the snow as he landed. Susannah took a step back, giving a nervous laugh. "Gracious! 'Tis a good thing that your study is on the first floor, sir."

"You say that you love me, little Susy? Oh, my darling." He swept her into his arms, quite off her feet, and spun her around. "You've made me the happiest man on earth. I've loved you forever. Since we were children together, I suppose."

"You have? I've loved you forever, as well, Daniel. 'Twas just hurt feelings and pride that have kept me a prisoner all these years. I loved you so much that when you left, it hurt more than I could say. But now you're back, and I can't dissemble any longer. It would not be fair, not to either of us."

Daniel's heart leaped, and he enfolded his future bride in an embrace that left them both breathless. When he allowed his beloved enough room to breathe, she chuckled. "You're the one who will catch your death out here. We must go inside."

"I am not cold. I am warm through and through now with the knowledge that the woman I have loved all my life loves me in return," he teased.

"Your lips are turning blue," she rejoined. "Come, let us make haste."

They wandered around to the front porch, her arm tucked in his. As they mounted the steps, Baxter held the door open, his face registering confusion at both Susannah's flushed cheeks and his master's lack of appropriate winter clothing. But Baxter was not well-bred for nothing. He simply held the door open and bowed as they passed through.

Good man, that.

"In the past I would have fixed a cognac tincture to warm us both up," Daniel remarked. "But as it is, I would like you to bring us some tea, Baxter. Boiling hot, if you please."

Baxter bowed and made his way to the kitchens as Daniel led Susannah to his study. Once inside, he helped her remove her cloak and tam. Then he drew her down beside him on the settee.

"Why did you look so terrified when you came to tell me?" He must know. She'd seemed so much on the verge of saying goodbye, and yet she had told him everything he'd dreamed of hearing. Everything that he had planned to wait for, the rest of his life.

"I'm embarrassed to say," she admitted, hiding her face on his shoulder. He placed his arm around her. He half expected her to push him away. She had always done so in the past, leaping away from him as though his touch burned her. This quiet acceptance, and even encouragement, of his touch was wonderful, but it might take a fellow a few days to get used to it.

"Tell me, anyway," he murmured, bending his head close to her ear and tightening his hold around her waist.

"Well, I was afraid. I'm not blaming you for the decisions you made as a boy, Daniel. Nor do I still harbor a grudge in my heart for all your years at sea. But the truth is, I am an independent person—"

"Quite independent," he teased.

"Yes, quite." She nestled closer to him. "And 'tis difficult for me to surrender all of my past airs, my stubborn belief in how right I am—all that sort of thing. And it's hard for me to give up my shop so completely. It's my own creation, and my own livelihood, and I am giving it all up for—"

"For me." He paused a moment. Yes, he could well

understand how very difficult that might be, especially when he had betrayed her trust so callously in his youth.

"But all this I would do for you. After all, you have given up drinking. And if you are brave enough to do that for me, then I would be brave enough to give up my shop."

He closed his eyes for a moment. Never had he realized the enormity of what they were embarking upon until Susannah, in her simple and direct fashion, stated matters so. He had relied upon liquor to take him away from the cares of this world while she had created her shop to help her endure the hardships of the world. And out of love, they were relinquishing their hold on both of those things.

"So…I suppose you could say that though we are both scared, we can be brave together." He kissed the top of her head, breathing deeply of her scent of orange blossom. "Does that sound like an adventure to you, Susy?"

"You're scared, too?" She pulled away from him and fixed him with a keen, searching look.

"Yes, of course, my darling." It was so much easier to say the words aloud than to carry them in his heart. "Afraid that I shall fail you, again. Afraid to give up liquor forever. Afraid that in asking you to help me with all the myriad duties and responsibilities of Goodwin, I am asking more of you than I should. But there is no one I would rather start this grand exploration with than you, Susy."

Susannah cast him a gentle smile, one that curled the corners of her rosy lips. "Then we shall be brave together in this new adventure, Daniel. There is no one I would rather set sail with than you."

Chapter Twenty-Four

Only one matter still preyed upon Daniel's mind. He'd admitted the truth to Susannah a week before, when she'd confessed her love to him as she'd stood shivering in the snow. But there was a feeling that still pervaded his entire being. A feeling that somehow, in some fashion, he was not coming to Susannah as a whole man. Yes, he was determined to conquer his drinking. And his emptiness was filling as he quietly accepted his newfound faith. But was it enough?

He paced the floor of his bedroom. His wedding was a week away. But he could not, in good conscience, bring Susannah nothing more than the husk of a man. He had to be real, vital—a flesh-and-blood presence in their marriage. When drinking, he had embraced the void. But now he must be certain that the void was entirely filled.

He dressed himself quickly, warming up by the fire. In a week or so he would bring on a valet, as tradition dictated, and yet he had sidestepped tradition by promoting one of the footmen to the position. Baxter spoke well of the young man and indicated that he would be willing to train him in the formalities his position would entail.

And Susannah had promoted one of the female tenants, a shy young lass with slightly crossed eyes, after seeing how well she did with the sewing bee. This new gel was nimble with a needle and had a dignified manner that would suit Susannah well.

So once again, while they had deferred to tradition on the surface, the two of them had sought their own path.

No need for a cravat. If he went outdoors, he'd simply bundle up in a long coat.

But even as he attended to the routine of dressing for the day, the gnawing feeling of panic would not abate. He must do something; try harder to become a better man for his bride.

He couldn't talk to Paul about this. Paul embraced the emptiness of a dissolute life, as well. His friend would guffaw, offer him a drink and then tease him for turning the liquor away. And he couldn't talk to Susannah about it. He'd confided in her once before. But while she understood—to some extent—his fears, he didn't want to alarm her. No need to make her feel more nervous about their impending nuptials.

And, of course, he had no father still living, nor a brother. And if they were alive, 'twas unlikely they would offer sympathetic counsel. Neither one was compassionate to the failings of the human race.

To whom could he turn? For he must speak to someone. He couldn't continue as matters stood.

There were people in this world that had to listen to you, no matter how lax your history had been. Their profession demanded it of them, for it was their primary purpose. And they guided lost souls and wayward sheep who strayed from the flock.

The round, kindly face of Reverend Kirk drifted into Daniel's mind.

Of course. He could go to Crich and discuss the matter with the reverend. He was to marry them in a week's time, anyway. Under the pretense of seeing to the details of the wedding, he could speak with their gentle country pastor for just a moment.

He couldn't ride out today, for the wind was howling and the occasional dusting of snowflakes whooshed by his window. Yet, as he drew back the curtain and rubbed his sleeve across the pane to clear it of frost, he saw that the roads were clear. He would order the carriage, drive out to Crich and return in time for his dinner.

Funny, even though Baxter had always seen to the efficient running of Goodwin, 'twas quite amazing how much more punctual everything had become once Daniel took an active interest in the household. For from the moment he pulled the bell and ordered his carriage, till the moment he rolled out across the moor, was less than ten minutes. And he even had the luxury of a warmed brick at his feet and a fur lap robe. Even the cook had packed a variety of eatables for him to partake of on this brief journey.

He was well taken care of now that he'd seen to the welfare of others.

That thought did lessen the feeling of inadequacy that plagued his very soul.

He shut off his mind as they rolled out over the moors. The last time he journeyed to Crich he had spent most of his trip occupied with intense soul-searching. Now, however, he would spend the time merely looking out over the frozen hills. The moment for introspection would come when he had someone to guide him, to listen and to offer wise counsel.

Why, was that the spire up ahead? Daniel withdrew his pocket watch. Astounding. They had traveled for the better part of an hour and it seemed as though only a few moments had gone by.

The carriage wound its way into the clearing between two hills and slowly rumbled into the churchyard. The coachman drew to a stop beside the rectory. Yes, since it was Saturday, it was quite likely that Reverend Kirk was in his home, preparing for the morrow's service. He would try here first rather than the chapel.

He allowed the coachman to open the door. No more leaping out on his own, disdaining his own servant's help. The man had a job to do, after all. It would be demeaning for him not to have a chance to do his duty, just as Daniel was taking care of his duties and responsibilities in managing Goodwin.

Daniel took the rectory steps two at a time and gave the door a sharp rap. Nervousness made his gestures more short than usual, and he took a deep, steadying breath. He couldn't very well barge his way into Reverend Kirk's home simply because he was a bundle of nerves. He must calm down.

The door opened, and a stout, older housekeeper smiled as she wiped her hands on her apron. "May I help you, sir?" Her voice had a strong Liverpudlian accent—it reminded him of the seas and of voyages he undertook when adventure sang through his blood. And it was appropriate, too, because this was his latest and greatest journey.

"I've come to speak with the reverend, if he is available." Daniel removed his hat and twirled it in his hands. The gesture might conceal the fact that they were shaking.

"He is. He is upstairs writing, but if you'll come through to the parlor, I shall let him know you are here, Mr....?" She gave a discreet pause.

"Mr. Hale. The reverend is presiding over my wedding next week."

Her broad face broke into a sunny smile. "Of course! Mr. Hale. Do come in." She ushered him into a pretty but plain parlor, where a fire crackled and popped in the grate. "Make yourself comfortable. Shall I bring anything to you? Tea, perhaps?"

"No, thank you. I don't wish to take up too much of the reverend's time." He set his hat on a worn oak table and sank into a chair near the hearth.

"Very good, sir." She bustled out of the room, and her footsteps echoed up the stairs. "Reverend! Mr. Hale is here to see you. I put him in the parlor. I expect it's about his nuptials," she called cheerily. Even though the door to the parlor was shut, Daniel heard every word as though she'd spoken directly to him. He smothered a smile and waited for the reverend to appear.

It didn't take long. The reverend's footsteps rang out over his head and echoed down the staircase. Daniel rose as the parlor door opened.

"Good day, Mr. Hale! So nice to see you." Reverend Kirk extended his hand and shook Daniel's with a cordial gesture. "I must say, I am surprised. This weather is so cold, I certainly did not imagine anyone would travel four miles to see me."

"Well, it is cold, but the roads are clear," Daniel explained. Then he paused. He could continue making polite chatter, which would ease the social awkwardness of the situation. But, in truth, he was more concerned about easing his troubled mind. "I hope you don't mind my frankness, Reverend. But I have a great weight pressing on my mind, and I feel the need to speak with you before my marriage."

"Of course, my son, of course." The older man waved him back over to the chair. "What is troubling you?" He sat beside Daniel, drawing his chair up closer so that his mere presence was a comfort.

"Well, you see, this is the problem." Now was the time to empty his soul. He'd spent the whole day avoiding the thoughts that had roiled his mind, and now was the time to give them full rein. "I've embarked on my spiritual journey and yet—sometimes—I feel like I am merely the shell of a man, and it pains me to offer Susannah so little. I worry there is a void in me that cannot be filled, and I don't want to come to Susannah as an empty, useless waste of a man."

"My son, I can tell you right now that you are not a useless man. Nor are you a waste. You've done an admirable job of taking over Goodwin Hall. Even though I live miles away, I have heard tales from my parishioners about the good work you are doing there. For the lives of the people who depend upon Goodwin and its master, you are working profound changes, and it will improve all of their lives." Reverend Kirk laid a comforting hand on Daniel's shoulder. "You should give yourself more credit, Daniel."

"But—it's not just the outward appearances," Daniel protested. "I do realize that the changes I have installed at Goodwin are helpful. And most of them were wrought under Susannah's supervision, so I cannot even take full credit for their implementation. My fear is for what I am on the inside. If I am an empty vessel when I am alone, then how can I be a good husband to my wife?"

"Susannah is a woman who is very strong, very spiritual in nature. I've known her family for a long time. She can help you, and so shall I. Don't close yourself off and tell yourself that somehow you are unworthy of Susannah and unequal to the task of this marriage. You can— and you will—see this through and become a stronger man because of it."

Daniel nodded, staring into the fire. Yes—he had allowed liquor to be his world. And he'd never sought to deepen his experience by developing a sense of spirituality. No, he had chased after excitement and thrills and then used liquor to deaden his pain.

Now he was on the precipice of a grander experience than any he had ever known, and he was embarking without the safety of knowing that he could drink until the pain was gone.

And yet, back then, he had been alone. Now he had so many people who loved him, or who supported him, or who wanted him to do well. Susannah. Her sisters. The servants and tenants at Goodwin. Even Paul, in his own way. And even Donaldson, who'd continued to love and care for Goodwin even when its master could not.

Now Reverend Kirk was telling him that he had even more than those precious things. The reverend himself was there to help him on this journey. And he had God's love. And though the thought of it was still too enormous for him to comprehend, 'twas comforting nonetheless.

"Reverend, you've helped me more than words can say. Thank you so much for your kindness and patience." He paused, the inkling of an idea beginning to form in the back of his mind. "I wonder, though, if I could prevail upon your kindness and patience a little longer? I have a special favor to ask…."

Susannah waited, her arms stretched upward, as Becky and Nan lowered her gown over her head.

"Don't look yet," Becky scolded as Susannah turned toward the looking glass. "Wait until we have the tapes tied and the skirt fluffed out." She tugged the gown into place around Susannah's shoulders as Nan poufed the skirt with an expert hand.

"Very well. Now you may look." Taking Susannah by the shoulders, Becky turned her toward the looking glass.

Susannah squinted at her reflection in the mirror. Her natural instinct for perfection rose to the surface, and she touched the neckline with an experimental gesture. "What do you think? Does the neckline suit me? Does it make my neck look too short?"

"You look like a swan," Nan protested. "And that pale green just brings out the auburn of your hair."

"I have time to change things before the wedding, you know," Susannah muttered. Nan was a fairly direct judge, so perhaps there was no need for further alterations to the gown. "A week to go—I could redo the neckline if need be."

"There's no need," Becky added in her sweet voice. "You look lovely, Susannah. Like a portrait come to life."

"What are you going to do with your hair?" Nan stepped back and gave a critical tilt to her chin. "A Grecian style, perhaps?"

"Yes, I thought I might." With one swift gesture, Susannah wound her hair on top of her head. "I have a velvet ribbon in a darker shade of green. I thought I might bind my hair with that."

"Or wind it through, and let it peek out from your tresses here and there," Becky added, working her fingers through the thick knot atop Susannah's head. "That would look quite subtle and elegant."

A small avalanche of—what on earth? Hailstones?—pinged against the bedroom window. Susannah gasped and whirled around. Was someone in the village teasing her again? Things were much quieter now that her engagement was public knowledge...but still...

"I'll go see what that is," Nan pronounced, stalking over to the window and throwing up the sash. "Daniel Hale! What on earth are you doing down there?"

"I need to speak to Susannah." Her beloved's voice rang up to her. "Where is she? I tried knocking on the door, but no one answered."

"You can't see her now. She's trying on her wedding gown," Nan shouted. Susannah rolled her eyes. Soon the whole village would be talking of this incident, unless she put a stop to the nonsense right away. She turned and walked downstairs, grabbing her cloak from the peg as she went. Her hair tumbled about her shoulders, but she had no time to pin it up.

"Susannah! Come back upstairs," her sisters implored. "Don't let him to see you in your gown!"

She arranged the folds of her cloak so that no peek of the pale green fabric showed through. "I have matters well in hand," she called up to Nan and Becky. "Do compose yourselves." She wrenched the latch and pulled open the door to reveal her fiancé.

"Susannah—I..." He paused and laughed like a schoolboy. "How very strange all this is."

It was good to see Daniel laugh again. So often lately he had been very serious. While 'twas good to know that he was becoming the sober and respectable master of Goodwin Hall, she had to admit that she'd missed the mischievous twinkle in those green eyes. She leaned against the door frame, barring his passage inside. "State your business and be quick about it," she ordered. "I am standing here in my unfinished wedding gown talking to you."

He cleared his throat and stood tall, assuming an air of mock solemnity that provoked her to chuckle. Dear Daniel. What a fine husband he would be. "It's simply this, Miss Siddons. I wish for you to come by Goodwin Hall on our wedding day. In the morning. I would rather meet you there and drive out together than to meet at Crich."

"All right…if you say so," she agreed with some hesitation. She furrowed her brow. What was he about? Was he intent on making mischief on their wedding day?

"Don't fret," he added swiftly. "I shall make all the necessary arrangements. But this is for the best, I promise. Will you indulge me?"

She turned the matter over in her mind. Very well. If he said he'd make arrangements, then she could trust him to keep his word. "Yes." She shut the door in his grinning face and could not suppress her own delighted smile.

Marriage to Daniel was going to be a grand adventure indeed.

Chapter Twenty-Five

Daniel turned his mother's necklace over in the pale morning sunshine, allowing the sun to send prisms of light bouncing around his room. Today was his wedding day. His stomach roiled as it did when he would wait to embark on a ship bound on its next voyage. 'Twas a strange mixture of nervousness, newfound energy, hope for the future and the tiniest twinge of fear.

He took a deep, calming breath. With time, and with Susannah's help, he would learn to pray. As it was, his recent chat with Reverend Kirk echoed in his mind. He was secure in the knowledge that he would always have the support and the love of Susannah and the steadfast resolve of the reverend.

A knock sounded on the door. "Enter," he called.

Baxter popped his head round the door frame. "Miss Siddons's carriage is coming through the park gates," he announced.

"Very good, Baxter. Remember to show her into my study. Don't ask to take her cloak. She wants to remain completely covered so that I cannot see her gown," he reminded his stalwart butler.

Baxter bowed. "Of course," he replied with a grave air.

"And everything is prepared? The wedding breakfast? All my arrangements—everything is well in hand?"

Baxter nodded. "Of course, sir. The breakfast will be held in the dining room after the service. Cook is waiting until after the ceremony starts to begin preparing the bacon and eggs. No need to let everything grow cold, especially on a frosty day like today."

"Excellent plan. I trust that all the fires are at full roar in the grates?"

Baxter raised his eyebrows, as though he might be growing impatient with his master. "Yes. The house is in perfect order, sir."

"Good. I expect nothing less from you, Baxter. Now, I shall go down to the study. Send Miss Siddons in upon her arrival." Daniel draped his mother's necklace back into its leather-bound case and shut it with a snap. There was nothing more to do. All of his plans had been executed to the merest detail. Even a captain running a ship couldn't ask for more efficient attention to his plans.

Baxter bowed and left, preparing to welcome the future mistress of Goodwin. Daniel rushed down the back staircase so that he would not somehow encounter Susannah before he had a moment to compose himself in the study.

What if she didn't like his plan?

Well, then. They'd just have to postpone the wedding, wouldn't they?

He burst into the study and tossed the box containing his mother's necklace onto his desk. Then he paced the worn Aubusson carpet. Baxter was right—the fire was blazing in here. 'Twas enough to make a fellow broiling hot. He stuck one finger under his cravat. Would he ever get used to wearing these things? 'Twas enough to choke a fellow.

A soft knock sounded on the door. 'Twas unlike Baxter's sharp rap—how strange. "Enter."

Susannah poked her head around the door frame. "Daniel? Baxter sent me back here to see you."

"Yes." Funny, he expected more formality from Baxter. But the old fellow must know that something was afoot. He was too shrewd to let matters slide. "Come in, Susannah. And shut the door."

She slipped into the room and leaned with her back against the closed door. "Have you gone mad?" she protested. "You're not supposed to see me—not yet."

"If I am mad, then it must be with love for you, my darling," he replied. Then he coughed. How ridiculous that sounded—as though he were a Romantic poet. And judging by the subtle lift of Susannah's eyebrows, she wasn't that impressed by his flight of fancy, either. Better to press on, try to cover the moment. "I brought you here because I have a gift for you."

He took the leather box from his desk and held it out to her. She remained still, with her back pressed flat. "Do humor me a little, Susy."

She relented, allowing him to draw her farther into the room. "Very well. But we must hurry. The drive to Crich will take the better part of an hour and we don't want to be late."

"I promise this won't take long." He directed her over to the settee and knelt before her. "This was my mother's. And now it is yours." He opened the catch on the box with a flick of his thumbnail.

"Oh," Susannah gasped. Her eyes deepened to a sea-green shade as she gazed at the necklace. "Oh, my."

"Here. Wear it for the wedding," Daniel insisted. He reached forward to unbutton her cloak, but she pushed his hand away.

"You're not supposed to see me," she warned.

"And this is the other part of my gift." He sighed. Here it was—his whole plan laid out. If she didn't like it—well, no matter. He would be sunk. "We're not going to Crich today."

Susannah's face paled. She blinked rapidly. "Why not? You…you've changed your mind?"

"No, Susy." Bother, what an idiot he was. He pulled himself onto the settee and tucked her into his lap. "My apologies, darling. I did not mean to startle you. I just thought—we could be married here, at Goodwin."

"Here?" Tears trembled on her lashes, and Daniel swiped them away with his thumb. "Of course, Daniel."

"You see, I arranged it all with Reverend Kirk last week," he rushed on. Perhaps if he could explain it all quickly, things wouldn't be quite such a muddle. "I asked him to come and officiate at Mother's chapel. It's all decorated. Your sisters are waiting. Paul is there. I thought—why not embark on our journey together, at the very spot that means so much to both of us."

She leaned against him, her eyelashes, still damp from unshed tears, brushing his cheek. "Oh, that's lovely. I agree wholeheartedly, Daniel. What a delightful plan."

He drew her closer. "So I didn't create a muddle?"

She laughed, and his heart hitched in his chest. What a wonderful laugh she had. Just like a bell. "No, not at all. Mind you, I was a bit worried at first."

"It's not the wedding we might have had—with all the villagers present. But it is the wedding I think we'd like most. In the place we love best, with the people we love best." He patted her back with the flat of his hand.

"Oh, I love it. Thank you, Daniel." She drew away from him a bit, studying him with eyes that were both grave and warm. "But I worry—I have nothing to give you. Here you are, giving me that beautiful necklace of your mother's, and the most delightful wedding I could have hoped for—and yet I have nothing to gift you in return."

"This is what you may gift me," he requested, his tone humble. "Stay by my side forever, helping me to become a better man. Will you?"

"Yes, dear Daniel. I should like nothing better."

"There's one more thing I ask of you, Susy. Let's walk into the chapel together. We're starting this adventure together, and I want to start it by walking in on each other's arm. Will you do me the honor?"

"I will. May I keep my cloak on until we get there? Not to hide my dress from you—but to stay warm? 'Tis quite chilly out today, you know." She gave him her loveliest smile.

He laughed. "Of course you may. Let us hurry. Your sisters will think I have tried to convince you to elope, or some such." He set her on her feet and grabbed the leather box. "And once we get there, I shall endeavor to convince you to wear this."

"Endeavor? I should think not. Those emeralds will look just right with this pale green, and I am so glad I didn't change the neckline of my gown. As an expert in millinery and in women's attire, I think this will look rather brilliant." She gave him a wink and took his arm.

Together, they strolled down the hallway of Goodwin and out the front porch to the little chapel in the clearing.

* * *

Arm in arm with her fiancé, Susannah entered the chapel that his mother had built, and that he had so lovingly restored in her memory. After briefly divesting herself of her cloak and allowing Daniel to clasp the emeralds about her neck, she strolled down the aisle on his arm.

Her sisters smiled up at her, their faces reflecting their delight at the change in plans. Paul smiled, too, but his was a wan, man-of-the-world type of grin. Poor worldly Paul. Perhaps someday a woman would come along and encourage him to think beyond himself.

And there was Reverend Kirk, beaming with his kind, round face. He'd traveled all the way from Crich just to make their day more special, and her heart swelled with gratitude. She was so fortunate. What a blessed day this was. She darted a sideways glance at her handsome husband-to-be—he who was already beginning to sport a little darkening around his angular cheeks and chin, though it was still morning.

How incorrigible he was.

As Reverend Kirk began the ceremony, she could not stop marveling at the circumstances that had brought her to this very place on this very day. Her parents would be so delighted at this match. They'd always admired Daniel's mother. Her sisters would be well taken care of. Why, she'd even hired a few of the tenant girls to help out at the shop. Their nimble fingers, so skilled at the sewing bee, would be a great benefit to the Siddons Sisters Millinery Shop. In no time, Nan and Becky would be able to cease their constant toiling and be able to have lives beyond the store.

'Twas the last thing she had done for her sisters before releasing her claim on the shop.

And she would spend the rest of her days with Daniel. Helping Daniel, listening to Daniel, talking to Daniel. They would be partners on this journey to the end of their days. 'Twas a much more delightful, fulfilling prospect than toiling away at her bonnets for the rest of her life. She was trading her needle for Daniel and Goodwin and being a wife.

But it was also still a little frightening. A little strange. Giving up all she'd ever known to be with the man whom—she now knew—she'd always loved.

For inasmuch as Daniel needed her, she needed him. She knew that now. Without Daniel, she would have been alone—and lonely, which was even worse. In his company, she blossomed as a rose bloomed in sunshine. She needed him, as he needed her. Why, they had even committed great sacrifices for each other.

This was no longer a rumored engagement.

This was the kind of companionship she had craved for years.

They repeated their vows, and as the ceremony ended, sealed their troth with a kiss that caused her toes to clench within her kid slippers. She was Daniel's in truth now, the mistress of Goodwin Hall, a Siddons sister by birth but a Hale by name.

Nan and Becky cheered as Paul clapped his hands heartily. Then Susannah looked at her husband, who clasped her gloved hand and kissed it.

"Our first voyage together, Susy," he murmured. "Are you frightened?"

"A bit," she admitted. "But there is no one I would rather be brave with than you, Daniel."

Daniel tucked her hand into the crook of his arm, in

the familiar and comfortable fashion she'd come to love. "Good," he replied. "Then let's go home."

She cast him a smile and nodded. What she'd said was true. There was no one she would rather embark on such an adventure with than Daniel Hale. Daniel, with his mischievous green eyes, his dark, tousled hair and his teasing ways. Life would never be dull or lonely. No— it would be a bit frightening, and a bit exhilarating, and altogether wonderful.

Together, they marched up the aisle and out of the chapel, the keen air biting her cheeks. Ahead, the blond stone walls of Goodwin beckoned, as stalwart and strong as a fortress on the moors. And yet, in its windows, she could just pick out the glimmer of the chandeliers, the lamps and the candles, glowing with warm welcome. Goodwin was warmth and strength combined. Just like Daniel.

She was never so ready to start a journey in her life.

* * * * *

Dear Reader,

This book marks my first time to write about a family other than the Handleys. New series, new books, new characters. I could have set the story anywhere in England, but Tansley Village holds a special place in my heart. It is a real town in Derbyshire, and while I have never visited Tansley, I hope to go there someday. I'd like to see the moors and the sweeping vistas for myself, and to see the spire of St. Mary's church in Crich. Did I do the descriptions of these places justice? I hope so. For me, Tansley remains a blessed place, a place for new beginnings—which is quite appropriate for the Siddons family saga, as it marks a new beginning for me as a writer and for them as a family.

The next book in this series is all about Rebecca Siddons, known as Becky. She is everything Susannah isn't—romantic, soft, indecisive and sweet. Will she continue as a hopeless romantic, or will life deal her a difficult hand? I am afraid that, like Sophie Handley, Rebecca's path to true love must involve the development of some maturity. Her girlish ideals will have to go through the wringer a bit, but I have faith that in the end she will be much stronger for it.

You can learn more about my upcoming releases by following me on Facebook at facebook.com/LilyGeorge-Author, on Twitter as @lilygeorge2, or on my website at www.lilygeorge.com. Thank you, my dear readers, for staying in touch with me. I sincerely appreciate every opportunity to interact with you.

Blessings,
Lily George

Questions for Discussion

1. Susannah has a difficult time moving forward with any kind of friendship with Daniel because she feels he betrayed her, and she cannot forgive him. What advice would you have given Susannah for learning to forgive and moving on?

2. Daniel feels like a failure because he shirked responsibility when he was a young lad. What advice would you give him about learning from the past and moving forward?

3. Paul is often a bad influence on Daniel, provoking him to drink and gamble. How would you deal with a friendship that, over time, seemed to cause more harm than good?

4. Susannah is determined to be independent in an age when women were not encouraged to make their own living. What do you think this says about her character? Is it an admirable trait?

5. Daniel begins rebuilding his mother's chapel as a way to honor her memory. Have you ever created a memorial to a loved one? If so, did it help you with the grieving process?

6. When the truth comes out about Susannah and Daniel's engagement, some of the townspeople begin snubbing Susannah. Why do you think they behave in this manner? And what could Susannah do to change their minds?

7. When this does happen, Susannah reacts by breaking off her friendship with Daniel. Was that the right way to handle the situation? Could she have allowed their friendship to continue, even if it meant standing up to the gossip?

8. The Siddons family is very tight-knit, whereas the Hale family was not. How do you think this affected Susannah and Daniel's relationship?

9. Susannah helps Daniel when he is at his lowest point, and Daniel tried to help Susannah when she was at hers. Then they finally admit they will be scared but brave together. What do you think this says about how their marriage will progress? Are they up to the challenge?

10. Daniel goes to Reverend Kirk because he feels as if he's too empty inside to marry Susannah. How would his spiritual development change the void he's always tried to fill with alcohol?

11. Becky finally tells Susannah that it is all right for her to get married, which relieves Susannah of all the guilt she's felt in raising her sisters. In what ways can "letting go and letting God" help a person like Susannah?

12. Should Daniel be held responsible for his actions when he was a boy, or was he too young to know any better?

13. Susannah wants to make the lives of the tenants better at Goodwin Hall. Is her plan to work with the

tenants to make new clothing a good one? Is breaking away from tradition the right call for both Daniel and Susannah as they embark on their new lives?

14. In the Siddons family, Nan is the practical one, Becky is the dreamer and Susannah is the doer. In your family, does each family member fill a special "role," or do you find that people's roles overlap?

15. Susannah's faith has always seen her through her difficulties. How can she encourage Daniel to grow in his faith so that he can become the man he feels he should be?

REQUEST YOUR FREE BOOKS!

2 FREE INSPIRATIONAL NOVELS
PLUS 2
FREE
MYSTERY GIFTS

Love Inspired
HISTORICAL
INSPIRATIONAL HISTORICAL ROMANCE

YES! Please send me 2 FREE Love Inspired® Historical novels and my 2 FREE mystery gifts (gifts are worth about $10). After receiving them, if I don't wish to receive any more books, I can return the shipping statement marked "cancel." If I don't cancel, I will receive 4 brand-new novels every month and be billed just $4.74 per book in the U.S. or $5.24 per book in Canada. That's a saving of at least 21% off the cover price. It's quite a bargain! Shipping and handling is just 50¢ per book in the U.S. and 75¢ per book in Canada.* I understand that accepting the 2 free books and gifts places me under no obligation to buy anything. I can always return a shipment and cancel at any time. Even if I never buy another book, the two free books and gifts are mine to keep forever.

102/302 IDN F5CN

Name	(PLEASE PRINT)	
Address		Apt. #
City	State/Prov.	Zip/Postal Code

Signature (if under 18, a parent or guardian must sign)

Mail to the **Harlequin®** Reader Service:
IN U.S.A.: P.O. Box 1867, Buffalo, NY 14240-1867
IN CANADA: P.O. Box 609, Fort Erie, Ontario L2A 5X3

Want to try two free books from another series?
Call 1-800-873-8635 or visit www.ReaderService.com.

* Terms and prices subject to change without notice. Prices do not include applicable taxes. Sales tax applicable in N.Y. Canadian residents will be charged applicable taxes. Offer not valid in Quebec. This offer is limited to one order per household. Not valid for current subscribers to Love Inspired Historical books. All orders subject to credit approval. Credit or debit balances in a customer's account(s) may be offset by any other outstanding balance owed by or to the customer. Please allow 4 to 6 weeks for delivery. Offer available while quantities last.

Your Privacy—The Harlequin® Reader Service is committed to protecting your privacy. Our Privacy Policy is available online at www.ReaderService.com or upon request from the Harlequin Reader Service.

We make a portion of our mailing list available to reputable third parties that offer products we believe may interest you. If you prefer that we not exchange your name with third parties, or if you wish to clarify or modify your communication preferences, please visit us at www.ReaderService.com/consumerschoice or write to us at Harlequin Reader Service Preference Service, P.O. Box 9062, Buffalo, NY 14269. Include your complete name and address.

LIH13R

Love Inspired
SUSPENSE
RIVETING INSPIRATIONAL ROMANCE

Hometown secrets

Was the explosion that took the lives of Sarah Russell's parents an act of murder? Her teenaged daughter thinks so and is determined to seek answers in their sleepy small town. Sarah fears her daughter will uncover a secret she's not ready to share: everyone—including Sarah's daughter—believes the girl is Sarah's kid *sister*. Even the child's father doesn't know the truth. But as Sarah reunites with Nick Tyler to look into the mysterious deaths, she knows she'll have to tell him—and her daughter—the truth. Yet someone wants to ensure that no one uncovers *any* long buried secrets.

COLLATERAL DAMAGE
by
HANNAH ALEXANDER

**Available June 2014 wherever
Love Inspired books and ebooks are sold.**

Find us on Facebook at
www.Facebook.com/LoveInspiredBooks

LIS44599